SPECIAL MESSAGE TO READERS

After a childhood spent acting professionally and training at a theatre school, Laura Madeleine changed her mind and went to study English Literature at Newnham College, Cambridge. She now writes fiction, as well as recipes, and was formerly the resident cake baker for Domestic Sluttery. She lives in Bristol, but can often be found visiting her family in Devon, eating cheese and getting up to mischief with her sister, fantasy author Lucy Hounsom.

You can discover more about the author at www.lauramadeleine.com

WHERE THE WILD CHERRIES GROW

It is 1919, but the end of the war has not brought peace for Emeline Vane. Lost in grief, she is suddenly alone at the heart of a depleted family and can no longer cope. Just as everything seems to be slipping beyond her control, in a moment of desperation she boards a train and runs away . . . Fifty years later, a young solicitor on his first case finds Emeline's diary. Bill Perch is eager to prove himself, but what he learns from the tattered pages of neat script goes against everything he has been told — and he begins to trace a story of love and betrayal that will send him on a journey to discover the truth about what really happened to Emeline all those years ago.

Books by Laura Madeleine
Published by Ulverscroft:

THE CONFECTIONER'S TALE
THE SECRETS BETWEEN US

LAURA MADELEINE

WHERE THE WILD CHERRIES GROW

Complete and Unabridged

CHARNWOOD
Leicester

First published in Great Britain in 2017 by
Black Swan
an imprint of Transworld Publishers
London

First Charnwood Edition
published 2019
by arrangement with
Penguin Random House UK
London

A catalogue record for this book is available
from the British Library.

ISBN 978–1–4448–4282–1

Published by
F. A. Thorpe (Publishing)
Anstey, Leicestershire

Set by Words & Graphics Ltd.
Anstey, Leicestershire
Printed and bound in Great Britain by
T. J. International Ltd., Padstow, Cornwall

This book is printed on acid-free paper

For Terry and Iris
The most unlikely of allies

Prologue

April 1919

We ran through the darkness. My shoes were lost to dancing and the dusty road was cool beneath my bare feet, though the night air was warm. I laughed, tried to ask the young man who held my hand where we were going, but he only turned to me and smiled, teeth glinting in the deep tan of his face.

I followed him, jumping down on to the beach. It was high tide and the sea was rich with the scent of minerals. The surface was calm, but I knew that beneath it was teeming with life, with fins and scales and flashing silver eyes.

He stopped walking, so abruptly I almost collided with his back. We had reached the cliff at the end of the beach. When I tried to get his attention, tell him that we couldn't go any further, he dropped my hand, leaving a tingle of disappointment in its place.

It was damp here, smelled of wet sand and drying seaweed. He ran his fingers over the surface of the rock, pulling aside a plant that was making a valiant effort to grow in a waterless crevice. Behind it, a chunk of stone was missing, almost like a foothold. Another piece of stone had been prised out further up. Above that, a little way past his head, was a ledge.

I tried to protest that I was in no state to

1

climb, but he responded with a grin that I imagined had not changed since he was a lad of thirteen, delighting in trouble. He stooped and tapped my ankle, until I raised my leg, hesitating.

His hands enclosed the sole of my foot. His fingers were warm, coarsened from years of salt and rope. He was looking up at me through his black hair, with those eyes that always saw too much.

Then I was boosted high and I yelped in surprise as I scrabbled at the uneven rock. My foot found purchase in one of the holes, and I clung there, breathless with laughter, not daring to look over my shoulder. Behind me, I heard the breaths of his own quiet laugh, at my ungainly pose, at my skirt close to splitting.

With a burst of effort, I hauled myself up, and twisted, until I sat on the ledge. I gave a mocking salute down to the ground below. He swiped at my foot and began his own scrambled ascent. For a moment, he rested beside me. The stone beneath our hands retained a trace of the day's fierce heat.

He went ahead, feeling his way around the cliff face. The path was steep, and I tried not to think about the sea, lapping at the ragged rocks below. Wine was flowing through my veins; it made me reckless. Together, we edged our way around the curve of the cliff. This near, I was engulfed in his scent, cotton dried in sunlight and warmed by skin, woodsmoke in his hair, spice on his breath and always, always, that mineral tang, like the sea on a winter's day.

The path twisted, taking us high above the

dark waves. Finally, I felt grass beneath my feet, smelled sweetness upon the air and we emerged on to a tiny plateau beneath the brow of the cliff. Here, a single, twisted tree was growing: a wild cherry, its fruit flushed pink. The forbidding rock walls sheltered it from the winds, like a fierce creature guarding something precious. The young man ran a hand along the shining bark. This was his secret place, I knew then, in a town too small for secrets. I wanted to ask him why, but he only smiled, rested his hands upon my shoulders and turned my body to look.

Behind us was the town, all of it, stretching around the bay and up into the hills. I could see the café we had fled with its strings of flickering electric bulbs, could see the silhouettes of people dancing, stomping and spinning, kicking up the wine-soaked dust.

The wind carried smoke from the bonfire up here. I breathed deeper, closing my eyes until I could pick out other scents: coal from the railway track and tar from the boats, the powerful reek of fish scales, drying on nets and traps. I could smell sun-baked stone, wild herbs, myrtle and olive trees on the hillsides above. I caught a wisp of the food we had eaten that night, heady with spices. And above it all that single cherry tree, a drop of sweetness, just shy of ripe.

His hands shifted upon my shoulders. Once, I would never have stepped out alone with a man like this, but *once* did not exist any more. I leaned back and felt his cheek rest against my hair. Above us were stars and behind us in the darkness, a soul took up singing.

'There's a nightingale,' I whispered, but I knew he couldn't hear it. And I knew, too, that I was lost.

Part One

June 1969

It's the smell of kippers that wakes me, rather than the gut-wrenching jangle of the alarm clock. Kippers mean one thing.

Swearing, I stagger out of bed, the blanket and sheet tangling around my legs. Two steps down the corridor to the bathroom. The door is closed but I barge in regardless, hoping that Louise isn't sitting on the toilet. Serve her right if she is, she *knows* I have to be out of the house at this time.

My dad looks up in surprise, chin and neck half-lathered, handle of the razor clenched.

'Bleeding hell, Bill, could've stuck myself like a pig.'

I aim a hasty stream at the toilet, not without a few splashes — sorry, Mum — while Dad grunts behind me.

'Told you to get that clock fixed. In my day, we didn't need one, up at dawn . . . '

Ignoring his monologue, I make a grab for the face-cloth hanging by the sink. Dad drawls on and on, shaving slowly just to wind me up, I'm sure of it. Between his rinse-and-drag motions, I wet the cloth under the tap, rub at my face, neck, armpits. It rasps over my chin, but not too much. For once I'm glad that my manly grooming rituals are limited to a few pitiful attempts per week.

Toothbrush from the mug, a bit of paste and

I'm out. I brush with one hand, searching the drawer for a pair of pants and a vest. The suit is waiting on its hanger. I grimace at it. Some day, I'll buy myself a new suit. One that actually fits. One that isn't *brown*.

I thunder down the stairs in a cloud of Aramis — the same bottle Mum got me for my eighteenth — and spit toothpaste into the kitchen sink.

Louise is ignoring a bowl of cornflakes as she tries to re-animate her week-old hair-do, Mum is flipping Dad's kippers. There are toast corners in the rack, so I grab one, despite Mum's attempts to stop me. On with the hated, squeaky leather shoes, and shoelaces. Oh, for a world without shoelaces.

Outside it's warm and by the time I make it to the corner, I'm already sweating. The bus is at the stop, primed to trundle off like a greyhound at the track. I leap for the steps just as the driver releases the brake.

It's packed, as always. Men in suits far better than mine, with briefcases and umbrellas balanced across their knees, though when was the last time it rained? There's a spare seat at the back by the stairs and I collapse into it, a mess of sweat and toast crumbs. I'm so grateful to have made the bloody bus, it takes me a minute to see who I'm sharing a seat with. When I do, I realize why this space was free.

A child is staring back at me, a boy. He has fine, pale blond hair plastered to his head in a bowl cut, and enormous, bottle-bottom spectacles — the worst the NHS has to offer. He's one of those children who always look sticky. I grimace out a smile and glance away, pretending to be fascinated by the advertisements above. He's still staring, I can feel it. From the corner of my eye I see him raise a hand, slow as a snake, and wipe his nose.

I'm an adult now, aren't I? I should say something to this kid about manners, produce a handkerchief from my well-equipped pocket and brandish it at him. But there's nothing in my pockets, save for the loose change that makes the lining sag, a wrapper from a toffee and my house key, still proud on its own ring, the plastic one with a grinning sun that my aunt got me from Margate.

'You — ' I start weakly, staring down at the boy.

'What are you?' he interrupts.

The words of reprimand dissolve on my tongue. He is still looking up at me, but now his mouth is closed, lips pursed and appraising.

'What?' is all I can manage.

'I said, what are you? And you should say 'pardon', not 'what'.' He sniffs again. 'Mummy says.'

As I gape helplessly, I notice a book held tightly on his lap. It's a thin, cardboard-covered thing about the size of an almanac.

'What have you got there?' I ask, attempting to summon the false jollity that adults talk to children with. 'Is it a picture book?'

'No.' He still hasn't looked away, not once. Has he even blinked? 'It's the latest issue of the Palaeontology Society's Members' Journal. I'm

9

not a member, yet, but Uncle Alan is. He said I could have it.'

'Well, that's . . . ' Of course, I'd get stuck next to the weird kid. Up ahead the traffic is thickening, crushing itself on to the roads that lead into London. We'll be here for some time. 'That's, uh, groovy.'

The boy frowns. 'What does 'groovy' mean?'

'Groovy, you know, something cool, interesting.'

'Groovy,' the boy tries out, and nods. 'So, what are you?'

This again. I look around for the boy's mother or guardian or anyone, but no one meets my eye. In fact, the two businessmen in the seats opposite are studiously ignoring us, obviously relishing the fact that *they* do not have to sit next to the sticky, eccentric child.

'What do you mean?' I sigh at last, giving up. 'Am I what? Animal, vegetable — '

'I mean what *are* you,' he repeats patiently, helping me along. 'As a job. What *are* you?'

'Oh. Right. I'm a solicitor.' I feel a wave of pride at those words, and brush a few crumbs from my polyester lapel. 'Well, I'm a solicitor's assistant, really, but in a few years I'll be — '

'What's a solicitor?'

This is like being back at the grammar school, under the eagle-gaze of the old headmaster, who distrusted anyone who came from the new part of town.

'We, uh, we sort out legal things for people. Help them with problems, fill in the right paperwork.'

'So what do you do all day?'

10

'I help my boss, Mr Hillbrand. I make copies for him, and sometimes he trusts me to visit our clients and take them papers to sign.'

'Why?'

'What do you mean, 'why'? Because they need signing.'

The boy shrugs, as if to say, *Have it your way, pal*.

'I'm going to be a palaeontologist,' he says, careful to pronounce every vowel. 'And dig up dinosaurs and the oldest creatures in the world and build them again.'

'That sounds cool,' I admit. The boy nods sagely. 'Much cooler than papers.'

I sink back into my seat. The traffic is moving again. We'll be in central London in twenty minutes.

'When I was your age,' I tell him, taking the crumpled tie out of my pocket, 'I wanted to be Scott of the Antarctic.'

★　★　★

'Late, Perch.'

'Traffic, Mr Hillbrand, sorry. That A13 was murder this morning. Hello, Jill.'

'Morning Billy, good weekend?'

I show my teeth in what I hope looks like a smile and nod. No one calls me Billy. Not even Stephanie.

I sit down at the desk squashed into the corner, behind the stack of triplicate forms that are waiting for me. Almost immediately, I stand up again.

'Tea?'

'Yes. But let Jill do that. Jill? Need to go through a client file with you, lad. They're coming in at eleven.' Hillbrand cracks his neck importantly. It makes me shudder to think that some day I'll be a crackly necked old bastard. 'They're interested in one of the dormant case files, believe it or not. Right back from when Great-uncle Durrant ran the firm. Never looked at it twice, to be honest. Reckon it's a straightforward enough job, though. Some papers need locating, power of attorney transferring to the relatives, and what not.'

He suppresses a belch. Hillbrand's one of those people who looks thin, until he turns to the side and you see his belly. I've seen the man eat enough for a family of four, but for some reason, not an ounce of it ends up on his limbs.

'Anyway,' he says, 'thought it was about time you got a client of your very own. I'll let you walk it, feed it.' He laughs at his own joke, and I smirk along dutifully, until the reality of what he's said hits me.

'Wait, what? You mean that I . . . that I'll be in charge of the casework?'

'Jesus, Perch, close your mouth, you look like Larry the Lamb. Don't get excited. You'll start on the easy stuff. Might mean a few late nights, though. Reckon you're up to it?'

'You bet!'

I sound like a Boy Scout. Hillbrand looks pained. He digs around in his pocket for change.

'There's two and six. Go and get some biscuits, will you? Nice ones, with chocolate bits,

12

not the rubbish your granny buys. This lot we've got coming in aren't short of a few bob. They'll know the difference.'

I'm halfway down the dark staircase when I hear his yell. 'And I wouldn't say no to an egg bap!'

★   ★   ★

The woman sniffs when I offer her the plate of biscuits. She bypasses them with a tight smile and a flick of her hand, even though they're Cadbury's best. She's wearing short gloves, an immaculately tailored cream dress.

The man next to her is already on his third cigarette, though they've been here all of ten minutes. He slumps back in his chair. His belly and Hillbrand's are facing each other like boxers at opposite corners of the ring.

It's clear that Hillbrand & Moffat Solicitors is *not* what they were expecting. I know the feeling. I too walked trembling up to the grand building several months ago, only to discover that the solicitor's office is nothing more than a couple of broom cupboards on the second floor. The rest of the building is, in fact, a gentlemen's club. One that Hillbrand has never been invited to frequent.

This pair are obviously used to finer things. I, on the other hand, have no cause to complain.

'Mr Hillbrand,' the woman says, setting down her cup of tea, untouched, 'as my attorney mentioned in his letter, expediency in this matter is of great importance. My father's condition is,'

13

she presses a hand to her lacquered hair, as if it just threatened to move, 'unlikely to improve, but nevertheless, we have a limited amount of time in which to act.'

Her accent is strange, somewhere between American and British. Hillbrand offers a buttoned-up smile of his own.

'I understand, Mrs Mallory. I'm sure we can have this done and dusted for you by the end of the month.'

He holds out a hand and I fumble with a stack of cardboard files. Two of them slide out of my grip and into his lap. He manages to keep down most of a grimace.

'From what I know so far, it seems like a simple matter,' he says, opening the topmost file. 'Power of attorney over your father's assets, transference of ownership of a property to you, the next of kin. And a subsequent sale to a developer?'

Mrs Mallory shifts in her expensive tailoring.

'In essence, that is the case.'

'The law doesn't deal in essences, Mrs Mallory.'

Is Hillbrand trying to be funny? The woman shoots him a disdainful glance.

'I'm aware of that, Mr Hillbrand. Just as you are no doubt aware it would have been preferable for my own attorney to deal with this from Boston. However, changeover processes are lengthy and since your firm once represented my family *and* have possession of the relevant historic files, we have decided to place ourselves in your hands. Do I make myself clear?'

I've never heard such polite hostility. Hillbrand has the grace to take the hit.

'Of course, my apologies, Mrs Mallory. I have to ask, though, what cause do you have for hesitation?'

'We're missing something vital to the settlement. Our father has suffered a severe stroke, and the doctors tell us that even if he does survive, it is unlikely he will ever regain speech or movement. So we cannot simply ask him. As you can imagine, this puts us in an awkward position.'

'Indeed. And it's my job to get you out of it. What have you lost?'

The lady stiffens. Is she blushing? Seeing this, the man beside her laughs out a mouthful of smoke. It's the first noise he's made other than a grunt of greeting.

'Not *what*,' he says. 'Who.'

Rather than elaborating, he only laughs again and finishes his cigarette.

'What do you mean?'

The words escape my mouth. Hillbrand cuffs me over the head with his eyes. The woman, meanwhile, notices me for the first time. Did she think that the biscuits floated up to her?

'Who is this?' she asks. 'Not the other half of 'Hillbrand and Moffat'?'

'No, no, Mr Moffat passed away several years ago,' Hillbrand says smoothly. A lie. At the end of my first week, in the pub, he told me that Mr Moffat never existed. When Hillbrand took over the business from his great-uncle, he got the name 'Moffat' off a jar of mayonnaise and added

15

it to his own because he thought it sounded better. 'This is Mr Perch, my assistant. He's capable.'

Mrs Mallory looks dubious, but addresses me properly this time.

'What my brother meant, Mr Perch, is that we are short one family member. Unfortunately it is her name on the deeds to Hallerton House. Without her, even if we are granted power of attorney, we cannot sell.'

'By 'short', do you mean . . . ?'

'Missing. Gone,' the man mumbles as he lights another cigarette. 'One day she's there, the next, nothing. Mind you, people say she was mad.'

'I'm sorry?' Hillbrand is trying to regain his grip on the situation.

'Our father's older sister,' fills in Mrs Mallory. 'Our aunt, Emeline Vane.'

'Ah . . . and how long has she been missing, exactly? Have you contacted the authorities?'

The man starts laughing again, harder this time. At least, he seems to be laughing. He might be coughing. I wonder whether I should offer him some water.

'The authorities,' he wheezes to himself, wiping his eyes with a handkerchief. 'There'd be no use in that. She's been missing for years.'

'Fifty years, to be exact,' the woman says, before either of us can ask. 'Emeline Vane disappeared on February twenty-seventh, 1919.'

I don't know who is more stunned. Hillbrand is turning red from the neck up, staring at them as though they're crazy. I feel my mouth go clacking off on its own again.

16

'Well, if that's true, then there's no problem.' My cheeks burn under the scrutiny but I can't stop gabbling. 'I mean, that long, she has to be presumed dead. So there's nothing to stop you from being granted probate — '

'You think we haven't tried?' the woman interrupts. Her brother is watching me from behind his cigarette. Slowly, she smooths an invisible crease in her skirt. 'It isn't that simple. Our father would never declare the death. He has some letter or other from after her disappearance, secreted away. He's always said that it proves she's alive.'

Her eyes, cool as smoke, meet mine.

'It will be your job, Mr Perch, to prove him wrong.'

19th February 1919, Hallerton

Durrant came to see me today.

Outside, the hail fell like words. Small, mean, unwelcome ones that stung. Not enough to bruise or cause pain but enough to serve as a reminder of skin and frailty. I know them well.

Infirm. Afflict. Attend. Cold words. They have to be, to withstand the use. I don't want to say them any longer. I've been waiting for the time when I will be their subject, rather than their owner. Before, it seemed inevitable. It seemed only fair. But it has never come.

I could smell the freezing glass of the window, loose in its frame. Once, on a winter's day, Timothy and I licked frost flowers from the panes. I remember the bitterness on my tongue. How many years ago was that? Freddie and Albie were home from school, so it must have been at Christmastime. The memory has the scent of cloves about it. If we were in the study, it must have been after father died.

It was a mysterious place then, an adult world of leather ledgers, with rows of numbers and abbreviations that were as impenetrable as a foreign language. But they are mine now, and I shall have to learn to decipher them.

Durrant was looking at me oddly, the way everyone in the village does these days. How long had I sat there thinking? I tried to concentrate, told him I was sorry. He smiled, the way he has since I was a child in a smock and he a man with a twist of barley sugar in his pocket. But then, the smile collapsed at the corners.

'It is I who should apologize, Miss Emeline. I would rather have waited another few weeks before forcing business upon you, but there are bills, and death duties . . . '

I nodded as he spoke. In truth, I do not remember much of it now, but at the time he looked so wretched that I tried to summon up the appropriate words. I told him that I would like to settle matters. That Mother had hated debt.

Durrant, if possible, looked more wretched than before.

'Your . . . ' He made a habit of clearing his throat. 'Your mother came to me some nine years ago, to change her will after your father's passing. It has not been altered since then. You must know already, it leaves everything to her children, surviving. The house and the grounds . . . '

The fire sputtered and died, drowning in smoke. Swiftly I took the poker, tried to shake a flame back into the coals, but they only tumbled, useless in their coats of ash. Durrant knelt beside me, took the poker from my hand. He smelled of cologne and some kind of liniment.

'Thank you,' I said, as he blew a coal into redness. 'I never was much good at lighting them.'

'Emeline, how have you been coping?' He did not speak like a solicitor then. 'I do not think

19

you should be here alone.'

I told him that Edith came to help me almost every day, though I only paid her for two, I watched the flames spring back into being.

'This is my home. I do not want to be anywhere else.'

I began to feel the shifting of the warmth across my face, across the clothes that had not felt dry for weeks. Durrant sighed. We knelt like a pair of children, shoulder to shoulder on the hearthrug, staring at the flames.

'There's no money.' His voice was flat. 'I should not be telling you as much, before the official reading, but it's true.'

Outside, far off, something tumbled in the wind.

'Nothing?' I asked.

'The bills, the estate duty, it amounts to more than what is left.'

He made to take my elbow, to help me rise, but I stood alone and returned to the desk, to the leather chair stiff with cold. I asked him when the will would be read.

He blinked at such a straightforward question, made an examination of my face before answering.

'Friday, at two o'clock.'

He told me that my uncle was coming to stay for a time. To keep an eye on me, his look said. Timothy would come with him, his first visit home in over a month. The first time since Mother's funeral.

I nodded. Behind Durrant's shoulder, I could see Father's crystal decanter. It had stood on its silver tray for as long as I could remember. How long did brandy keep? I wondered idly. My mother never drank it and I don't think my brothers ever dared. Eight years? Ten?

Durrant began to speak again, but I couldn't make out the words. Instead, I recall standing, walking to the sideboard. His voice petered out as I picked up one of the matching crystal glasses. It was thick with dust.

'Do you think this stuff is still good?' I cleaned the glass with my sleeve. The velvet gathered up the grime. If Durrant answered, I didn't hear him. I poured out a little of the liquid and sniffed and asked if Timothy needed to attend the reading of the will.

Durrant watched my actions, and told me that I could witness on Timothy's behalf.

'Good. I do not want to send him off to school again with that on his mind.'

Then, I remembered what I wanted to ask, the request that had nagged at me for the past few weeks. I placed the glass down.

'Mr Durrant,' I told him, 'I should like to make a will.'

His face curdled between red and white.

'Please, Miss Emeline — '

'It only need be a simple one. I have nothing of value, it seems, but my share in this house. What if something were to happen to me? I should like to know that Timothy will be taken care of.'

'Emeline, we do not need to do this now. Might it not wait until you are — '

He stopped himself. Until you are better, he

was *going to* say. Until you are in your right mind again. *I looked into his eyes and almost laughed at what I saw. At the people we had been: a girl-child and a kindly, occasional visitor. At what we were now, at the pair of us, alone in this echoing house, alone because there was no one else left. There was a high colour to his face as he turned away.*

'We will talk more on Friday.'

He gathered up his hat, his coat, clipped shut his bag. He told me that he would ask his wife to send up something hot, for my supper.

I felt the first tear burn the corner of my eye, but would not look at him. Instead, I took up the glass and drank down the old, hard spirit.

June 1969

I walk back to my desk in a daze, listening to Hillbrand's repeated pleasantries as he ushers Mrs Mallory and her brother down the stairs. Jill makes a *what happened?* face from her desk in the corner, but I just shake my head and shrug. Where would I even start? The clock on the wall reads quarter to twelve. I can't believe it's only been forty-five minutes.

Limply, I select one of the triplicate forms waiting for me. I haven't even placed it into the typewriter when Hillbrand sags against the door, loosening his tie with one hand.

'Put that down,' he puffs. 'Anyone else expected, Jill?'

'Not that I know of, Dicky.'

He opens his mouth to correct her over-familiarity — once again — but gives up mid-breath. Instead, he points at me.

'Cow. Now.'

The Old Cow is Hillbrand's favourite pub. I'm not sure why. It's narrow and dark and jammed into an alleyway between grander buildings like a filling in a tooth. It smells of fag smoke and forty-year-old beer-soaked carpet. It's only just past opening time and Norm, the landlord, is still pottering around, clinking glasses.

'Morning, Dick,' he calls. 'You're in early. Good Monday, is it?'

'Two of the usual, Norm,' says Hillbrand,

struggling out of his jacket. 'You want an egg?' he asks. I eye the huge, murky jar of bobbing shapes and shake my head. 'Suit yourself. And an egg.'

A quarter of the pint and half of the pickled white globe have disappeared down Hillbrand's gullet before he lets out a hefty sigh.

'Well,' he leans on the bar and casts an eye at me, 'what did you make of that, eh?'

I swallow down a mouthful of bitter. It's warm and faithful to its name. Hillbrand has never asked me if I like it. I don't, but he's buying, so I suppose it doesn't matter.

'I think . . . they, er, were unusual.'

'Mad as a bag of badgers,' snorts Hillbrand, chewing the rest of the egg. 'That what you mean? I'd agree. *But*. They're not short on funds. Paid the consultation fee upfront, didn't even blink when I said it was probably a month's work. Who'd have thought that damn old file would turn out to be a goldmine?' He waves his pint heaven-ward. 'Thank you, Uncle Durrant.'

'But it's impossible.' I brace myself for another sip of bitter. 'They said themselves, no one's seen this aunt for decades. And they must've tried to find her before.'

'Haven't had much luck, then, have they? But you reckon it's impossible? Shame, I was going to hand the files over to you this afternoon.'

The sly bastard, he knows I can't refuse. This could be my chance to escape the endless triplicate forms, my first step towards handling real business, towards becoming a *real* solicitor.

'Well, maybe not impossible,' I concede. 'How much have they told you?'

24

Hillbrand looks pleased. He glances over at Norm, who's absorbed in counting out a roll of pennies, and lowers his voice.

'Enough to get started. I looked back through the file; turns out Great-uncle D was the Vane family solicitor for donkey's years. Old Man Vane moved most of his business to some big city law firm in the thirties, but he left the property bumf with us, for some reason. Relates to a big old house, out east. Mallory said they've had a juicy offer to knock it down, turn it into one of those holiday camps.' He sucks down another mouthful of bitter. 'They need to move quick, though, or the developer will bugger off and find another site. And they'll never find a better buyer. It's a dump, apparently. Never been there myself, though it's near where Great-uncle D used to live. Think he must have mentioned it before. Damned if I can remember the details, but it seems like it hasn't been lived in for years, never been on the market.'

'Why?'

'Who knows? Sentiment? You know what old folk are like.'

I try to imagine my own grandparents, clinging on to a crumbling mansion out of sentiment when there was money to be had. Wouldn't happen.

'All right, so the old man's never wanted to sell,' I say. 'Isn't it a bit, *underhand* of them, going behind his back when he's so ill?'

Hillbrand laughs. I catch a waft of egg vinegar.

'Use your head, lad. If Pa dies before they

prove this aunt is officially out of the picture, what will happen?'

'They won't inherit the property?'

'They'll inherit *half* the property. Can't sell half a house any more than you can eat half a whelk.'

'But if they can get power of attorney while he's out for the count, they can declare her dead — '

'*And* flog the house.'

I nod. My head feels light from the beer. They don't sound like the most compassionate family in the world, but I suppose that's none of my business.

'So what am I meant to do?' My voice sounds too loud. 'Contact Interpol and ask them the whereabouts or last known location of some mad bat from fifty years ago?'

'Who do you think you are, Harry bloody Palmer? No, Mrs Mallory mentioned a load of family papers. You'll start with them. See if you can't rustle up something useful, like proof that this Miss Vane was barking. It'll be easier to get her declared dead *in absentia* then.'

'Where are they, the papers?'

Hillbrand drains the last of the bitter through his teeth, and grins.

'How'd you feel about taking your first business trip, Perch?'

'You mean, stay away?' *Travelling for business or pleasure, sir?* the man at the ticket booth will ask me. *Business,* I'll say with an important sniff. Back home, Stephanie will tell everyone that I'm working away, on urgent solicitor matters. 'Where?'

'Norfolk. Thereabouts.' He eyes my pint glass, still half-full. 'Same again?'

★ ★ ★

A thousand years pass before I find myself boarding the bus once more, among the early-evening traffic. That's the last time I ever go to the pub with Hillbrand during the day. How the hell does he do it? A quick, ten-minute snooze at his desk and he was off again, digging out the old file on the Vane family, making calls. I nearly nodded off over the triplicate forms a dozen times before he slapped an envelope down on the desk in front of me. It contained the terrifying prospect of two five-pound notes.

'Baby's first business expenses,' he said. 'Ask for receipts and don't muck it up.'

I can feel the money now, burning a hole in my pocket. I check it again, just to make sure it's still there. There's a seat free at the back of the bus. I half expect to see the sticky child staring back at me, feel an odd flicker of disappointment that it's only another businessman, who acknowledges my presence with a disgruntled shuffle.

I grip the briefcase tightly on my knee. It's second-hand. The leather is loose-bellied and the clasp is held together by string, but it's mine, and inside is my first ever client file. Ahead, the traffic rumbles; the bus jerks and slows, jerks and slows, and my stomach resents me for the second pint of bitter. The man next to me has wrestled his *Evening Standard* into a manageable square,

27

so I slip the dog-eared cardboard file out of the briefcase, and open it on my knee.

It's full of typewritten pages with neat, inked signatures. The dates are from forty or fifty years ago. A few sheets down, something heavier slips out on to my lap.

It's a photograph printed on thick card. It shows a house, large and square with rambling wings to either side. Bare creepers cling to the pale stone. There's a white wrought-iron table on the terrace, a few weeds struggling through the paving. The garden looks wild, but in a pretty sort of way. It must have been taken before it was abandoned.

Hallerton House, someone has written across the bottom, *Saltedge, 1919.*

21st February 1919, Hallerton

Last night I found a photograph I had never seen before, while I was searching Father's desk for ink. It had been placed carefully between two sheets of card. I felt guilty, taking it from the drawer, as though Father or Mother might appear and chastise me for prying.

But of course they did not. There is no one here but me.

I remember the day the photograph was taken. The Blackberry Day, we called it, my brothers and me. It was before Timothy was born, so I must have been eight or nine. One of those rare, stolen weekends when my brothers were home from boarding school and all three of us were allowed to play together; when duty and decorum were flung aside at the door of the boot room and we ran wild.

It was autumn, cold enough for mist to fill the garden in the morning, before the sun burned it away. I remember my brothers standing in the dim corridor outside the kitchen, eyes shining, scarves looped around their necks. Freddie's cheeks still round and childish, Albie tall and awkward as a heron, his voice beginning to boom and pitch. He was the oldest so, of course, he was our commander. He sent me to the kitchens to barter with Cook. She always did like me the best.

I must have looked like mischief itself, but she took pity on me. By the time I ran back to my brothers, my arms were laden with spoils: a jam tart each, a slab of cheese, freshly baked bread, a few cold sausages. We tumbled it all into the pannier of an old bicycle and set off, me between the handlebars, Albie pedalling, Freddie balancing precariously over the back wheels, We whooped and wobbled down the drive, and soon we were free, rulers of the country lanes, of the woods where the bright leaves flamed and fell like sparks.

We ate our picnic by the side of a little stream. It was as glorious as a feast; we drank cold water straight from our hands, filling our bellies with the taste of ancient stone and winter to come. It was when we were on our way home, the sun sinking low and golden, that we found the blackberries. Hedgerow upon hedgerow, heavy with fruit.

They squashed between our fingers, upon our tongues, I still remember their taste, perfumed and sweet. Not the bright May sweetness of a strawberry, but deeper, more mysterious, as if they'd drawn the cold smoky nights into their juice, as if they'd seen midnight. We ransacked the brambles, scratching our arms and pulling threads from our clothes, filling the pannier to the brim and never thinking about the stains.

That's how we look in the photograph, standing all together on the front steps, three dark-haired wild things, windswept and smeared with berries. Father had laughed, called us his savages and fetched the box camera. That evening Cook made a crumble with the berries. I remember it so clearly, I can almost taste it.

I looked for blackberries today as I walked to Saltedge. Of course, there are none; the brambles are bare. The air was icy and stung my throat, but my blood pumped and my body felt strong. It seems impossible that the influenza, which raged so violently through Mother, never touched me. I quickened my steps, remembering summers spent racing this path, the scent of sap and earth and the boisterous sounds of two tumbling young men and Timothy clinging to my back like a monkey, shrieking in delight.

I staggered to a halt. The memory had taken me over so rapidly . . . I blinked it away. The path before me was empty and beyond it lay the salt marsh. The water was thick with cold, shifting like mercury between the mud-trapped reeds, I could smell its odd rotting scent, saltwater meeting fresh.

I could see the path that led to the village. I knew that Uncle Andrew was expecting me there, waiting in Durrant's office with the local magistrate, waiting to make official what the solicitor had whispered to me beside the fireplace.

. . . what remains of my estate shall be split equally between my children: Albert William Vane, Frederick George Vane, Emeline Clara Vane and Timothy John Vane.

Before I could move, the church bell began to toll, tearing those cold, official names to tatters.

31

One, it called, for Albie. Two, for Freddie.

The mud of the marshes came up over the tops of my boots. At any other time I would have looked for thicker clumps of reeds, for firmer ground, but I didn't think of it then.

A February wind was shrieking from the sea; it bent the grasses low and whipped tears into my eyes. The icy sludge splashed my face but I didn't care, all I could think of was pressing on, across the flat, brown expanse. Did it ever end? I couldn't remember.

In summer, the marsh is as green as forest glass, the air heady with salt and seed, the sky dead still and maddeningly blue. Sea-lavender foams in clusters of pink, marsh marigolds are livid yellow and Albie and Freddie pull the old farm cart between them, like a pair of sunburnt packhorses, Timmy is in the back, me out in front, the dry stalks scratching at my legs. There are stems of salty glasswort to chew on, and a white egret flashes in the sun like a question mark.

But that world is buried and this new one is sombre as a flagstone. I do not want the cold comfort it offers, the brassy bugles and the new-cut medals with the tang of the engravers still upon them.

I remember reaching the dunes. The stinging wind made my face numb, but when I crested the top I am sure I cried out in relief. Before me spread the sea: spray-frenzied and empty. Blessedly empty.

June 1969

The tantalizing scent of salt and haddock and batter hits me as I open the door. The tinkling of the bell is drowned out by the radio. The Beach Boys oohing away like happy ghosts.

Steph bounces along, her back to me as she wraps a portion of chips. I glance into the back room, and sneak behind the counter.

'I have had,' I murmur into her ear, 'the strangest day.'

She jumps, but a moment later clobbers me on the head with a heap of rolled-up paper.

'You bugger!' she laughs. Grinning, I slip my hands around her waist, and the apron tied there, reaching for one of the chips in the paper. My face rests against her hair, in its dark, blunt bob that she's always trying to get straight. She smells of hairspray and powder, perfume and grease from the fryer.

She turns a blind eye as I eat a chip, then offer her one.

'Eurgh,' she says, 'no fear.' She twists out of my arms. 'And you'd better get over that side. Malcolm's out back.'

Reluctantly, I shuffle to the other side of the counter and lean there, watching as Steph finishes wrapping the chips, stretching sideways to fetch a bag. Bending in a normal way would be asking too much from her mini-dress. Hundreds of guys must try it on with her, working here. I've still got no idea why she said yes when I asked her to the dance in our last year of school; she was — is — one of the best-looking girls around, and the sharpest.

'So you going to tell me about this day of yours,' she says with a mocking smile, 'or just stand there looking at my legs?'

'Can't I do both?'

She rolls her eyes at me, but is still smiling as she deftly shapes a sheet of newspaper into a cone and fills it with chips. A flick of vinegar, a hail-scatter of salt.

'Here.' She hands them over. I fall upon them. 'You're the best.'

'If Malcolm comes in — '

'Then I'll pay for them. Here, look at this.'

Juggling the chips with one hand, I fetch the envelope that contains the five-pound notes and lay it carefully on the tiled counter top.

Steph's eyes go wide beneath thick, black lashes.

'Where'd you get ten pounds?' she demands, taking the notes in her hands like playing cards. I can see her making a mental inventory of exactly which things she would buy in exactly which shops on the King's Road.

'I can't really spend it,' I say, as she unwillingly returns the money to its envelope. 'It's for expenses. I'm going on a trip.'

'What trip?' Her face falls. 'Without me?'

'It's a business trip, Steph. My first one ever.'

'When?'

'First thing tomorrow. To some godforsaken place in the middle of the Fens.' I try to sound

34

casual, but the words come with a shiver of anxiety. Do I really know what I'm doing?

'But we were going to the pictures, remember?' Steph is saying. '*The Italian Job* is on. Everyone's been raving about it.'

'We can go next week.'

She's looking cross now. 'I might be busy next week.'

'Steph, I have to go, this is my first real client.' She turns away and clangs about the fryer, emptying the chips out of the basket, dumping in new ones. I check over my shoulder; most people buying supper have been and gone and there's no sign of her boss Malcolm, so I catch her arm, turn her to face me.

'What if it was the other way around,' I say, brushing a strand of hair back into place, 'and someone sent you off to some fashion house in Paris?'

'That's different,' she swipes at me lightly, but she's smiling again, 'that's *art*. This is business.'

'True, but I want to do well with Hillbrand, Steph. If he starts giving me my own clients I'll make more money, and then maybe, we could . . . '

'What?'

She's stepped closer to me, her fingers linked into the collar of my shirt.

'Well, you know, maybe, move to town. Or something.'

'Or something?' she murmurs, one eyebrow raised.

What am I supposed to say? *Just stop talking, you idiot*, my brain instructs and I lean down to

35

kiss her hurriedly. I'm strangely grateful when I hear the plastic strip curtain behind me rustle and have to leap away.

Malcolm peers suspiciously out into the shop, his fingers wedged into the accounting ledger.

'Everything all right out here, Stephanie?'

'Yes, Mr Tiller.'

He sees me and his mouth turns lemon-sour.

'Paid for them, have you, lad?'

'Just about to, Mr Tiller.'

'Be sure you do.'

I make a face at his retreating back. Stephanie swallows a giggle, barely.

'That'll be sixpence, sir.'

I dig a coin out of my pocket. She drops it into the till and — after a brief glance behind her — leans forward, far over the counter.

By the time I pull away I'm flushing, right to the tips of my ears. Stephanie is smiling deviously.

The evening breeze cools my cheeks.

'Bill!' she calls, before I can shut the door. 'Bring me back something nice!'

22nd February 1919, Hallerton

Uncle Andrew is here to watch me. He hasn't said as much but I can tell, the way I catch him looking, examining my every word and movement. Did Durrant send for him? Or someone from Saltedge? They tried to make me go to London, after Mother's funeral, but I refused. They see me as a child, do not understand that I'm the one who has been holding Hallerton together for the past year, ever since Albie died.

I see the way they stare, on the rare occasions I go into the village, the way they whisper to each other. They want to see me taken in hand by someone responsible, they don't think it's seemly for a woman to be living alone in a place like Hallerton. I'll not bow to their ridiculous notions.

By the time I returned from the marshes yesterday it was dark, I was shivering, and I must have looked a state, my coat covered in mud and sand. Andrew stood waiting at the front door. He was furious — I had expected him to be — but I saw he was also frightened. What do any of us have left to be afraid of?

I told him that I had not meant to cause concern; that I had only gone for a walk on my way to Saltedge and got lost. That I must have been more tired than I realized. He knew it was a lie. He swore. He had never done so in front of me.

'I thought you had — '

He stopped. His hair isn't as dark as I remember. It is as neat as it always was, slicked away from his temples, but peppered with grey now. Mother's did the same, turned grey quickly after the war began.

He strode about the kitchen, clattering open cupboards — in search of something to steady himself. A noise from the doorway made me turn.

Timothy stood there, his small face pinched and pale. He wore Albie's old university scarf. Even wrapped three times around his neck it was still too long. His eyes were dry, but so solemn that my heart began to crush itself in my chest when I thought of how I might have scared him. If fear still existed for me, here it was.

I held out my arms and he hurtled into my chest. His fingers were cold, digging like claws into my filthy coat.

'There is brandy in the study,' *I told my uncle, over my shoulder. He was livid still, but had the grace to leave us.*

My little brother clung to me. The same hair as mine, heavy and brown as a bulrush, I leaned my cheek against his head and held him, as though he were a baby again and I a child of ten.

'What were you doing?' *Timothy whispered. His voice was muffled in the fabric of my coat.* 'You would never lose your way on the marsh.'

'I didn't lose my way.' *His hair smelled like soap and soot from the train.* 'I wanted to see

38

the sea. I'm all right now.'

'Were you trying to run away?'

I pulled back. Timothy's eyes were serious. There was a muddy smear on his cheek from where he had held me. I wiped it away and as I did so a memory returned, of wiping the sweat from my mother's face. Of her eyes, burning with fever, spilling over with tears as the doctor voiced the dreaded name of her illness. She'd sent for Uncle Andrew that same night, to take Timmy. She'd been too frightened even to kiss him goodbye. She tried to make me leave too, but I didn't. It seems like years ago, rather than a mere six weeks.

'Can I come home now, Emmy?'

Timothy's eyes were on the kitchen tiles. I wanted to smile, wanted to tell him that of course he could, but Uncle Andrew appeared in the doorway, one of the crystal tumblers clutched in his hand.

'Emeline,' he said, 'I suggest you get cleaned up.'

★ ★ ★

There was no food in the house, which made Andrew more suspicious than ever. He eyed my clothes, the way they hang loose now. I suppose I haven't given much thought to eating recently.

They went to fetch provisions, he and Timothy. I resolved to try my best, to be neat and sensible, to prove that he should not listen to whatever the village gossips are saying.

There are no maids here, any more. Edith has

been trying to teach me how to run the house, but we barely have time to keep a few rooms clean, let alone starch and iron linens, I found an old dress at the back of the wardrobe, made from heavy grey velvet. It does not fit well any more, but at least it is clean. I pinned up my hair and pinched some colour into my cheeks and tried to smile for Timothy. When they came back, Andrew piled what he had bought on to the kitchen table, and asked me to make supper.

Perhaps he thought it would do me good, remembering how much I used to love cooking, I ran my fingers over the packages and parcels. It was all simple, wholesome food. A pat of butter, primrose yellow; fresh eggs nestled in a box of straw, a string of sausages from the butcher, a loaf of farmhouse bread.

Timothy sat with me as I prepared it all, talking of this and that, of his school and his room in London at Uncle Andrew and Aunt Olivia's house, and for an hour, I was almost happy. I cut the loaf into doorstop slices and spread them thickly with butter. At the back of the pantry I found a jar of Edith's jam. Blackberry.

We ate supper in the parlour, I knew that the food should be delicious; soft-boiled eggs and golden-brown sausages, sticky and savoury, bread and jam for pudding, and yet I could not taste it. To my relief, Timothy ate like any nine-year-old boy with a good appetite, and his chatter warmed me, more than the tea did. In turn, I tried to cut into the food on my plate, to raise it to my mouth and swallow, as I should.

Uncle Andrew caught my arm as I shooed Timothy towards the doorway.

'When he is settled,' he said, voice low, 'come back here. We must talk.'

I helped Timothy find his pyjamas in his little travelling case, sent him off to wash his face and brush his teeth in the bathroom while I lit the fire. The water in the pipes clattered and gurgled and I heard him yelp at its iciness. Tomorrow I will have to discover how to make the boiler work. The bedclothes in Timmy's room felt cold and clammy so I stuck my hands beneath the blankets and rubbed the sheets warm.

I stayed with him until his eyes drooped and his breathing deepened. It seems impossible that this draughty old house, marked by the scuffs and scratches of generations, should come down to we two.

Six years ago, Hallerton would have been filled to the seams with people, the way it used to be every Christmas. Albie and Freddie would invite their friends, and they'd play billiards for hours and entertain us all with their new songs and dances. They would slip me glasses of sherry, even though Mother said I wasn't yet old enough to drink. We'd light all the candles on the Christmas tree, just for the delight of seeing Timothy's excited smile. I remember the smell of fir and wax, cinnamon and port, and all of us happy, ignorant of what the next five years were to bring.

Piece, by piece, it unravelled. First Albie called up, then Freddie, then friends and neighbours. The war took them all and gave us back soldiers, unfamiliar in their stiff uniforms, with stiff words embedded in their minds. And we were left to wait, those of us who were too young or old for use, as the money trickled away and the comfort of the world was lost in the violence of necessity.

By the time I went downstairs again, the house seemed darker than before. Uncle Andrew was waiting; he'd brought the decanter of brandy into the parlour. It glowed amber in the light from the lamps. The papers were already spread upon the cloth.

'Clara's will,' he told me, as though those two small words did not hold pain. 'I presume you know what it says?'

On one of the pages I found Mother's signature. I traced it with, my thumb. Andrew hesitated, leaned over to take my hand.

'You need not worry about Timothy's education,' he said, making his voice kind, 'I will see to that. I promised your mother as much. And he may continue to live with us, during the holidays.'

'Why should he not live here?' Andrew did not rise to the challenge in my voice. Of all things, there urns pity on his face.

'You know why. And I cannot let you stay here alone any longer. You should be where people can care for you.'

I told him what I told Durrant. That this is my home, that I had no desire to leave it. Andrew's voice was patient.

'You might not have a choice, Emmy.'

Although I hate to admit it, deep down I know

he is right. How can I stay here when there is no money, when there are debts to pay and nothing to pay them with? Unless I sell Hallerton, I have no future. But if I sell . . . what future can there be for me? Shall I live alone in a flat in London until the money from the sale runs out, and I am left to fall upon the charity of family too distant for love? Too respectable for work, too poor for society, Timothy will be raised up into business, and I will be left, trailing the past, like a rope with nothing at its end.

June 1969

'Now remember, use the trouser press if they have one, and hang your spare shirt up as soon as you get there,' Mum says, knocking away my hand to tighten my tie another fraction of an inch.

'Mum,' I choke, 'I'm going to Norfolk, not to Ascot Races.'

'All the more reason.' She squints at my shoes for any trace of dirt. 'You'll be showing them what a proper London businessman looks like.'

Louise snorts from the breakfast table. 'Who's he going to impress in the middle of nowhere? A load of farmers and fishermen?'

'Don't go eating at Berni Inns every night, now.' My dad winks, stripping the last flesh from his kipper.

'Like there'll be a Berni Inn for a hundred miles,' grumbles Louise, but I can tell she's jealous. I shoot a smirk over at her, as Mum takes down the house savings jar from the shelf.

'Here's ten bob,' she tells me, pressing the note into my hand.

'He's already got *ten pounds*!' Louise bursts.

'Well, just in case. Put it in your sock, then even if the rest gets stolen — '

'Stop fussing, Mother,' Dad interrupts. 'Bill's big enough and ugly enough to look after himself. Might have a family of his own to worry about one of these days, if his Stephanie has

44

anything to do with it.'

'Well, see you then,' I say loudly over Dad's guffaws, making my escape before Louise can start taunting and Mum can offer any more sage advice.

It feels strange to watch the bus come and go at the stop, to take a different one that toils through the heart of London all the way to Liverpool Street.

Outside, it's another brilliant summer morning, but inside the station is dark. The bricks are dark, the wooden benches are dark, even the glass of the huge old clock is dark with grime. The crush of commuters is ebbing, but still, the place is overwhelming. Footbridges cross and criss-cross the space, labelled with conflicting arrows and soot-blackened signs that are of no help to anybody. Finally, I find my way to the ticket booths. There's a long queue; with the rush hour over, most of the staff seem to have sloped off for tea breaks and second breakfasts.

When I reach the front, I heft my briefcase importantly and ask the woman behind the desk for a return to Saltedge. She does not look impressed. In fact, she looks blank. I repeat the request, and she rolls her heavily made-up eyes at me.

'Never heard of it.'

She pulls out a ledger and idly turns the pages. Her hair is so blonde it's white, coiffed and crisp as a meringue.

'Reg,' she calls over her shoulder, 'ever heard of Saltedge?'

I'm turning red now, as customers in the

45

queue behind me start to shift, annoyed by the delay.

'Saltedge?' a thickset man replies, shuffling into view, mug of tea in hand. 'Never heard of it. Where is it?'

'Norfolk,' I stutter, 'somewhere in Norfolk, I think.'

The ticket lady's look says, *Well, why didn't you say so in the first place?* Her finger flicks faster.

'Saltedge,' she says at last, pink nail on an entry. 'Here it is. On the North Norfolk Line.'

'Right,' I say, 'could I have a — '

'Closed.' She smiles tightly. 'Two years ago.'

'Closed?'

'You can thank bloody Beeching for that,' Reg says, after another slurp of tea. He doesn't seem to care about the ten or more people in line behind me. 'Nearest station's probably Shering-ham, ain't it, Pam?'

'Sheringham,' she agrees, slapping the book shut. 'Return or single?'

'I, um, return, please. It's for business — '

'Eight shillings and six.'

I hand over one of the five-pound notes. Pam gives me a withering look.

'Haven't you got anything smaller?'

'I — '

'Don't have much change,' Reg says cheer-fully, 'busy morning, and no one's done the bank-run yet.'

If my cheeks were red before, they must be close to spontaneous combustion now. I glance back at the line of people. Most of them are pointedly checking their watches and huffing and not quite catching my eye. Gritting my teeth, I bend down and fish the ten bob out of my sock. It's warm and slightly clammy. Someone behind me suppresses a laugh as I offer it up. Gingerly, Pam takes the note between her finger and thumb.

'Platform four,' she tells me, tearing off two tickets, 'the nine-fifty train to Norwich. Change there for Sheringham.'

Before I board I find a kiosk and buy a newspaper, a packet of fudge and a box of matches, just to break up the damn five-pound note. The train is waiting. I open the first compartment, but there's a man in there from the ticket queue so I hurry back out and walk to the very end of the train. The last compartment is empty. I shove my suitcase on to the luggage rack and settle with my briefcase by the window. Eventually, a whistle blows, the brakes hiss and clatter and we lurch like a belch from the throat of the station.

Soon we're passing through Bishopsgate, through the brick and smoke and washing of the East End. Briefly, the Bryant & May factory tower appears, exhaling phosphor into the flawless June sky.

The sun shines straight through the glass on to my face as we travel east. Stratford, Forest Gate . . . The fabric on the seats is rough and scratchy. Ilford, Romford, Brentwood . . . The light is making me sleepy. Joggled by the train, my eyes droop closed over an industrial landscape.

I awake with a start, for a reason I can only

47

guess at. It's warmer now. I lean forward to shove the window down and stop in surprise. The warehouses and grey, stilted roads are gone. Instead there are fields, stretching green and yellow to either side. London is all behind. I've spent my whole life within a bus ride of its smog; never left the city on my own. There, I'm Bill Perch, solicitor's assistant, but where I'm going, I'll be a stranger. It's an odd thought.

The compartment grows hotter as the day gets going. I wish I was wearing a T-shirt. I can just imagine Mum's face. She still thinks that wearing them in public is shameful. My mouth is gluey with thirst. I should have bought something to drink, but all I have is the fudge and that only makes my tongue more claggy.

★   ★   ★

At Norwich there's a station café, full of passengers fanning themselves, rail workers with their overalls tied around their waists. I buy a lemonade and it's warm and sugary but washes the dryness from my throat.

The train to Sheringham is tiny: one open carriage filled with lumpy bench seats. It's painted green and crawls like a caterpillar through banks of dry grass. It's flat here, so flat that the sky looms pale and parched over everything. I'm the only passenger, except for a few old ladies. At last, the brakes squeal on the hot metal track and we drift to a standstill. SHERINGHAM, says the sign, above a narrow platform. A few children hang over the barrier gate to gawp at the train. End of the line. End of the bloody world, it feels like.

I try to shake off the torpor of the journey and hurry after the driver, struggling with my luggage and briefcase. He's abandoned his train and is making a bee-line for the ice-cream van that's parked on the corner.

'Excuse me,' I gasp out at his shoulder, 'do you know how I can get to Saltedge from here?'

The driver squints at me, as if I've just asked him to recite Pythagoras' theorem. His waistcoat is hanging open, hat and jacket missing. He takes out a handkerchief, wipes his face and drapes it over his bald head.

'Saltedge?'

'Yes.'

He nods slowly and starts fishing in his pockets for change.

'I'd say y'ent above a walk, down that way.' He jerks his head. 'Train used to come all the way to Saltedge at that time of day, but it were mostly for Hallerton. Course there e'nt no point now.'

His accent is broad, all strange-sounding vowels. I hope I've understood.

'Hallerton, as in Hallerton House?'

'Zackly.'

'And it's not far?'

I feel like I'm melting in the sun. I'm tempted to spend more of the expenses on trying to find a bus, or even a taxi, to take me to Hallerton, but that seems extravagant for such a short trip.

He shakes his head. The damp handkerchief doesn't move, stuck to his scalp. 'Y'ent far.'

'All right, thank you.'

'Mind how you go, bor,' he drawls, returning to his contemplation of the ice-cream truck. My mouth waters at the thought of a strawberry split, or a lemon ice, but what if someone saw me? I'm a professional solicitor and solicitors don't eat ice-lollies.

The path isn't signposted. It runs across the train track and down the edge of a field. I set off, thinking explicit thoughts about cold lemonade and a cool bath. It's nearly two now, and the sun is hammering down, the air stifling. *Mad dogs and Englishmen*. I have to stop to remove my jacket and loosen my tie an inch. I'd roll up my sleeves, but I want to arrive looking like a businessman, not a holidaymaker.

Five minutes later, I come to the end of the field. Ahead, there's a track, gravelly and dusty and barely wide enough for a car. Still no signs. It can't be much further. I switch my suitcase into the other hand and plod on.

Every time I look up from my feet I expect to see buildings, houses and a sign declaring 'Welcome to Saltedge!' but there's nothing. No fields even, only an expanse of cracked mud with clumps of reeds. Is that buzzing noise the sound of insects, or the blood pulsing through my head?

I wipe my face with my tie. My shirt has turned translucent, plastered to my back, and I'm sure that if I took my vest off I could wring it out. Have I taken a wrong turn? Why the hell did I listen to the train driver? He's probably having a good laugh with his friend the ice-cream man, about how he sent the idiot from the city off on a wild-goose chase. He's probably on his third orange Mivvi.

I stop dead. Ahead is a crossroad. The same pitted track. I look around for a sign, a road name, *anything*, but there's nothing. I want to cry with frustration, and almost do, until I hear a different sound, a juddering rumble, growing louder by the second.

I barely have time to leap into the hedgerow as a filthy green monster rackets round the corner and bounces to a halt, showering me with grit. As I cough through the dust, a woman's head appears out the driver's window. At least, I think it's a woman. Her hair is long, sun-bleached and tangled, her face is tanned, not a scrap of make-up. She's staring at me, smiling as the dilapidated Citroen 2CV wheels slowly backwards. There's a strong smell of petrol and burnt rubber.

'Hey,' she says.

I croak out a 'what?' but am reminded of the sticky bus child and turn it into a 'pardon?'

The woman doesn't seem fazed. She looks cool — in both senses — in a thin T-shirt of some indeterminate colour. A leather necklace dangles to her chest. She looks older than me, by about ten years.

'Hey,' she repeats. 'Sorry I missed you, man, didn't realize the time. Jump in.'

What would my mother say? No doubt she'd whisper about drugs and the danger of taking lifts from hippies.

'I'm OK walking,' I tell her haltingly. 'I'm only

51

going to Saltedge. The train driver at Shering-ham said it wasn't far.'

The woman at the wheel snorts and leans an elbow on the sill.

'Not far if you're a train. It's about two miles, down this way.'

I stare at the arid farm track, swimming with heat.

'Oh.' Her previous words finally trudge into my brain. 'What do you mean, you missed me?'

'At the station. Was supposed to pick you up, two o'clock sharp, give you the keys to the place. Dicky fixed it. I mean *Mr* Hillbrand.' She's grinning.

I can't help but smile in return. 'He didn't tell me.'

'Just like him. So you want to jump in? Frying out there.'

She shunts open the passenger door. I twist to put my suitcase in the back seat. There's barely room. The car is cluttered with boxes, gardening twine, bits of pipe, old newspapers. The briefcase I keep on my lap. It takes two attempts to slam the door closed behind me but the shade is an instant relief. Sitting down has never felt so good.

'All right,' breathes the woman to herself, and the car jolts forward again. Soon, we're rushing down the country lane, the wind streaming through the open windows. Hippy or no, I'm swamped with gratitude.

'How do you know Mr Hillbrand?' I yell over the clattering of the car.

'He's my cousin,' the woman yells back, 'once

removed or something. Haven't seen him for years.'

The thought of this woman and Hillbrand being in the same room, let alone the same family, is almost too much to comprehend. No wonder he didn't mention her.

'I'm Bill,' I remember to say, 'Bill Perch.'

'Yeah, I know.' She grins. 'I'm Jem Durrant.'

24th February 1919, Hallerton

Someone from the village told Andrew they saw me on the dunes, near the sea. Although I said that I was only walking, that there was no harm in it, he has made me promise not to go out alone any more. Sometimes I think all he does is frown and ask me how I am feeling. How can I tell him that there are times when I feel like my mind is not my own . . . ?

Of course, I cannot. I can see his face now, horrified, looking at me like I am a stranger rather than his niece. He tells me that I am overtired, that I should rest. He doesn't know that the only time I sleep is when I take a few drops of the morphine that Dr Lewis left for Mother. She could not swallow by then, so there is almost a full bottle. I have hidden it beneath my pillow and am grateful for it.

Andrew has invited guests for dinner. To what end I wasn't sure at first, until I heard him on the telephone, describing the house, the grounds, the proximity to sea and rail. He found me shortly afterwards, in the boiler room with Edith, both of us with our sleeves rolled up, shovelling coal into the furnace to try to make it work. I will admit I was shovelling with greater fervour than necessary, I dug the spade furiously into the coal. Andrew wanted to talk. I did not.

'Emeline,' he said eventually, over the scrape of metal and the roar of the flames, 'come up to the study, please.'

I heaved in one spadeful, then another, my back muscles cramping and protesting until I heard him leave. Edith laid a hand upon my arm.

'Go on, miss,' she told me, 'there y'ent much left to do here.'

Andrew was seated behind the desk. Why did my jaw clench to see him there? He told me that some of his acquaintances would be coming for dinner, the day after tomorrow. They are all in a position to purchase property and have expressed an interest in Hallerton.

'So soon?' I could not help but ask it.

'It's as we agreed. A swift, private sale to a trusted party will be in your best interests. That way, we may be discreet about your financial situation, in the event of . . . ' He trailed off, fingers shuffling through the papers before him.

'Of?'

'You are out in society now, and with no one to . . . no other companionship, I wondered if you had thought about marrying. The sale of Hallerton will provide you with financial security for a time — '

Beyond the window, movement caught my attention. A crow was limping around the lawn, looking for all the world like a jaunty ne'er-do-well with his hands in his pockets. When I was a child I used to leave them things, the crows; bits of coloured paper or ribbon. Once, I left them a tin ballerina. They took her too. I liked to imagine her, leaving the playroom behind, soaring into the trees in the safety of their claws, up into the clouds and on, to the secret places only the birds knew.

Silence brought me back into the study. The lawn was empty, and I found that I was staring instead at my reflection, a thin face, ghost-pale and streaked with coal dust, hair loose and tangled. Andrew was looking at me in that desperate way, the same way Durrant had.

'You are right about the dinner, I am sure.' I tried to summon words that made sense. 'How many are we to host?'

His pause made me realize that I had missed something, something important, but there was no help for it.

'Four,' he said eventually, 'Mr Thorpe and Mr Granson from London, they are both in business in the city. Captain Johnson from Harwich and Mr Rossiter, who has concerns in the North. I was saying, I thought you might like to cook us a little supper, the way you used to. But if you do not feel strong enough then it is no matter.'

Andrew was watching closely, watching for weaknesses. A dinner could be my chance to prove that there is nothing wrong with me; that he can trust me to look after Timothy, to run Hallerton. I gave him my best smile and told him that I thought it was an excellent idea.

'Do you think quail might suit?' I asked him. 'And fish to start? There are eggs in the pantry for a dessert, but I do not know about sugar.'

'Emeline,' he took my hands in his, black with

56

coal dust as they were, 'should I call for the doctor? You do not seem well.'

I told him that I was fine. He spoke again, but all I could think about was the bottle of morphine, cold beneath my pillow. I do not think he suspected me, even though I almost ran up the stairs. Timothy called to me from the playroom as I passed, but I didn't stop. My hands were shaking so much I was barely able to lock my bedroom door. My breath was too quick, too hard, but the little bottle was there. I upended it over a glass of water, more drops than usual.

I have slept, half the day since then. It is dusk as I write this. The bottle stands, un-stoppered, next to me. Timothy will be wondering where I am.

June 1969

'Sure you don't want to go straight to the village? You look dead beat.'

Jem holds the wheel loosely with one hand, green stains embedded in the grooves of her nails and knuckles.

'Thanks,' I tell her, feeling awkward and stuffy in my sweat-soaked polyester. 'I'd prefer to make a start at Hallerton. We're on a deadline, you see.'

'All right,' she says easily, turning into a narrow opening with brambles encroaching on either side. A pair of oak trees dapple the light as the tyres crunch on what was once gravel, now thick with weeds. The shade deepens as a building looms before us.

'Here we are,' Jem says, slowing to a halt. 'Hallerton House.'

The pale stonework is streaked and dark with mildew, crumbling at the sills. Most of the windows have been boarded up and the glass in the others is cracked or broken. Part of the roof is missing; a small tree has sprouted between bare rafters. The only thing that looks new is the door, heavy, plain wood with a brassy keyhole. When Hillbrand called this place a dump, I thought he was exaggerating. I thought it would look the way it does in the photograph, shabby yet elegant. I didn't expect this.

'What happened?' I murmur.

Jem leans her chin on the steering wheel, looking up.

'Time,' she says, not quite so cheerfully. 'And neglect. This is what happens when people leave. Give it ten years and the trees will have the whole place down.'

It'll come down sooner than that, if Mrs Mallory has her way. I try to imagine the place as a holiday camp: no house, just row upon row of chalets, a packed swimming pool, sun-loungers and music blaring and the smell of hot sugar. Now, it's utterly quiet. The glaring heat of the afternoon is held at bay.

'You're really going in there?' Jem says, making a face.

'Yes.' I try to sound firm, businesslike. 'I've got work to do.'

She slides down in her seat until she can reach into the pocket of her denim shorts. Her legs are as tanned as her face, shins scratched and scuffed all over, right down to her feet, in their open sandals. There's a ring on one of her toes. I try not to stare.

'Here.' She drops a pair of keys into my hand. 'That one opens the front door, that one's for the study. All the other doors are bolted from the inside.'

The splutter of the engine breaks the quiet.

'I'll come back for you in a few hours,' Jem shouts through the window, over the noise. 'There's a path to the village at the end of the garden, but it runs next to the marsh, not a good idea if you don't know your way.'

'Thanks,' I call after the car, but she's already

wheeling around. She winks in return and then she's gone, the mud-spattered back bumper disappearing around the corner. Gradually, the noise of the engine disappears into the distance, the scent of petrol fading from the air.

Alone at Hallerton. For one unnerving moment I'm convinced that this whole bizarre day has been a dream, that any second I'll wake up in my narrow bed, the London suburbs outside the window.

I can *feel* the house. It's as if something is watching me from behind the shattered glass, from within the stones that have sucked at the seasons. Something that wonders why I'm here, waiting to see if I have the nerve to enter . . .

I shrug away the prickling at the back of my neck and march up the steps. It's just a house. An old dump of a house, like Hillbrand said. The front door is stiff. I have to shove it hard before it bursts open in a flood of stale air and a noise like frantic wings that is swallowed by the silence. I peer inside. Daylight needles its way through the boarded-up windows. I can make out a hallway, stretching off into the gloom, rooms opening to the left and right.

I leave the door open, for fresh air, I tell myself. In the first room, the floor is thick with dirt and leaves, with chunks of plaster that have fallen away from the ceiling. It must have been grand once. The windows are high, scraps of faded red fabric clinging to the curtain-rail above. The wallpaper has bubbled and peeled away, hanging down in great strips. My footsteps crunch across the floor, absurdly loud.

At the far end of the hall I come across a second closed door. It must be the study, the place where — according to Mrs Mallory — her father kept the old family papers. She told Hillbrand that it was the only room in decent repair, even though her father never came here more than once a year, to 'see to business'.

I try the handle but it rattles uselessly, shut tight. As I bend down to check the keyhole, the light within the room flickers with movement, a shadow crossing the doorway. Someone's inside.

For a second I'm frozen with uncertainty, but then I remember the keys. Hurriedly, I fit the second one to the lock. This time the handle turns. I shove the door wide.

A rushing of feathers, dark shapes leaping in alarm beyond the window. Crows. Only crows. I laugh with relief as they flap off down the garden from their perch on the sill, cawing outrage.

26th February 1919, Hallerton

Today I have cleaned and scrubbed and dusted, making the house ready for the dinner party. I want everything to be perfect, for Andrew to see that I am fit and well and able to run the place.

There is so much to do! We have not received dinner guests here for over a year. Edith and I started by polishing the silverware, whilst Andrew took Timothy to fetch the food, The list I gave them was almost a full page long, but I shall need it all if I am to impress. It is not only a question of hospitality; it is my claim to Hallerton.

When they returned, they were laden down with food. The war must truly be over if fresh meat, butter and sugar are so readily available again. Timothy was beaming from ear to ear. He had been bought a chocolate bar, for being a good boy, and ran to share a piece with me.

This afternoon I laughed for the first time in months, as I hoisted Timothy on to my shoulders, so he could dust the pictures in the dining room. Every so often, one of his swipes would send fragments of plaster raining down on to our heads, but he only laughed and spluttered and swiped again. Andrew found us there, giggling, He frowned as though I was doing something wrong, but he said nothing. He only peered critically at the walls, stained with damp, at the mildew on the window frames, the old red curtains, bleached by the sun.

'We'll keep the lights low,' he said. 'The less they can see of this, the better.'

I think I hated him then. I know this house as well as my own skin. I know its imperfections, its creaking floors and uneven walls, as well as one might know the signs of a hard life on a person's face; weathered but beloved, nonetheless.

My anger did not last long. It soon faded into sadness. Timothy does not yet know why Uncle Andrew has invited men for dinner. He does not know that I am preparing to sell his past from under him. Andrew says that he will understand, one day. I am not so sure.

In the kitchen the food was waiting, spread out on the big table. It has always been my favourite room, the kitchen; when I was a child it was like a fantastical bazaar. The deliverymen would bring crates of oranges and lemons from far away, chocolate from London and wine from Paris. Fishermen from the village would sell us gleaming fish, cold from the North Sea, the dairy would bring churns of cream and freshly made butter, local farmers would bring jars of honey thick with the scent of wild gorse and heather . . .

Sometimes, Freddie and Albie would raid the pantry. Once they made me steal a jar of caviar, to see what all the fuss was about. I remember the three of us, scooping it out with our fingers and grimacing at the taste. The stable cats enjoyed it, even if we did not.

When they were away at school I went to the kitchen on my own. The maids would give me offcuts of pastry to play with, would laugh as I sucked the sugar from sour pink rhubarb in spring or made a mess of myself with ripe berries in summer. They made wonderful things then, especially when my mother had friends to tea, Plump cornucopias, piped full of cream and jam, just begging to be squashed between the teeth. Strawberry turnovers, with pastry that crumbled to nothing. Towering blancmanges that emerged like magic from the copper moulds, before being bedecked with candied flowers, with borage and honeysuckle and roses collected from the gardens, every petal sparkling with sugar.

In the heat of summer there were ices, and the maids would sweat and toil, filling the freezing machine with ice and rock salt and turning and turning the handle until the custardy mixture turned firm and blissfully cold. They'd let me scoop a little straight from the pail, before they buried it in ice or took it away to be sculpted.

Sometimes, Cook herself would let me sit on the work surface beside her so I could watch the dance of activity across the kitchen, surrounded by the smell of baking bread and roasting meat and boiling fruit. She knew full well that my governess would be in a rage when she found me there, but she never cared. She told me that the kitchen was the beating heart of a house, and that if I could appreciate that, I was welcome.

One by one, we had to let the staff go. The deliveries became smaller, then stopped altogether. The maids departed for other work.

Finally Cook was the only one left. She stayed as long as she was able. Now, it is quiet. No movement, no steamed-up windows or clanging pans. Now, it comes down to me. If this kitchen is the heart of the house, I am the blood and must make it beat again.

★ ★ ★

So, I have sliced and simmered and whisked and hoped. Before the war, a lifetime ago, I begged Mother to send me to cooking classes in Norwich. They were not exactly what I hoped, taught by a tight-lipped woman who thought that ladies should know how to manage a kitchen, rather than cook in one. But I learned some basic skills there and have tried to remember them.

I have cooked Dover sole fillets in a sauce made from herbs and butter and lemon. Guinea fowl roasted in a pot with red wine and chestnuts, parsnips baked with honey. A dessert made from rhubarb stewed in Madeira, custard flavoured with golden saffron.

I was so occupied that I did not hear Edith come into the kitchen. When I finally noticed her, I saw that she was smiling, her pale blue eyes losing the look of concern they so often wore these days. She said she was glad to see me happy. I did not wish to correct her.

Eventually, she shooed me off to dress for dinner. Andrew caught up with me in the hall, asked me to fetch out Father's best crystal glasses. There are six of them, paper-thin, engraved with a pattern of leaves and the letter 'V', Father once told me they were brought back to Hallerton from Venice over two hundred years ago, by a great-great-uncle who was a sea captain, He only ever used them on the rarest of occasions, I would have left them where they were, but I want Andrew to think well of me, so I smiled and did as he asked.

I have put on the dress that Mother bought for my coming-out season a year ago, kingfisher-blue tulle. I have never worn it, We received the news of Albie's death the day before we were due to go to London, He had been granted leave, was supposed to be joining us there to toast my birthday. We were still devastated, all of us, by the loss of Freddie, but I believe my mother was trying to hold herself together, for Albie's sake. After he died, she did not have the strength any more.

The dress is too loose now. It made me look like a child, masquerading in adult clothes, which would not do.

I have not been into Mother's room since the day they took her away. I couldn't help lingering at her dressing table, where she used to brush my hair. I took a string of pearls from her drawer, a pair of matching drops for my ears. I suppose we shall have to sell her jewellery, to pay our debts. But not tonight.

Timothy made a face when I called at his room to say goodnight just now. He is not used to seeing me dressed like this. He clung to my neck when I kissed his forehead.

'You smell like Mama,' he whispered, and I

held him all the tighter. Her perfume still lingers on these pearls, the scent released as they warm against my skin. The loss of her hit me with such force when he said that, it was all I could do to stand, I had to come back here, to try to calm myself by writing, My hands are still shaking, and I fear an attack will come upon me, but our guests are due at any minute. I must be strong, I must show Andrew that he can trust me with my own future.

I will take a drop or two of the morphine, to compose myself. The bottle is small enough to fit into my pocket. I hope it will see me through the evening.

June 1969

The hot afternoon is sliding over the edge of evening by the time I look out of the study window, sweat-stained and dusty. A 'load of family papers', Hillbrand said. I was expecting a filing cabinet, maybe an archive box or two. But it isn't a load; it's a *mountain*.

Decaying boxes fill the room from floor to ceiling, shoved into corners, jammed on to shelves alongside yellowing ledgers. Some of the boxes split when I move them, the seams crumbling to dust and spilling an avalanche of papers. There are receipts and bills and stock certificates, letters and notes and contracts, some of them over a hundred years old. Even a quick glance tells me that they're a mess. A couple of newer archive boxes sit on a sideboard; they must belong to Mrs Mallory's father. They mostly contain letters from the local council written over the past ten years, a couple of invoices from builders and locksmiths.

I scoop another handful of papers from a teetering pile. Is this Hillbrand's idea of a joke? It'll take me days to even begin looking through all of this, let alone to find anything useful. Why bother to send me out here, to the middle of nowhere, on the vague possibility there might be some clue about the fate of a long-dead aunt? He must be desperate.

No, a dry voice at the back of my mind tells

me, picturing expensive tailoring, guarded expressions, perfectly lacquered hair; *they must be desperate.*

Grimly, I roll up my sleeves and drag out another box, trying not to inhale dust and dead flies. Everyone starts somewhere, I tell myself, picturing that first, fat solicitor's cheque. It'll all be worth it.

An hour later and I uncover a rickety chair from beneath the boxes, the leather seat cracked and crumbling. I lower myself into it with a sigh. As soon as I stop moving the silence returns, slowly at first and then in a rush, sweeping down from the empty rooms, making my ears hum. I must be the only living and breathing human for miles. The hairs stand up on my arms. I rub them back down.

To be doing something, I tug at one of the desk drawers. It sticks and has to be wiggled open. Inside, it's the same story. Hundreds of loose sheets, some clipped together, others crumpled at the edges. A page is stuck between the drawer and the wood. I tug it free, ripping the top corner. Sod's law it'll be something important.

I straighten it out. It looks like a bill, hastily scribbled on paper torn from a pad, the name DR B. LEWIS and an address in Saltedge printed at the top of the page. It's for a visit, for medicine of some kind, dated February 1919.

A flash at the window makes me jump. One of the crows again. I don't think they know what to make of my presence. They keep coming to eye me and strut about on the sill and eye me again.

Maybe they've worked out that humans mean food. Even London pigeons know that and these crows look a lot brighter. I should bring them some bread tomorrow.

Abruptly, the crow takes off. For a moment the window is empty, but then I realize that I am being watched. Eyes are looking back at me from the glass. A woman, her hair hanging loose, the skin of her face streaked with something dark . . .

★ ★ ★

'You sure you're all right?' Jem asks as I slide into the passenger seat. 'Thought I'd killed you for a second there.'

'I'm fine.' I rub at my neck. 'You just surprised me.'

Jem snorts and turns the key in the ignition. It takes three attempts to start.

'Sorry, man, should've thought. I'd be jumpy as hell after being in that place on my own too.'

We jolt away from Hallerton, down the shadowed path and on to the road. The warm evening flows over the car like syrup. I take a breath of it, petrol and hot tarmac and drying grass. It all seems so alive.

'It's just a house,' I say, trying to sound relaxed, 'and I'll have to get used to it. I'm going to be spending a lot of time there over the next few days.'

'That bad, huh?'

There's a smear of dirt down one of her cheeks. I wonder if she knows about it.

70

Something tells me that she wouldn't much care if she did. She smiles and I feel like someone's cut a rubber band from around my chest.

'You wouldn't believe it,' I tell her, 'it is *chaos*. This whole thing might be a waste of time, but I have to look.'

'For what?'

'For — ' I pull myself up short. I'm tired and starving and my brain feels like it's been through a mincer. 'I, um, I'm not sure I'm meant to say. Client confidentiality and that.'

Jem shrugs. 'Whatever. But it's about Emeline, right?'

The question takes me by surprise. Should I admit it? Feign ignorance?

'What do you mean?'

'You're the first person who isn't a handyman to be given the keys to that place in *years*,' she says. 'The only one who ever comes here is old Mr Vane, and the only reason he comes at all is to check the place hasn't fallen down. He hasn't lived there for decades. In the village they say it's because his wife divorced him and took their kids to America, and he couldn't stand to be there alone. But he's never sold. Because of Emeline, right?'

I gape. She's scratching absently at the mud on her cheek.

'How do you know all that?'

'The whole town knows it, Perch. This isn't London. If you fart, someone has something to say about it.'

'In that case, do you think there might be someone I can talk to, for a testimonial or

71

something? I'm going to need all the help I can get.'

We turn a corner and I see buildings, crooked houses and cottages around a tiny village green. I guess this is Saltedge. The heat of the day lingers, but here at least there's a breeze. It smells strange, like the muddy banks of the Thames and the sea all at the same time.

Jem swings to a halt outside the village pub. *The World's End*, declares the faded sign. She turns off the engine, but makes no attempt to move, tapping her fingers against the warm, bug-spattered metal of the door. I think she's forgotten my last question until she half-turns her head.

'Asking people here about Emeline isn't such a good idea.'

'Why not?'

She twists her lips into what isn't quite a smile.

'Small places like this, they tend to hoard their memories. Pass them down, generation to generation like bloody heirlooms. And every year, they embellish them a little more. Sometimes it's hard to tell where the truth begins and the exaggeration ends. Especially when the story is as dramatic as Emeline's.'

I scrub at my eyes, stinging with dust and tiredness.

'Look, I don't understand why everyone is making such a fuss about this woman. Old people lose their marbles all the time, what's so dramatic about that?'

Jem looks across at me. In the deepening

shadows of the car, I can't make out her expression.

'Emeline wasn't old,' she says slowly, 'that's what was so awful, she was only nineteen or twenty when she disappeared. And as for losing her marbles . . . ' She squints out through the smeared windscreen at nothing in particular. 'I don't know. People here will tell you that she was mad, that she couldn't cope after her brothers were killed and her mother died. They'll tell you that she tried to hurt herself, more than once, and that in the end, she probably succeeded.'

26th February 1919, Hallerton

I did not mean to. I swear I did not mean to. Can hardly hold a pen now but they won't talk to me, won't let me tell them it was an accident so must write it down here. Words are swimming. Must try — concentrate on the letters and stay calm. One at a time.

Dinner was going well. Captain from Harwich ate enough for six people. Smiled at me with his eyes that had seen so many oceans, and I almost begged him to take me away when he sailed; set me at the front of his ship until my skin turned to wood.

But the captain is retired now. Talked about the Navy, and Thorpe and Granson about London, Rossiter looking my way — a thirsty man at a public house — asked my accomplishments.

Such a meaningless question, Andrew answered for me, said I sang and spoke French and was fond of cooking, as they could see. He was speaking of a stranger. Once, someone with my name had done those things, but she was as lost as if I had drowned her on the marsh.

Could not eat. Edith saw, took my full plate without anyone noticing. Sometimes I think she is the only one who understands. She lost her son, Jeremy. He was our delivery boy. He used to share his apple with me.

Dessert served, Andrew nodded in approval. Thought my plan was working. I could not eat that either, refilled my glass instead. Wine pale as elderflower. I drank it, poured more and drank again.

They rose to go to the study, talk business. I rose too. Their business was Hallerton and Hallerton is mine, and Timothy's. Andrew stopped me. He looked alarmed, asked in a hushed tone what I was doing, said I didn't know my place. Do not remember what I said. The gentlemen were watching from the door so he relented, said I might join them if I behaved like a lady, served the port in Father's glasses.

The pain is dreadful, hot and smarting. Wish I could rip off the bandages, plunge my hands into the pitcher — must be brief, can barely form letters.

Glasses in the kitchen, Edith in the dining room. A mouthful from the bottle in my pocket, terribly bitter.

I pulled the cork from the port, angry with Andrew. Ruby liquid flowed into fragile glass, but then it was blood, dark and draining from a vein, from a hole no bigger than a coin in the stomach of a boy, pouring into mud, so much of it that his body must have been a husk, without all that liquid to fill it.

Next a scream, Edith's. Do not know how much time had passed, only wondered why she should scream about spilled port. Then, warmth against my palms, and weakness. I looked down at the glasses.

No glasses. Only broken shards on the tray, in my hands. No pain, just surprise. Blood on the tiled floor.

Faces, Andrew's, Rossiter's, dear Captain's, jolly no more. They carried! me, found the bottle in my pocket. Took it away. Perhaps doctor will give me more. He is coming soon. He must, I can tell him I did not mean it.

June 1969

Nineteen or twenty when she disappeared, Nineteen or twenty.

As tired as I am, I can't sleep. I don't know if it's the heat, or the strange place or the distant sound of the sea across the dunes, but even though I sparked out as soon as my head touched the pillow, now I'm wide awake.

A quarter to four in the morning, according to the clock beside the bed. Why should it bother me that Mrs Mallory's Aunt Emeline wasn't some doddery old lady who went a bit doolally? *Nineteen* . . . The same age as Stephanie and me.

It makes no difference. I'm going to go back to Hallerton as planned, dig up what I can to prove that Emeline is long dead, then leave. Even Jem implied that she probably killed herself years ago. The fact that she was my age doesn't change anything.

It changes everything, says a quiet voice at the back of my mind.

Resolutely, I shut my eyes and try to sleep. The pub is quiet. Unsurprising, seeing as I'm the only guest. Stan and Betty Throgmorton, the landlords, must be snoring somewhere. Stan seems all right, but Betty's eyes needled me from across the bar, and I heard her snort with disdain when I called Jem 'Miss Durrant'.

Four o'clock. I peek through the curtains. It's

not-quite dawn, the sky pigeon grey. Across the village green, movement catches my eye: an old man in an oilskin coat stepping out of a dilapidated cottage. A white cat slips out behind him, and he bends to scratch its ears. For one, bewildering instant, I want to be him, with a boat and a cat and the dawn on the sea to call my own.

God, I need sleep.

Four thirty. The room turns pale and the seagulls start up an almighty racket. No point in sleeping now. I wish I'd brought a book or something. There isn't even a radio in the room. Eventually I retrieve the file on Hallerton from the briefcase. It's a strange mix of old documents from Uncle Durrant's days and new ones from Mrs Mallory. Might as well do something useful and sort them out.

It makes for dull reading. There's the proposal from the holiday camp people, land reports and valuations and official correspondence. Behind that is a page of Hillbrand's notes from the meeting, deciphered and typed up by Jill. At the bottom, a line catches my eye: *E.V. last seen 27 February 1919.*

February twenty-seventh. Why does that date look so familiar? I'm sure I've seen it somewhere recently. In a desk drawer, on a crumpled bill, above the details of a doctor's visit . . . I'm sure of it. Or am I? I forgot about everything else when Jem scared the daylights out of me. What did I think I had seen, there at the window? Either way, I'm not going to find any answers lying in bed.

Five o'clock. I creep down the stairs and out of the pub. I should wait for Stan and Betty to be up, but there's something restless in my chest, clattering around. I think it's excitement.

Across the village green, a bakery is just opening. The smell of freshly baked bread is too much to resist. A couple of old ladies are gossiping by the door, but they fall silent as soon as I approach, hissing about 'the Vane girl' and 'the house'. I try to ignore them as I buy a couple of rolls.

Outside, I follow Jem's directions towards Hallerton. Away from the village, the land opens out. This must be the marsh. Clumps of reeds, froths of pink and yellow flowers. There's a flash, and a great white bird takes off, trailing toothpick legs towards the sea. I wonder if the old fisherman will watch it, from his gently rocking boat.

Eventually, the path disappears into a wilderness of green, a jungle of brambles and hedges that must once have formed the boundary of Hallerton. I wade through the tall grass of the garden, disturbing clouds of insects and startling the crows on the old terrace. They watch with their quick, black eyes as I take a seat on the steps.

Dad will be working through his kipper soon. Louise will be prodding at her bowl of cornflakes. They seem centuries away. Even the bread here tastes different: chewy and floury, nothing like the sliced white we have at home. The crows limp and loiter nearer, pretending they aren't interested. Smart buggers. I tear up the remaining roll and scatter it their way. They stab up the pieces and carry them off to who knows where.

In the morning light the house looks sad, softly decaying. The yellow stone around the doors and windows is crumbling and green with lichen, but once it must have glowed, radiating the heat of a summer's day. The creepers choking the walls must once have been climbing flowers, the wilderness of grass a lawn for games and picnics. All around, the trees echo with birdsong. Would Emeline Vane have heard the same songs, fifty years ago?

I pick my way through greenery around the side of the house. My neck doesn't prickle *quite* so much when I let myself in, but still I can't shake the feeling that I'm being watched. The study is as I left it, stuffy as ever. I loosen my tie, already reaching for the piece of paper that I left resting on top of the drawer. A crumpled bill, the handwriting smudged and hasty:

Dr B. Lewis
26th February 1919
Night call: 2/6
16 fl. oz. lithium bromide: 3/6
Two drams as needed

There was a visit from a doctor the night before Emeline went missing? I stare at the old paper, fragile in my fingers. *Rustle up something useful*, Hillbrand said, *like proof that this Miss Vane was barking*. Slowly, I smooth out the note and place it in the folder of papers, wondering why I feel so strange.

27th February 1919, Hallerton

Edith sleeping, so can write . . . Will have to hide this book. Pencil, almost blunt, Can't unscrew pen. Doctor gave me something, stronger than the morphine. Drags me down. Sand in a bottle.

Timothy cried. I remember that. Wish I did not. Wish we were playing. I held him tight but Edith came with the glass, made me let go.

I am not well, they tell me, Andrew, Dr Lewis. He bandaged my hands. Not well. Too much, Mother and Albie and Freddie and the house. I need rest, they say. Andrew found a place. On the continent, in the mountains. Name of a saint . . .

St Augustine's. Clean air and quiet and no more worry about Hallerton, Do not want to go. Must. What if I lose myself again? What if next time I can't stop, a step too far on the marsh?

Will go. Andrew says better soon, that Hallerton upsets me.

Nearly dawn. Today then. Edith will wake soon. Pour sand into a glass. It drowns me. Maybe better, maybe I

June 1969

By noon, the study is like a furnace. Sweat drips from my forehead on to the papers, the text blurring before my eyes. Finally, thirst forces me to explore the rest of the house. My tongue feels like a big, dry toad in my mouth. I'd give anything for a drink, even a pint of warm bitter from The Old Cow.

I wander through the rooms. Some are thick with plaster fragments, others are musty and blooming with fungus. At the back of the house I find the huge, old kitchen, all shattered tiles and corroded pipes. Once it must have been a hive of activity, but now it's silent. A shiver runs down my back. No wonder Mrs Mallory wants shot of this place.

There's a door to the outside, secured by a rusted bolt. Sunlight hits me as I step on to the terrace. I peel the shirt from my back and tie it around my waist. I find a tap on the wall and turn it hopefully. It chokes and hisses and clanks, until water explodes from the end. It's brown and cloudy at first, but soon clears.

I stick my wrists under the stream. It's cool, and I decide I don't care where it comes from. I gulp it straight from my cupped hands, until it fills my empty belly with an earthy, metallic chill. Distantly, I hear a church bell toll one o'clock. Jem said that if I gave her a crown for the week, she'd bring me lunch every day. It *must* be lunchtime soon. I'm just about to head back inside when I hear the crunch of tyres pulling on to the drive.

We sit on the terrace, in a patch of shade cast by a woody old lilac tree. The stones are cooler here, and belatedly I think of my suit trousers.

'Forget it,' Jem says as I try to brush grit from the fabric, 'there's no one here to look smart for. Be cool.'

She's abandoned her sandals and sunglasses, and is rooting through a canvas bag with quick, green-stained fingers.

'Here.' She flings something at me. I fumble a catch. A bottle of beer, the glass cold against my palm. I've never seen anything so enticing.

'I'm supposed to be working.'

'Too hot to work,' she says, opening her own, 'for a few hours at least.'

I don't need persuading. The beer is nothing like the ale or bitter I'm used to. It's light and fresh and sparkles down my throat. We sit in silence for a while, chewing through ham and tomato sandwiches the size of dinner plates, with only the high hissing of the leaves and the drone of the insect-filled garden for company. I think of Steph's radio, blaring out music over the fryer in the fish and chip shop. It'll be sizzling in there today.

I lean back on my elbows. The ghost of a breeze drifts past, stirring the greenery above. Drinking the last quarter of the beer, I start to relax. Jem produces a punnet of strawberries. They're rich and red and explode on my tongue like sherbet.

83

'These are delicious.'

'Thanks, man. Having a good crop this year.'

'You grew these?' It occurs to me that I don't know anything about Jem. Do hippies have jobs? I can't imagine her walking into an office, or a shop. 'Is that what you do?'

'Yeah, I guess.' She flicks the strawberry top off into the shrubbery. 'The fruit and veg are for fun. Most of the time I'm over at Heathwicke, doing the roses.'

I have no idea what she's talking about. She notices and smiles.

'Heathwicke's a country estate, inland a ways. Still lived in, unlike this place. The old man there is *crazy* about his roses. Won't let anyone touch them, except me.'

There's a note of pride in her voice. I try to imagine what it must be like, out under the sun all day, surrounded by flowers, no need for ties, or briefcases or lace-up shoes.

'Cool.'

She nods, opens another beer and passes it to me. I take a swig without thinking.

'How's your work?' she asks softly, as if someone might hear.

'All right.' I twist the bottle in my hands. 'I think I found something today, but I'm not sure ... Don't suppose you know what lithium bromide is?'

She takes a deep drink, pushes the beer around her mouth, thinking.

'You probably get it by mixing lithium carbonate with hydrobromic acid. Why?'

Not the answer I was expecting.

'I, er . . . The thing I found, it mentions lithium bromide, two drams.'

She's watching me now, alert. I wonder if I've said too much.

'Sounds like a prescription. They used to use it as a sedative, back in the day. Nasty stuff.'

Proof, Hillbrand wanted. Looks like I've found it. Despite the heat, a shiver runs through me as I wonder what could have happened to Emeline, to merit a night call from the doctor, strong sedatives.

Jem must see the change in my face. 'You still haven't told me why,' she says, frowning.

How much has Hillbrand told her about why I'm here? Does she know that it's my job to dig up dirt? To prove that Emeline Vane was out of her mind and leave Hallerton open for a quick sale, for the wrecking ball and a developer to scour its presence from the land? My cheeks are hot with shame. I realize that I don't want her to know.

'It's probably nothing.' I tip the bottle too far and spill beer down my chin. 'How do you know all that stuff anyway?' I say hastily, wiping it away. 'You sound like a scientist.'

Jem laughs, pulling a cloth pouch from her bag.

'Got a degree in biology. Half a degree, anyway. I was only interested in plants, but they made us do some chemistry. Speaking of which . . . ' She smiles over at me. In her lap, there's a small heap of dried green stuff, some rolling papers. 'You game?'

*   *   *

'What's Jem short for?' I watch the smoke drift into a parasol of leaves and branches. 'Is it gem, like a jewel? Short for Gemma?'

I can't see her face, lying on my back as I am, but I hear her laughter, warm and dry as hay.

'Jem, short for *Jemima*. Like the Puddle-Duck. Can you believe that?'

'Jemima Durrant,' I repeat, and laugh. My eyes are heavy. 'Have you always been here? In Saltedge?'

'Nah. Used to visit my granny here as a kid. Came back to look after her when she got ill a few years ago. She died last spring.'

The breeze plucks weakly at the hem of my trousers. Jem nudges my arm, the smoke between her fingers.

'Better not,' I mumble, 'work to do.'

I think about Hillbrand, cramming down an egg sandwich at his desk as the traffic exhausts itself on London's melting roads. I think of the expenses for my first business trip and all of a sudden I'm laughing, at the ridiculousness of it all, at Berni Inns and trouser presses when I'm here, flat on my back beneath a glorious blue sky, drinking and smoking with a hippy.

Jem's laughing too, and I realize that I've found a friend here, albeit an unlikely one. We laugh ourselves out, until all I can do is breathe in the scent of the summer afternoon: warm stone and lilac blossom, grass and pungent smoke and the distant earthiness of the marshes. I close my eyes and feel myself slip into a doze, watched over by the strange, silent house . . .

The sound of wings wakes me, frenzied beating. I lurch upright, breaking instantly into a sweat, but there's nothing. The terrace is absolutely motionless, and for a second, it's like the world has stopped altogether.

Gingerly, I turn my head. No Jem. No bag. How long have I been asleep? My head feels like it's filled with cotton wool. The sun smoulders, the leaves droop. Impossible to tell what time of day it is.

I'm reaching for my watch when there's a cry, ragged in the stillness. Two crows flap down on to the terrace, grease-black and ungainly. One of them has something in its beak that the other one wants. They caw and dance around each other, wings half extended. Someone else might laugh, watching them, but I don't. It wouldn't be right.

Whatever the crows are fighting over, it's small and thin and metallic. Shaped like a figure, maybe, edged with faded pink ... The second crow screams in protest as the first shoots into the air, still carrying its prize. It doesn't fly to the usual perch on the study window sill but banks sharply upward, fluttering into the house through a broken second-floor window. Maybe it has a nest inside.

I squint up at the remaining panes, green with mildew. The sun is shining into my eyes, making me aware of a slowly spreading headache. Thanks a lot, Jem. I should be getting back to work, but instead I stare, summoning up the will to move.

Behind me on the steps, the second crow makes an odd noise. As I turn to look, I could swear something flashes in the corner of my eye, movement, a hand at the glass, eyes staring down, a pale face streaked with something dark . . .

Jem, the logical part of my brain insists, but I know it isn't her; her car is gone. I'm the only living soul for miles. I peer closer and of course, the window is empty. Nevertheless, I find myself walking forwards, keeping my eyes on the glass. I don't know why, but I feel like something is pulling me on, a presence I felt from the first moment I set foot in Hallerton.

Inside, I can barely see for sun-blindness. I stop at the staircase, its wood-panelling falling into powder. Is there something up there? I could turn around now, go back to the study and get on with my work, shake off this strange impulse and put it down to too much sun and Jem's magic herbs. But I can't. A feeling in my gut tells me that up those stairs, something is waiting.

The first stair groans deeply but holds my weight, as does the next one, and the next. The decay isn't as bad up here. I can still make out the pattern on the wallpaper, the remains of a rug disintegrating on the floor. Somehow, that makes it worse. I listen, but all I can hear is the thundering of blood in my head, my own rapid breathing.

There's a long hallway lined with doors. Some of them have fallen in. It smells overwhelmingly of damp. I try to map where I am, which door belongs to the room over-looking the terrace. This one. Closed, of course, the jamb thick with leaves and grit. Through the crack, I see a shadow move across the light. *Crows*, I tell myself, *crows, crows*, and fling open the door.

A bird takes flight in panic, disappearing through the broken pane and out into the sunlit garden. The door rebounds from the wall, the noise booming through the entire house, until it settles with the faint cracking of plaster.

The room is empty. Why would it be anything else? There's no furniture, just debris from the broken window, a built-in wardrobe, its interior hollow. Then I see it, a mess of twigs and leaves scattered around the empty fireplace.

Every step is deafening as I crunch across the floor. I'm not sure if it's a bird's nest or a hoard: bottle caps and bits of coloured plastic, a bead, a shred of shiny foil, a twist of green fishing net, and there, dropped in the centre, the piece of metal the crow carried off.

It looks like a child's tin figure, a ballerina, pitted and scratched by beaks and claws. I prod it with my finger and see a flash of a painted eye as it clatters on its side and slips beneath a broken board.

I should leave it, should pull myself together, button my shirt and go back to the study and the documents. Documents, for a client. That's all this job is. Nothing more.

But I can't. The crows will look in accusingly from the window sill, angry that I've lost one of their treasures. The board's falling apart anyway.

Sighing at myself, I kneel down and work my fingers under the splintered wood. When did I start shaking? Jesus, Perch, you should be on the first train back to London.

The board comes away easily. I try not to disturb any more of the crows' collection as I lift it free. Beneath, in a blanket of old dust and bird mess is the figure. Disgusting, but it serves me right. As I reach in, my fingers scrape on something hard and leathery. It's as though all of my caution has been exhausted, because I pull the object free without a second thought.

A book. The pages are wrinkled and bird droppings have stained the leather cover, but apart from that it looks sound. It's secured with a ribbon, made colourless by time. I pick at the knot but it comes away in my hand, the book falling open to where a pencil has been wedged inside.

It looks like a diary; the handwriting is clumsy, finishing mid-sentence. *Maybe better*, it says, *maybe I*

I flick to the front to look for a name, and there, written neatly in ink are two words that I know are going to change everything: *Emeline Vane*.

Part Two

May 1919

The sea was quiet, the waves gentle as the breaths of untroubled sleep. He moved carefully over the sand and shingle, gently untying one of the boats, pushing it inch by inch towards the sea. For someone who lived in a soundless landscape, he made little noise. It still surprised me even now, weeks after we had first slipped away together on the night of the party.

Above, the moon shone, like silver warmed against skin, just enough to see by. The water was cool and the sand gave under my feet as I waded out to meet him, my skirt dragging heavy behind me, until we were face to face, just us and a boat and the night to call our own.

Somewhere past the end of the cliff he stopped rowing, put the oars up and let us drift, tiny as a leaf on the dark water. The moonlight caught upon the ripples and scattered, until it seemed we were floating through stars. As the town disappeared behind the rocky headland, he pointed. There, in a fold of the cliff I saw branches against the sky, a hidden plateau and a lone cherry tree, our only witness.

The current took us further, around the curve of the coast. If I could have made time stop altogether, it would have been then, as we sat, knee to knee in that tiny boat. But eventually, he picked up the oars and began to row to shore. We were heading for a cove; a tiny crescent of sand that mimicked the moon's shape, sheltered by dark cliffs, unreachable, any way but ours.

I helped to pull the boat into the shallows. I felt strong as I waded ashore, uncaring of the seawater that soaked my clothes. Impulsively, I reached behind me and unbuttoned my skirt, stepping out of the sodden fabric. My blouse was wet too. I peeled it from my skin and dropped it to the sand, followed by my petticoat and chemise. The night air swept across my bare skin and I stretched out my arms in the pale moonlight. He looked up at me and I laughed at his expression, before running headlong into the shallows.

The seawater ran from his hair, his skin and on to mine, into my mouth, richer than tears. His arms held me, weightless in the water, and I thought I would never get enough. But finally, breathless and chilled, we made for the beach. He lit the fire, and we spread our clothes around it to dry.

Wrapped in a blanket, I watched him unpack the basket he had brought. He took from it a leaf-wrapped bundle, a tiny jar of golden honey, a handful of almonds, a flask of sweet wine. The firelight flickered over his hands as he worked and I felt desire rising in me again; not just for him but for everything he was, everything that made him, that surrounded us here.

He must have sensed what I was thinking, for he glanced up at me and quirked an eyebrow, before sitting back from his preparations. The leaf-wrapped bundle contained cheese, I saw, so pale and white and soft that it was almost cream.

In the light of the fire, the honey looked like liquid amber, pieces of comb crystallized in its depths. I sat by, spellbound, as he poured it from the jar. It pooled stickily on to the leaves, and the almonds he scattered, warm from the fire's edge, sank slowly into its sweetness.

No need for hesitation or manners, I leaned forward and scooped up a mouthful with my fingers. The honey met my lips first, luxurious, heady and perfumed with orange blossom. Next, smooth, cool creaminess, then a single toasted almond, bringing warmth. I didn't know that I had closed my eyes until I blinked them open, the mouthful finished.

He was smiling back at me. He had given me the elements of the world, I realized: salt, bitter, sour, sweet and something else, something indefinable that dwelt in the head and the heart as well as on the tongue, like a certain spice that couldn't be named, but was nonetheless there, waiting to be tasted.

February 1919

'Mademoiselle?'

I blinked through the fine veil that covered my face. Outside, the light from a gas lamp formed a halo in the fog. Beads of moisture clung to its ironwork like a cold sweat. Odours swirled around me: coal and petroleum, horse dung and river water. A teasing wisp of cigarette smoke and perfume.

We were in Paris.

'Mademoiselle?' the man repeated, and I tried to make out his face. A stranger, a taxi-cab driver. I faltered, but Uncle Andrew was by my side, urging me out of my seat.

Paris. Despite everything, I felt an old thrill of excitement. I had come here once with Mother, to visit some friends of hers. It had been spring, the public gardens full of early flowers. I remember eating patisserie in an elegant café. It was like something from an enchantment; delicate confections that tasted of flowers, sugar spun into silk.

A motor car honked, startling me out of my memories. The fog had settled on my face and I shuddered, but Andrew took hold of my arm. It seemed like a hundred years since we had left England, though it could only have been that morning. A train to London before it was light. A boat, but no memory of the crossing. Andrew had given me a sedative to drink at the dock.

The pavements were teeming: porters, towers of trunks, ladies in furs, groups of dark-coated men. A row of weather-beaten sheds had been painted with the words BUREAU MILITAIRE. A woman surged up from the ground into our path, raising her hands to my face. When I only stared in shock, she sank back into a pile of cloth-wrapped bundles where a child held a baby, inert with cold.

Andrew pulled me aside.

'Refugees,' he muttered, 'don't look. If you help one, the others will see, then we shall never get away.'

'Away?' My thoughts were a hopeless jumble. 'Where?'

'To St Augustine's.' There was a strained patience in his voice. It was not the first time I had asked that question, I realized with a creeping horror, perhaps not even the second or the third. 'The place my doctor recommended. In Switzerland, in the mountains, remember? Where you can rest.' We reached a set of wide doors. 'See?' he said gently. 'We are at the Gare de Lyon. This is where you will take the train.'

I did not want to walk through. Beyond I could see bodies moving, hundreds of them, like a maelstrom. I tightened my fingers on his sleeve.

'You aren't coming with me?'

'No, Emeline. I told you this morning, I must return to London, to make the sale of Hallerton. A woman from St Augustine's will take you the rest of the way.'

The medicine was loosening its hold on me. I felt myself frown.

'The sale? Without me — '

'If there are papers to sign I shall send them on to you, of course. Do not worry about that.' He stopped and made a noise of frustration in his throat. 'How are we supposed to find the right platform? This whole damn place is chaos.'

Despite the late hour, the station was crowded with people, children crying and families trying to stay together. Their shouts echoed back from the glass panes of the roof, high above. The feeble electric lights were losing their battle with the winter darkness, the smoke and the soot.

Finally, Andrew spotted the platform. I clung to his arm. If I let go, I would be swept away and lost in the crowd. Part of me was tempted to do just that; disappear completely. It must have been the part of me that was unwell. I clung all the harder.

The train was painted black, heavy cloth nailed at the windows to keep all light out. One pale lamp illuminated the compartment, which was as stale and airless as a coffin. Andrew placed my valise on the seat, helped me to remove my fur cape so that I did not overheat, talking of how this train would take me to Dijon, and thence through a tunnel into Switzerland, and that by morning I would wake to sunlight and clean air and the mountains.

The veil that covered my face stirred softly with my breathing. Eventually, Andrew knelt into my eye-line.

'Emeline.' He lifted one of my bandaged hands in both of his. 'My dear, this is for the best. The people at St Augustine's will know how to care for you. You do believe me?'

He was waiting for something. A response. I forced myself to nod, my head heavy on my neck. He looked relieved.

'That's my girl. Now, your escort should be here soon. Will you take something to calm you for the journey?'

His hands were already busy with the travelling case, taking out the flask, the cup and the bottle. I watched the sands as they fell, as he swirled the water to dissolve them. Were they the same ones that lined the river of the dead? Had my brothers crossed that shore, leaving no prints? Had my mother followed? I felt a tear slide free from beneath my lashes. I took the cup when Andrew offered it, and drank and, waited for forgetfulness.

After a time, someone called Andrew's name. I turned my eyes to the ground. A woman stood on the platform, in a starched white cap and a black coat. Beneath, she wore a uniform, like a nurse. She looked back at me, her smile like a thin scrape of butter.

'Emeline,' Uncle Andrew told me, looking relieved, 'this is Madame Bovard. She will accompany you to St Augustine's.'

The woman nodded, said in broken English that she was pleased to meet me. I could not think of anything to say, but my silence didn't seem to trouble her. I let my head fall back against the cushions. I could feel the medicine sweeping up behind me, like a grey tide. Let it hurry, I thought.

A high-pitched blast startled me out of near-sleep: the guard's whistle. Madame Bovard and Andrew were still down on the platform. I couldn't hear their voices but I could see that she was speaking to him in a businesslike fashion, taking a packet of papers from her handbag. Andrew was unscrewing the lid of a pen. They walked away a short distance, so he could lean upon a stack of trunks.

I watched as his pen touched the paper, hand moving in the shape of a signature, on one page, then another. *Why should he sign anything?* a sharp voice asked, in the part of my mind still free of the medicine. *Why should they send a nurse, to take you to a place where you can rest? And why Switzerland,* the voice persisted, *so far away, if not to keep you out of sight, out of mind? You've made yourself an embarrassment. What if they mean to keep you there for ever?*

My heart was thudding, yet at the same time, the medicine was taking hold. I blinked hard, trying to fight it, to comprehend what was real and what was the beginning of an attack. I tried to breathe, to be calm, but at the same time every instinct was screaming that I should get off the train. The whistle sounded again. Down on the platform, Andrew glanced at his watch, scribbled all the faster.

Barely able to comprehend what I was doing, I lurched to my feet, clinging to the rack overhead. I risked a glance through the compartment window, my breath hitching, terrified that

100

Andrew or the nurse would look up and see me. But they were facing away from the train, still focused on the papers. I took one shaky step backwards, then another, making for the train corridor.

My head was spinning as I groped behind me, searching for the door handle. For one awful moment, I thought they would turn, thought my bandaged hands would slip on the metal. Through the haze in my head, I knew that I had to choose. I could sink back into the seat, give myself up, or I could run, I could risk everything . . .

The door sprang open and I staggered into the corridor, like an animal fleeing a cage.

People were boarding, but the medicine made my vision blur and I could not see details, only shapes in my path. I pushed my way down the corridor. From somewhere behind, I heard a shout that could have been my name, but I did not stop. My hat snagged on something. I ripped it free, tearing at the pins that held it.

Everything was tilting like the deck of a ship in a storm. A woman cried in alarm as I reeled into her. Beyond was a narrow wooden door. It opened on to the tracks. Gasping, I struggled towards it.

I had not reckoned on the drop, five feet on to the track. My knees hit the stones, then my hands. Pain burst behind my eyes as the cuts reopened. *Get up*, my body ordered, *keep moving*. But there was nowhere to go. To my left was another train; this one for freight. Behind and in front, the long wooden compartments stretched for ever. I was caught between one train and the other, with nowhere to hide.

Distantly, I could hear shouts, Andrew's voice demanding something in broken French. They would soon discover where I was. I hauled myself upright but didn't manage more than a few steps before collapsing against a freight compartment. My eyes flooded with frustration. I couldn't run any further.

The shouts grew louder; I would be found at any moment. But then, I heard a hiss and a heavy clank, like brakes releasing. The train beneath my shoulder shunted forward an inch, and began to roll. From somewhere, far away down the track, a whistle shrilled, a vast cloud of steam blooming from the engine. I stepped back, and watched as a running board came sliding towards me. The train was leaving. *Take one step*, some part of my mind begged, sane or not, I couldn't tell. *One step, and you'll be free* . . .

June 1969

Someone's knocking on the door. *It's the doctor! Don't let him in, he'll give you something, nasty stuff . . .* But it just carries on, louder now, and there's a sour voice too: 'Mr Perch? Mr Perch!'

I roll over, drag the blanket over my head.

'Mr PERCH!'

Shit!

I fling back the covers; the room's a tip. I can smell my own sweat. The hammering won't stop and a headache has just realized I'm awake. It springs into action, squeezing my temples.

' . . . minute!' I yell through a dry throat. I'm wearing only a pair of Y-fronts. No good. I wrap the sheet around my waist and make for the door, pulling the rest of the bedclothes with me.

I crack it open an inch. Betty Throgmorton's lips appear, then the rest of her. I didn't know it was possible to purse a whole face.

'Mr Perch, are you ill?'

Am I ill? I can't remember. I certainly feel ill.

'Sorry?'

'Stan tried to wake you for breakfast. We kept it as long as we could,' she sniffs, 'but the kippers turned.'

I can imagine her tipping the fish into the dog's bowl with relish.

'Sorry,' I mutter again, though I'm not sure why. 'What time is it?'

The corner of her mouth twitches, like she's enjoying herself.

'Gone eleven.'

'*What?*'

'We did wonder whether you were ill. Or gone out early like yesterday. If you aren't going to avail yourself of my breakfasts, Mr Perch, I would appreciate knowing about it.'

'I will. I mean, I won't.' The headache pounds away with gusto. 'I mean, I'll try to be on time tomorrow. I had a bad night.'

'A bad night,' she repeats, as though it's the most outrageous fib. 'Well. I'm sorry to hear it, Mr Perch. I'll leave you to get on with what's left of the day.'

Mean old trout. 'Thank you.'

'Oh and Mr Perch? Someone from London telephoned for you this morning. Twice now. A Mister Hill-something. I told him you would call him back when you got up.'

Hillbrand! Shitting shit! I slump into the room and look about hopelessly. He'll think that I'm skiving, having lie-ins and spending my nights in the pub . . . I hunt around for a clean pair of underwear. No time. Got to call him now.

My trousers are crumpled and my shirt is in an even worse state, but I jam my arms and legs into them, sweating as I am. Socks and shoes: I hate socks and shoes! The laces tangle around my fingers. In the end I just stuff them down the sides.

Stan Throgmorton's polishing glasses at the bar, where an old man is already working at a pint of bitter. My stomach squirms with

104

embarrassment. I bet they've been sat down here shaking their heads at city folk sleeping till noon, when decent people have been up for hours.

'All right, bor,' Stan greets me cheerily, thumping down a glass, 'thought you'd died up there. Bet said you had a bad night.'

'Er, yes, sorry,' I manage. The old man at the bar is staring at me like I'm a dog walking on its hind legs. 'She said that I had a call from London. Is it all right to use the telephone?'

'All right by me so long as y'ent all day,' Stan says. 'He's in the corner there.'

In the darkest corner of the pub, surrounded by yellowing advertisements, is the phone. I jam my finger into the dial and start pulling round the numbers. The mechanism heaves itself back between each one with agonizing slowness. Finally, I hear a click as the call connects.

'Good morning, Hillbrand and Moffat?'

'Hello, Jill.'

'Billy! How's Norfolk? Eaten any winkles yet?'

'Not yet. Is Mr Hillbrand in?'

'He was on his way out to The Cow, but I might just catch him, wait there, Billy.'

I can hear her shouting: 'Dicky! Dicky, it's Billy!' down the stairs.

'He's on his way,' she announces. 'You not well, Billy? He tried you a couple of times this morning, but the landlady there — '

She's cut off as Hillbrand snatches up the phone. I await the inevitable dressing-down, his anger, disappointment, the order to come back to London immediately, the dismissal that follows, saying that I don't have what it takes to

105

be a professional solicitor . . .

'Perch! Finally.'

'Mr Hillbrand, I'm so sorry, I — '

'What the devil's going on? Called three times this morning. Woman there told me you were still in bed.' He pauses to hiccup, or belch, I'm not sure which. 'You ill, lad?'

I swallow. I'm not going to add lying to my list of faults.

'No, sir. I was up all night reading. About Emeline Vane. I found something, a personal account. I don't think anyone else has ever read it before.'

'Good lad!' Hillbrand booms, swamping me in relief. 'Knew it'd have to be something like that. Not like Bill to play lay-a-bed, I said. Here, the landlady there sounds like a right piece of work.'

I can't help but smile.

'You can say that again.'

'So,' I hear a chair creaking in the background as Hillbrand sits, 'tell me about this account of yours. I was starting to worry you'd never find anything in that dump.'

'It — ' Abruptly, I feel strange, like I'm doing something wrong. I shake my head, trying to clear it. My temples give another thud. 'It has details of the last days before Emeline's disappearance. When her Uncle Andrew was trying to secure the sale of the house. She talks about your great-uncle, about making a will.'

Hillbrand sucks in air.

'And?' he says. 'What was the resolution?'

'I'm not sure. It cuts off on the date she went missing. But I found something else,' I say over

106

his huff of frustration, 'a doctor's bill for lithium bromide, the day before she disappeared.' Why do I feel like I'm betraying someone's secrets? I pull myself up and carry on. 'A sedative, apparently.'

'A sedative,' Hillbrand murmurs. I get the impression he's writing down everything I say. 'Promising, promising. Looks like I sent the right man for the job.'

Despite my rumpled state, some of the old pride returns. William Perch, Solicitor.

'Anything else?' Hillbrand is asking.

'Sort of.' The thought of taking Emeline's diary back to London and using it as evidence against her makes me wince, but there's Hillbrand's expectant silence, waiting for me to prove he was right to put his trust in me. 'There's mention of a place called St August-ine's. Emeline . . . hurt herself, or something. Whatever happened, it frightened her uncle, and he planned to send her there. I was wondering if it was maybe — '

'A nut house!' Hillbrand sounds like he's just struck gold. 'Could be! I'll get Jill to look into it. This is good timing, Perch.' Even down the line I can hear his neck crackling. 'Mrs Mallory's been on the phone. Our window's closing. Papa Vane's starting to come around and the developers are getting itchy feet.'

Realization clunks into place.

'Papa Vane — do you mean Timothy?'

'What?'

'Timothy Vane, he's Mrs Mallory's father?'

'Hold up.' I hear papers rustling. 'Yes,

107

'Timothy John Vane', says here. Why? Found something else?'

Timothy; a little boy with hair the colour of bulrushes, riding piggy-back, clinging to his sister . . . I scrunch my eyes closed to get rid of the image.

'No, sir. Just trying to piece all of this together.'

'My man in Havana. See if you can't dig up anything else while you're there.'

*   *   *

The room is as I left it, stifling and chaotic. I sink on the bed, feeling like I've run a marathon. The bedclothes are a mess on the floor. Half-heartedly I drag them towards me. There's something caught in the folds, dark and rustling. The book. Emeline's book.

I stare at it, lying there on the faded carpet. If I'd been doing my job properly, if I'd refused Jem's beers and smokes and gone back to the study like I was supposed to, I would never have looked up at the window, or seen the broken board. I would never have found it. It would have stayed hidden, guarded by the crows, would've crumbled into dust or been destroyed by falling brick when, one day soon, the house is torn down.

Gingerly, I pick it up. I don't want to touch it. I feel like the words inside will seep through the covers into me, and I won't be able to forget them, won't be able to transcribe them for the court case, for Hillbrand to preen over and Mrs

Mallory and her brother to nod at and say, *We told you.*

But Emeline . . . I've never heard anyone talk the way she does, about the marshes, the deaths of her brothers, her mother. In the middle of the night, I forgot that I was turning pages. It was like she was whispering in my ear, speaking to me from the darkness of her bedroom, fifty years ago. Sharing her private thoughts, her fears, as though she knew one day I'd be listening, and wanted me to understand.

I throw the book down on the bed. Get a grip, Perch, you're going as mad as she was. I feel guilty as soon as I think it, even though only hours ago she said it herself: *There are times when I feel like my mind is not my own.*

Not hours, decades. She's long dead and you're only here to look for papers. Whatever happened to her fifty years ago, it's just a case. Emeline Vane is just a case.

February 1919

I felt cold air upon my face. It smelled of frozen fields, of smoke, of rivers deep in winter's hold. It should have made me shiver, but my skin had long ago turned numb. At first, the blood coursing through me, the panic and the fear of being caught had kept me warm. I had watched the Gare de Lyon slip away, before the train gathered speed and the station was swallowed by night.

When I closed my eyes, I could remember what had happened, but only in disconnected moments. A drop to the tracks. Running like an animal. Someone shouting my name, a leap on to a running board, scrabbling up to a platform that connected two freight compartments, the wind rushing past, taking me away, far away from everything I knew . . .

What had I done? It was so hard to think. I could see the track flashing past below, ghostly in the darkness. I should move, should try to find some way to stay warm until morning, but I couldn't. The cold stole what remained of my strength. I let my eyes drift closed.

Was it a minute or an hour later that I became aware of noises? The sound of footsteps, the scrape of a latch, the shunting of wood. When the beam of a lantern swung full on to my face, it was all I could do to force my eyes open in the sudden glare.

'What the . . . ?' someone swore.

The bandages around my palms looked grimy, rust coloured in places where the blood had seeped through. Once these same hands had arranged flowers, had picked out melodies upon a piano, had poured tea, to my mother's instruction. They had held her hand, until there was no life left.

After a time I heard someone approach, quickly and confidently across the rocking floor.

'Mam'selle?'

It was the man with the lantern, the one who had hauled me to my feet, half-carried me across the adjoining platform, through a pitch-dark freight compartment and into another that was far warmer.

'Mam'selle, can you hear me?' An accent licked at his words, rough and rounded.

I gathered the strings of my concentration, moved my head up and down.

Yes.

'Française?'

No.

'Allemande?' he asked tightly. 'Russe?'

I shook my head, trying to think of a lie, an explanation. *I misplaced my ticket. My case was stolen. I fell at the station and lost the way. I was with my uncle. My uncle . . .* I shuddered at the memory of what I had done. The next moment I felt warmth surround me. A musty greatcoat had been draped about my shoulders.

I looked up in surprise. Through the shadows I made out the man's face. It was lean, hair shorn close to the scalp. He wore a ragtag outfit of military remnants: a cloth cap, faded red trousers, cavalry boots, a moth-eaten woollen comforter, an old waistcoat. He was a boy, really, eighteen at most, but his eyes were quick and appraising.

'English?' he said, accent thick.

I steeled myself, pressed my hands together to stop them shaking.

'Yes.'

'What has happen?' he persisted, struggling with the words. 'Something bad? You are lost?'

It took me longer than it should have done to organize my thoughts.

'I am sorry to trouble you,' I finally told him in French, 'I was unwell, at the station. I must have fainted.'

His eyes widened when I spoke, but he was quick to recover.

'Where were you trying to get to, when you fainted?' He was alert, weighing up the situation.

I faltered. Switzerland, St Augustine's . . .

'Home,' I lied, 'to England.'

The boy shook his head.

'Not at the Gare de Lyon you weren't. Wrong station for England. Try again, Mam'selle.'

'I . . . I have been away.'

'That so? For a long time?'

'Long enough.' My heart was hammering in my chest again, making my breath short.

'Where are your bags?' the boy pressed. 'Or your coat or your papers?'

I couldn't think; panic was doubling and redoubling even as I tried to push it down.

'Please,' I heard myself whisper.

'You're putting me in a sticky spot, Mam'selle,' the boy was saying. 'War might be over but we have to stay vigilant. Think the train guard better hear about this.'

'Wait!'

I knew what I had to do. The boy fell silent as I struggled with the bandages on my right hand, pulling away the layers of cotton. My palm looked bad, swollen and scored by cuts, but I ignored it, began to work at the ring on one of my fingers. Finally, it slipped free.

'Here,' I told him triumphantly, thrusting it forward. 'The stones are only garnet but the rest is gold.'

The sharpness on his face was gone. Hesitantly, he took the ring.

'Please,' I said, searching his face. 'Please, it's yours if you will help me, I cannot go back.'

June 1969

It's noon by the time I stump across the village green on my way to Hallerton. The sun is hidden behind clouds, the air hot and heavy as wet wool. A group of men outside the bakery fall silent as I pass. Their stares add to the pressure in my head, where the ache has taken up residence.

I hear Jem's car before I smell it, smell it before I see it come clattering over the bridge that leads into the village. For a second, I consider ducking down the path that leads to Hallerton, pretending I haven't seen her, but I don't. I stand at the edge of the green and wait for her to pull up alongside, wondering why I feel so guilty.

'Hey,' I say, before she can.

'Hey yourself,' comes the answer, the quirked smile as she peers over her sunglasses. Her hair is frizzier than ever; the fraying gold ends make her look like an eccentric lion. 'Heard you had a bad night.'

'Yes,' I say, a little curtly, 'I did. Is that really the news of the day?'

'Just asking.' She's looking closer at me now. My cheeks feel hot as I squint off over the village, avoiding her gaze.

'What is it?' she says.

'Nothing.' I try to sound normal. 'I'm on my way to Hallerton. Work to do.'

'Hop in. Got something to show you first.'

'I can't. I'm late enough already. Hillbrand told me to find — ' I stop. Jem still doesn't know why I'm here. It just makes me feel worse. 'I have to work.' I finish pathetically.

'This is work. Honestly, Perch, you'll want to see this. It's about Emeline.'

Say no, walk away, go back to your deeds and documents.

'What about her?'

'Easier to show you.' Jem pushes her sunglasses back into place. 'Come on, it's at my place.'

We putter off towards the edge of the village. Whatever it is, it won't take long, then I can get back to the papers. Besides, Jem might have some aspirin. We stop beside the last cottage in a row. The front windows are squat and dark, paint peeling, the roof sloping down, low enough for me to touch.

Jem shunts open the thick wooden door.

'Don't you ever lock it?'

'Not really,' she says over her shoulder, disappearing into the dark interior. I have to duck to follow. 'Mind your head.'

After the blinding, overcast day, the house is pitch dark.

'Wait a minute,' she says, 'I'll let in some light.'

Tentatively, I take another step forward. The floor is made from flagstones, covered here and there by rugs worn to threads. It smells strange, of old wood and long-faded spices. I catch a glimpse of a huge fireplace before a rectangle of light bursts open in one wall, filled with green.

'This way,' Jem calls.

I should've known. At home, the gardens are like pocket squares, lawns ringed by prim marigolds, but this one is a riot. Rose bushes stretch down the centre, some with perfect buds, others with bright blooms unfolded. Long purple flowers brush my head from above the door, trailing perfume. In the far corner I can see raspberries on bushes, strawberries tumbling from pots. An elderly, twisted apple tree oversees the boundary, branches furred with lichen and spangled with early fruit. Beyond stretch the fields, not a fence in sight.

'Wow,' I murmur. Jem reappears at my side. I hadn't even heard her leave. In her hand a glass is fizzing.

She hands it over. 'Here. Aspirin. You need it, right?'

I don't even bother to question how she knows, just drink the mixture with relief. As the sediment slides from the glass I remember Emeline, the way she describes the morphine, bitter in her mouth.

'Thanks,' I tell Jem quickly, trying to shake off the thought. 'Now, what did you have to show me?'

'One second.' She grins and disappears inside, her bare feet slapping the stones.

I sink into a rusting iron chair. Somewhere, there's a Bill Perch who does the right things. A Bill Perch who refused Jem's beers, who never found the diary and instead compiled a neat collection of evidence, of doctor's bills and land deeds, to present to Hillbrand. Who would be working at Hallerton, or on a train back to

London, rather than sitting here surrounded by flowers and growing things.

But then, who's to say the other Bill would be right? I made the choices, brought myself here. What if this is what I want?

Jem dumps a heavy object on the table, snapping me out of my thoughts.

'Had a look through Gran's stuff last night,' she tells me, using her T-shirt to wipe off a layer of dust. 'I found this.'

It's a photograph album, with black card pages that creak as she opens them. Inside are the usual family portraits: children in sailor suits, po-faced men wearing wonky spectacles and severe-looking women.

'What're you looking for?' I ask, even though I already know the answer. My heart is beating faster with expectation.

Jem just smiles her knowing smile and flattens down a page, swivelling it to face me.

11th November 1918. Armistice Day.

A group of people stand outside The World's End. Apart from a horse and cart at the edge of the frame where there would now be a car, it's barely changed. Union Jacks hang from the windows, are held clenched in fists. A child is sitting on the shoulders of a man, kicking his legs in the air with joy. A plump woman in a fussy blouse is beaming behind a table of food.

'That's my gran, Annie Durrant. Hillbrand's great-aunt, I guess.' Jem points but I'm not listening, because seated in front of her . . .

A young woman, her dark eyes looking straight down the lens of the camera, hair pinned back beneath a winter hat. A pale face, soft lips unsmiling, hands folded in her lap.

'Is that . . . ?'

Jem nods. 'Yes. That's her.'

Emeline Clara Vane. Beautiful, sad, alive.

February 1919

The young man sat, rifling through a bag. All around, freight stretched into the darkness. A small space had been left in one corner, just enough for a stove and a wooden seat and table built into the wall.

I presumed it was intended for the bagman, but the boy didn't look like he worked for the railway. The flickering light illuminated skin in need of a wash, scarred knuckles, the dark lines of a tattoo at the edge of his rolled-up sleeve.

Not for the first time I felt a jolt of fear. We had reached an agreement; at least, I hoped we had. He'd taken the ring without further questions, told me to make myself at home. Part of me felt weak with relief, even though I knew the world was not often so forgiving. The miles were rolling past outside, taking me further and further from Paris.

'You look done in,' the boy said. I tried to smile.

'It has been a long day,' I told him, my French stiff and formal.

He bared his teeth in a grin.

'Hungry?'

'No thank you.' It left my mouth automatically. In truth, I had no idea. My body still felt like something that did not belong to me.

He only snorted, went back to his search through the sack. 'You're thinner than a towrope.

When was the last time you ate?'

I stared, taken aback by his informality.

'I don't remember.'

Everything, from the beginning of Andrew's dinner party, before even, was a blur. My stomach dropped at the memory. I had taken the morphine recklessly, I realized, and on purpose. What else had been deliberate?

'Well then,' the boy said over my silence, 'high time for supper.'

Before I could ask what he meant, he began to unpack items from the sack, jars and packages of all kinds. I leaned closer. There was a block of chocolate, wrapped in silver paper, a tiny jar of caviar, a tin of coffee, peaches in syrup. Whistling through his teeth, the boy took out a knife and began to hack the top from one of the tins.

Clumsily, I picked up the caviar. It looked just like the kind we had stolen from the pantry. I hadn't seen any since before the war.

'Where did you get this?'

The boy looked smug.

'Fell out of a crate.'

'You stole it?'

'I redistributed it,' he said, taking the jar from my hand and cracking open the wax seal. 'This much freight, things are bound to go astray. Why waste them?'

'But this belongs to someone,' I protested.

'Certainly does,' he said, poking around behind the chimney pipe of the stove and pulling out a whole cured leg of ham. 'But they, Mam'selle, aren't here. We are and we're hungry. Least, I am.' He seated himself comfortably and started to carve at the meat. 'Care to dine?' he asked, around a mouthful.

Something was waking in me at the sight of that food, those distantly remembered flavours. An unfamiliar feeling: hunger.

'Thank you,' I murmured, reaching for a sliver of ham.

It was one of the strangest meals I had ever taken, scooping up the costly food with my fingertips. After months of tasting nothing, the flavours mingled and sang over each other. Chocolate, rich and dark, filling my mouth with its midnight bitterness. Candied almonds, roasted and sweet. Smoky, savoury meat, coffee like I'd never tasted before: poured strong and thick into a battered tin mug. It wasn't long before it all became too much and I sat back, stomach groaning.

The boy ate ravenously, though his body had not an inch of fat to spare. After a while, when it seemed he had eaten his fill, he took out a pouch of tobacco and fell to rolling cigarettes.

I drowsed, eyes half-closed, lulled by the rocking of the train and the spicy scent of tobacco smoke, like treacle and summer hay. It reminded me of Freddie, of how he used to sneak out to smoke on the terrace of Hallerton. Mother hated the habit. He would hide, leaning against the wall nearest the study, only the red end of the cigarette glowing in the darkness. I would creep out to keep him company and the night air would pull goose-flesh from my skin. I once pestered him until he allowed me to try a drag, and he laughed as I coughed and wheezed at the unfamiliar burning in my lungs.

That youthful laugh was gone, but the memory was precious. I was reluctant to break it when the boy spoke, to offer me a cigarette.

'Why not?' I heard myself say. He didn't hesitate, but finished rolling another, lit it from his own.

As before, the smoke made my throat burn, my eyes stream and I choked, trying to cover my mouth with my bandaged palm. The boy didn't laugh as I thought he would, only frowned.

'What happened?' he asked, when I caught my breath. He was looking at my hands.

'An accident,' I said. Was that the truth?

'With glass?'

My surprise must have shown, for he laughed out a mouthful of smoke.

'Got my own specimens,' he waggled his hand at me. Scars, some pink and shiny, others faded to white, criss-crossed the knuckles.

'How?' I asked, although I wasn't sure I wanted to know the answer.

'Had to deal with a stubborn window or two in my time,' he said. 'Wasn't always so prosperous as you see now, Mam'selle.'

'What about the war?' The cigarette was burning down between my fingers. 'Were you injured?'

'Never had the pleasure to be.' The boy took a last drag, flicked the remaining inch into the stove. 'As a guest of the Bureau of Corrections, my presence at the front wasn't desired.'

The boy saw the alarm in my face and smiled, the expression chasing away the shadows and the danger and the dirt.

'Despite what they say, Mam'selle, there's still some honour amongst thieves.'

I tried to nod, but the movement sent my head spinning and I caught the edge of the wooden seat. The boy was at my side, steadying me with his lean, scarred hands.

'Easy, easy,' he murmured, smelling of sweat and coal smoke and tobacco. I did not protest when he helped me to my feet, guided me towards a heap of sacks on the other side of the stove. They were filled with grain, dried beans or corn, and yielded as I sank on to them. From somewhere, the boy produced a blanket. It was rough and scratchy, but warm.

'Why are you helping me?' I mumbled, sleep already looming.

I couldn't see his face in the shadows.

'Knew a lady once,' he said eventually. 'She were a mademoiselle too. You remind me of her, a bit.'

'What happened to her,' my eyes were closing, 'the lady?'

When next I looked up the boy had returned to his place by the stove, a silhouette against the ochre glow.

'She married,' his voice was quiet, 'one of her own kind. But she weren't happy. She would've run if she could. We would've helped her run.'

'Monsieur . . . I don't know your name.'

'No 'Monsieur'.' The smiling reply found me before I slept. 'Just call me Puce.'

June 1969

I stare at the photograph for a long time. Eventually, the garden reappears around me, the sound of the bees, the distant noise of a radio from one of the other cottages. For an instant, I wish I could imagine myself into the photograph, into that November afternoon so I could step forward, take Emeline's hand and ask her . . . what?

I push my chair back with a sigh.

'You all right?' Jem asks. 'You've got the strangest look on your face.'

I want to tell her everything, about why I'm really here, about the diary, but for some reason I can't. How can I explain the impulse that keeps drawing me towards Hallerton, and Emeline, which insists that if I dig deeper, I'll find something important? I can't even make sense of it myself.

'Can I borrow this?' I ask instead.

Jem gives me a puzzled look, but slips the photograph from its cardboard corners and hands it over.

We drive to Hallerton in silence. I almost start to speak a dozen times, but at the last second I can't find the words. Jem says something about the weather breaking soon. I make a noise in reply, but all I can really think about is getting back to Hallerton.

'Don't worry about lunch,' I tell Jem as I slam

the car door outside the house. 'I'll have to work straight through today. To catch up.'

She shrugs, though not with her usual ease.

'If you're sure.'

I'm searching for the keys when she calls after me.

'Bill, what's going on?'

'Nothing,' I tell her. 'Thanks. I'll see you later.'

She's still watching as I close the heavy door behind me. The house is waiting.

'Hello,' I whisper into the silence.

In the study, I run my hands along the carved wooden arms of the chair. This is where Emeline sat, on a bleak, February day as she listened to Durrant speak. *I do not think you should be here alone*, he had told her.

Not alone, I wish I could reply.

The mantel above the fireplace is clogged with papers, but I clear a space, take the photograph of Emeline from my bag and set it there. Is she really gone, like Mrs Mallory thinks? Were the days after the dinner party truly her last?

I unwrap the diary from my spare shirt. As always, it falls open a quarter of the way through, at the point where Emeline's voice ceases and time takes over, with its own language of yellowing paper and water-stained edges.

Gently, I turn back to the previous page, to the hastily scribbled pencil lines. I trace the words, trying to grasp the mind behind them.

What if I lose myself again? What if next time I can't stop, a step too far on the marsh? Will go. Andrew says better soon,

125

that Hallerton upsets me.

Did they reach St Augustine's? Did her uncle send her there, sign away her life because he was afraid of what she might do, this girl who was coming apart through sadness? Did they want to keep her away from gossip, forgotten, out of sight, out of mind?

Until now, until money's involved. Now they send me, a stranger, not to find her but to bury her once and for all in an unknown grave, to dismiss her. I won't do it.

What about Hillbrand? William Perch, Solicitor, demands. *What about the developers, and Mrs Mallory and her brother? It's their case.*

They aren't here, I tell him.

The afternoon passes in a flash as I search through the labyrinth of papers for something, anything, that might help me turn the case on its head, prove that Emeline is still alive. A photograph, a ticket stub, an envelope with a foreign postmark . . . Didn't Mrs Mallory say that her father had a letter hidden away somewhere, one that proved Emeline wasn't dead? If so, it could be here.

But there's nothing, only bills and other demands for money. Outside the window, the sky grows darker. My eyes begin to struggle with the endless pages of cramped handwriting and typed print. The headache prowls, threatening to return.

I should call it a day and head back to The World's End. I should find Jem and explain everything. The photograph of Emeline urges me to try one more file, just one more, but resolutely I take it up, close it gently into the pages of the diary. There's always tomorrow.

Outside the air is greasy with moisture. A breeze has picked up, whipping the treetops into a frenzy, sending dust and dander flying. I'm barely more than halfway across the garden when the rain starts. One splash, two, and the sky opens, hurling down raindrops as big as water balloons.

I shove the briefcase beneath my suit jacket, but the fabric is drenched in seconds. I duck under a tree but it's no better there; by the time I get back to Saltedge I might as well have jumped into the sea. As for the briefcase, with its many holes and its precious cargo . . .

I hurry back towards the house, through a wall of grey water. The key to the front door is slippery in my fingers. Inside, the sound of the rain is amplified. I can hear it, finding its way through the broken roof, pouring on to floorboards that were once varnished and spread with carpets. Nothing to do but wait. Even as I think it, the rain gets heavier. I daren't go into the study, wringing wet as I am. There seems only one other place.

The roof above the room where I found the diary is sound. Was this Emeline's room? Movement catches my eye as I cross the threshold, but it's only two of the crows, sheltering from the rain on the window sill.

Instinctively, I nod at them, but they only look at me with their unfathomable eyes, and shuffle uneasily, croaking in their chests. Slowly, I sink down against one wall. After a while, they decide that my company is preferable to getting their feathers wet, and start to preen their fine, black wings.

My jacket is done for. I shrug out of it and dry my hands as well as I can on my shirt before taking out the diary. I turn back to the beginning, to follow Emeline's journey, her last days in this house, before the accident.

If not for that accident, she might have watched as Hallerton was sold off, might have been married, might still be living now, growing old somewhere in London. If not for that accident, I would never have heard the name Emeline Vane.

★   ★   ★

'Oh man,' Jem says when she sees me, sitting hunched and damp on the floor, clutching the diary. She helps me to my feet.

Outside, it's dark. I must have been sitting there, thinking, for hours. The rain still falls, but in a slow hush rather than a torrential battering.

'Been looking for you all over,' she says when we're in the car, brushing an oilskin hood back off her hair. 'Didn't you hear me calling?'

She looks unhappy, and I feel a pang of remorse for blundering into her peaceful existence; a city fool with his loyalties twisted.

'I'm sorry.' The rain patters on the roof of the car. 'I need to talk to you about something.'

'I know.'

As she drives, I tell her everything. About why

Hillbrand sent me here, about the people waiting to tear Hallerton down, about Mrs Mallory and Timothy Vane, about Emeline's diary. When I've finished, I have to force myself to turn and look at her.

Jem's face is serious. She says nothing, and I wait for her to stop in front of The World's End and order me out of the car. But she doesn't. She doesn't drive past the pub at all, but swings down the road leading to her cottage. Only when she's turned off the engine does she let out a small sigh.

'Dicky called,' she says, 'that's why I came looking for you. He said something about signing a deal, that Timothy Vane is conscious again. He needs you back in London. Tomorrow.'

I force myself to meet her eyes in the gloom.

'Jem, I don't know what to do.'

'Come in, for a start.' Her frown is gone. 'No use sitting here. You'll catch a cold.'

Inside, the cottage feels damp. Jem potters about, turning on lights and hanging up her dripping raincoat. From a narrow, twisting set of stairs she throws down a towel and a bundle of clothes. I retreat to a dark corner to dry myself off. It isn't cold, but Jem lights a fire in the huge grate, I suspect more for comfort than for warmth. The clothes she's given me are ancient and patched; a pair of men's corduroy trousers hacked off into shorts, a huge old Aran jumper. It smells fusty, but the minute I pull it over my head, I feel better.

'Suits you,' she tells me from the grate, as she stacks up kindling.

129

'Whose is it?' It seems the easier question to ask.

'My grandpa's, I think. Certainly not Dad's. He wouldn't have been caught dead in fisherman's gear.'

She sits back on her heels, watching the growing flames. It's a good fire, licking bright and fast at the wood. Wish I knew how to do it properly.

'We've always had a gas one at home.'

Jem doesn't reply, only rearranges a log.

'Why didn't you tell me?' she says at last, still staring at the grate. 'About the diary?'

I start to say 'I don't know', but stop myself mid-way. I do know.

'I was worried you'd hate me.' I force the words out. 'For being here, for it being my job to prove that Emeline was mad, or dead or preferably both.'

'I asked about the diary, Bill, not your job. I more or less guessed what you were doing here.' She raises an eyebrow. 'Don't look so surprised. Dicky wouldn't be chasing around one of Grandpa's old cases unless it was important; unless there was money involved. So,' she says, 'the diary?'

She is staring at me, expecting an answer, deserving one.

How do I put it into words that don't sound deluded? The feeling that these last few days have changed me somehow; that Hallerton and the marshes and home-grown strawberries might mean more to me than business expenses or promotions or new suits.

Jem laughs at my bewildered expression and climbs to her feet, padding over to the sink. She returns with a bottle, full of something dark and purple and gleaming.

'Sloe gin,' she says, pouring some into a chipped glass. 'Made it last year. You look like you could use a drink.'

I manage a smile, swamped by gratitude for this woman, so unlike any other friend I've had. The liquid in the glass is sweet and sticky and tastes of ripe fruit, splitting in the sun.

'What will you tell Dicky,' she asks between sips, 'when you get back to London?'

'I don't know.' It's the truth. 'I wish I didn't have to go back. I . . . I like it here.'

'Don't you have folk waiting for you?'

Stephanie. I promised to call, I realize, but I haven't thought about her for days. She seems as distant as a memory.

'My girlfriend. She won't like any of this.'

'Bill,' Jem says gently, 'I hate to say it, but I think Emeline's family are right. She's gone. In all likelihood, she died somewhere fifty years ago. You can't save her.'

'But I can try to find her.' I sound like a child, insisting on the impossible. 'At least I can do that.'

Jem just sighs, pours out another measure.

'Bill Perch,' she tells me, and leans down to clink her glass with mine, 'you're either a very good solicitor or a very, very bad one.'

131

February 1919

Through the open doorway, I watched the first light of dawn break across a provincial town. A new day: my first one alone. That thought should have been enough to terrify me. But it wasn't.

'Are we near the end of the line?' I asked, as the train pulled out of the station, taking me further from myself.

The boy who called himself Puce snorted a laugh. 'Not by a long shot. Why? This far enough from Paris for you?'

'Not by a long shot.' I smiled and he laughed again.

He called me only 'Mam'selle', though I looked less like a respectable lady than ever. Still, I made do. He did not ask me the why or how of my situation and I showed him the same courtesy.

Only when darkness fell and he dragged the door closed on yet another nameless railway siding did he turn to me in the gloom. His face was serious.

'We'll be in Nîmes by midnight. End of the line. You know where that is?'

I was concentrating on rewrapping the bandages about my hands, but shook my head. My knowledge of France was rudimentary at best. Certain place names had been etched into my memory by four years of newspaper reports and bulletins from the Front, two in particular by those ever-feared telegrams: Verdun, Epehy. All I knew was that wherever we were, it was a long, long way from Hallerton.

'Thought not.' I heard the smile in his voice as he stepped closer. 'Nîmes is a city in the south, Mam'selle, between the wild Cévennes and the sea. The sun shines bright there, even in winter, and they grow violets and mimosa and oranges, though in Paris it's cold enough to freeze your nose.'

I couldn't help but smile at his description. In the chill of a freight compartment, it seemed another world. 'You sound like an advertisement,' I said.

He shrugged. 'South's where I would go, were I not a railwayman. But for me, home's wherever I make it.' His smile had a rueful edge. 'Depot of the Gare d'Austerlitz more often than not.'

'Is that where you're from? Paris?'

'Belleville, born and raised. You?'

'Norfolk,' I told him after a pause; 'any further east and you fall off the edge of England.'

He made to reply, but I pulled the bandage I was winding around my hand too tight, the fabric cutting into my palm. I winced. The cuts were still raw and angry.

'Those need cleaning,' Puce said, stepping closer.

I blinked up at him through watering eyes.

'Do you have anything that will help?'

He raised an eyebrow before striding off into the shadows of the compartment. I heard the sharp crack of a lid being forced open. When he reappeared it was with a bottle, sawdust clinging to the glass.

133

'Only a ten-year vintage, I'm afraid.' He sniffed, pulling out the cork. Brandy. It looked expensive.

'Is that really all you have?'

'Beggars can't be choosers, Mam'selle,' he said, rummaging through the sack by the stove. He pulled out a cloth, squinted at it in the light, pulled out another. 'I suggest you sample some. For medicinal purposes.'

Hesitantly, I raised the bottle to my lips. Fiery alcohol flooded my throat. I swallowed, gasped and drank again.

'Will it do?' came his mischievous question.

The brandy served to clean the scabbing cuts, though I had to grit my teeth against the sting.

'I remember that feeling,' Puce told me, as he retied one of the bandages. 'Used to hiss like an alley cat when I had cuts cleaned as a lad.'

'Thank you,' I told him, testing the new bandage.

He took another swig of the brandy. His face was flushed beneath its dirt. I wondered if we were truly the same age. He seemed an old hand at the world already.

'How old are you, Puce?' I asked. My voice sounded strange, speaking familiar words to a stranger in a foreign tongue.

'Never known.' The boy cleared his throat after another swig. 'About nineteen, I reckon.'

'I'm twenty,' I said, holding out my swaddled hand for the bottle. 'That means I win. Your turn. You get one question.'

He added a few more coals to the stove, rattled the orange heat about before he spoke.

'What's your name?'

The words hung in the air before us. I'd forgotten about the noise of the wheels on the track but now I heard their every syllable. I wanted to drop everything I once was out of the door, let it fall behind me, piece by piece.

'Emeline,' I whispered bitterly. 'Emeline Clara Vane.'

The boy took it in. Did not repeat it, only nodded.

'You can find another name, you know.' He leaned his elbows on his knees, face sombre. 'If you can't live with the one you've got, the world has ways of giving you another.'

'Like 'Puce'?' I tried to make it a joke, but my voice was thick with emotion. ' 'Flea'?'

'Never said it would be a good name.' He took another drink from the rapidly diminishing brandy. 'But Puce is mine. I've worn it comfortable now.'

'What was it before?'

He pointed a finger at me, eyes bright from the alcohol.

'You got to promise not to laugh.' He grimaced. 'It was Gosse, Jean-Baptiste. After Moliere.' He smirked at my astonishment. 'My mother were an actress before she were a whore.'

It must have been the alcohol, for I let out a laugh. It built into an irrepressible giggle until my eyes were streaming and I was wheezing for breath. Puce was laughing too, wiping his eyes on the comforter he wore around his neck.

'Come on,' he said, hauling me to my feet. Still gasping with laughter, I obeyed.

'What are we doing?' I asked as we staggered across the compartment, towards the door.

'Brace yourself on that,' he told me, indicating the wall, 'and give me your arm.'

'Puce?'

His face was alive.

'We're getting rid of these old names.' He hooked his arm firmly through mine and reached for the handle. 'Ready?'

Before I could answer he had grasped the door and hurled it open. Cold air and night flooded in, the din of the wheels clacking and the bellow of the train as it pushed itself across the dark landscape. The wind whipped the moisture from my eyes, tore, at my breath. It was terrifying. It was electrifying.

As we plunged into a tunnel, I felt Puce take a deep breath beside me. Then he was yelling, a wild, joyous shout that was grabbed away by the rushing blackness, and I was yelling with him, pouring out my uncertainty, shredding the restraints I had kept in place for so long. I yelled until my lungs were squeezed dry of breath, until the noise faded to a croak.

Puce let go of me to close the door. My whole body shivered, like the bubbles in a glass of champagne.

'There,' Puce said, 'it's gone. Now you can go anywhere, be anyone.'

Emeline Vane, gone. Something within me stirred, something that whispered words of liberty.

'So where will it be, Mam'selle?'

I closed my eyes, tried to imagine this train,

hurtling across the country like fire across tinder, towards another land, another life.

'South,' I whispered with a smile. 'I think I'll go south.'

June 1969

I watch as the village green, The World's End, the rows of cottages cram themselves into the tiny rectangle of Jem's rear-view mirror. No warm farewells from Saltedge, just a 'Mind how you go, bor' from landlord Stan and a sniffy look from Betty.

At Sheringham a train is waiting to take me back to London. The gulf between the city and the quiet, cloud-strewn marshes seems infinite, separated by time and memory as well as plain geography. I remember hearing a story somewhere about a village that only appears once every hundred years. I have the dreadful feeling that if I leave Saltedge and Hallerton, I'll never be able to come back.

'It'll still be here,' Jem says when I tell her. 'Though I know what you mean. I don't like to leave too often, either. My dad lives in Nottingham, and my sister and her family, but . . . ' She trails off. 'It's like Narnia.' She smiles eventually, glancing at me from the steering wheel. 'Did you ever read those books?'

I turn to reply when a gateway flashes past, an opening in the hedge. Through the tops of the trees, a crumbling chimneystack is just visible, the edge of a blue slate roof. I have a train to catch, but I can't help craning around, trying to make this final glimpse last. In six months, less, it might all be gone.

The car begins to slow. I look over in surprise.

'Two minutes,' Jem says with a wry smile, putting the car into reverse.

The old gravel drive is green and cool as ever. It smells of vegetation after yesterday's rain. The house looms up to greet us. It seems smaller somehow, and sad, as though it is tired of being alone and wants us to stay, to wait with it in its slow decline.

'Dicky might send you back here,' Jem says quietly, 'to collect more evidence?'

I smile, but I know the highly unlikely when I hear it. No doubt a deal is being hammered out between Mrs Mallory and the developer as we speak.

'Maybe.'

The afternoon washes around us. I can't bear the thought that the days will pass here without me, that summer will tip over the precipice into autumn; that the plants will droop and the birds will flee as trucks move in, and the green silence is destroyed, replaced by machinery and rubble.

'Wait here, will you? I'll only be a minute.'

'Where are you going — '

But I'm already hurrying around the side of the house towards the terrace. Emeline's diary has given me an idea, a way that part of me can stay here no matter what happens, even after I've gone back to London. Like a tin figure, watching with painted eyes.

I search through my pockets. Change, bits of wrapper, and there, my house keys, on the plastic ring my aunt brought back from Margate.

Brightly coloured, yellow and orange. It'll have to do.

Jem calls me, saying that I'll miss the train. The breeze bends the leaves and I try to breathe it all in, the smell of salt and mud, damp stone drying in the sun, the sweetness of rot and wildflowers.

The colourful key ring clatters on to the steps of the terrace. As I walk away I hear a flurry of wings, the scraping of claws on stone, but I don't look back.

March 1919

The dark countryside receded behind me. I did not know where I was going, or what I would find when I got there. I only knew that I had to keep moving, that I would keep running until the road turned to dust under my feet.

Puce had smuggled me on to this train, sneaking me through the midnight bustle of the station at Nîmes. It would take me south, he said, south, towards the sun and the mountains at the very end of France. He had taken my bandaged hands in his, and I had tried to thank him as a shrill whistle blew. He wished me luck, made me promise to write to him at the depot, and then he was gone, sprinting away into the darkness, towards the train that would take him back to Paris.

For a long time I studied the passing tracks, watching them turn silver in the pre-dawn light. I didn't dare sleep. Puce said that by morning, the train would have reached the south. When I finally looked up again, I did not know if he was right, or if I was dreaming.

Mountains, there were mountains rising out of lilac shadows, capped with snow. I leaped to my feet on the narrow metal platform, and ran to the far railing. The wind blew the hair back from my face as we hurtled into that magnificent landscape, and I laughed because even as I watched, the sun was rising. A glow struck the peaks and turned them iridescent gold, raising the rest of the landscape out of obscurity.

I saw whitewashed houses shuttered against the night. I saw terraces of vines, sloping up into the foothills. Reeds grew along the track, clusters of purple and yellow irises. It was as though we had crossed through a portal and left behind the cold, grey world for one that was soaked in brilliance.

Even the air smelled different. I breathed deeply and took in sun-baked dust, night-cold leaves and salt; a marine promise entirely different to the icy North Sea. On the opposite side of the train, the hills dropped away and the sight of waves rushed up to meet me. The sun dazzled upon the surface of the water and sea birds called to each other, their voices high and thin, before we were swallowed up by the darkness of a tunnel.

A tunnel meant one thing: civilization. The train was slowing and I knew that we were reaching the very end of the line. I would have to try my luck in this unknown place. Cautiously, I peered ahead. A peeling sign with the name of the station was coming into view.

Cerbère.

In the distance, I could make out a mass of people waiting at a platform. If I did not move soon, I would be seen. Puce had warned me not to get caught; the train company did not look kindly on stowaways and would likely hand me over to the authorities. I shifted forward, took a breath, and jumped.

My muscles were stiff and I hit the ground

awkwardly, grazing my elbows. I crouched out of sight at the end of the platform and watched the train come to a stop. The people swarmed forward, flinging open the freight compartment doors, their barrows and carts at the ready. I heard voices, women's voices, talking and laughing together in a language that was not French. Where *was* I?

Beyond the station building I could see a road, a rough dirt track. If I could reach it, I could escape unseen. The women nearest to me had their backs turned . . .

I got my feet under me and ran. Over the rails I scrambled, over uneven stones and unfamiliar weeds, the breath catching in my lungs. Too late I heard the men's voices, too late I saw three figures walk around the corner of the building, heading straight for me. Instinctively, I ducked down behind a cart that stood, waiting to be unloaded.

The men came closer. Two of them were middle-aged, and had the signs of a hard life about them, their skin brown and shrivelled as winter onions. But the third . . . he looked like a different creature. He was young and strong, black hair glistening with water, pushed back from his forehead, eyes of such light blue they looked almost silver. He passed the cart, barely a pace away, and I must have moved or made some noise, for the next thing I knew, those eyes were looking straight into mine.

Crushed down in my hiding place, there was nothing I could do but stare back, hoping beyond hope that he had not seen me after all.

143

He frowned, looking at the train, then back to me and I saw him fathom everything.

I heard grunts of conversation, footsteps crunching around the side of the cart. I squeezed my eyes closed, waiting for the inevitable hand on my shoulder, for the three men to drag me off to the stationmaster's office. But nothing happened. I made myself look up. The young man was standing over me, a puzzled look on his face. There was no sign of the others.

Slowly, I felt my limbs unknot. He did not look angry, nor was he wearing a railway uniform, only a heavy blue jumper and a faded neckerchief. Perhaps he would not stop me from leaving the station after all . . . With as much dignity as I could muster, I stood, brushed myself off, and started to stride past him.

Not fast enough. He caught my shoulder, pulled me back. For an instant, I found myself separated from him by only a few inches. His lips were a little chapped, I saw, before I remembered myself and shrugged off his hold.

'Well?' I asked.

He stared at my mouth, and his own lips moved silently, as if trying to fathom my words. Why wasn't he shouting for the railway officials, for the stationmaster to come and take me away? After a while, he glanced at the rooftops of the town below and seemed to come to a decision. He reached for my arm again.

I jerked away, only for my foot to slip on the loose stones. Unthinkingly, I grabbed for the edge of the cart. The rough wood dug into my palm and I heard myself cry out in pain. Perhaps

144

it was shock, or exhaustion, but I couldn't find my balance again, couldn't let go without my knees buckling.

Everything was clouding in, like snow at night. There was a strong hand on my elbow, another around my waist and the last thing I noticed was a scent: cotton dried in sunlight, the sea on a winter's day.

June 1969

'Bill, I'm talking to you.'

Stephanie is staring. Behind her, people are jostling at the sticky bar; the sunlight is streaming in, making everything hotter. All I can smell is stale beer and cigarette ash. I try to loosen my sweat-damp collar.

'What?'

'You're doing it again!'

She looks annoyed. Obviously she expects an answer. On the radio, Nancy and Frank are crooning about saying something stupid. I know the feeling.

'Sorry, Steph.' I reach for the glass of shandy. It's still almost full, growing warmer by the second. 'You know I came straight off the train. I'm knackered.'

I swallow down a sip. The beers I drank with Jem on the terrace tasted ten times better. All I want to do is get home and close my door, where I can be alone, where I can think about Hallerton.

'You never even called me.' She finishes her snowball, careful with her lipstick. 'Four whole days. You going to tell me they don't have telephones in Norfolk?'

'Only in the pub. And I did mean to, but this thing with Emeline, it took up all of my time.'

'Emeline?' Is that hostility in Steph's voice? I can't tell. She's looking down, false lashes screening her eyes. 'Who's Emeline?'

'Emeline Vane, the person I'm trying to find, for the case. For the client. The person I'm trying to find for the client.'

'Oh.'

Never has one syllable been more baffling. I should've gone home, shouldn't have gone to meet her at the chip shop just because I felt guilty.

'Hey, I brought you something!' I reach for my suitcase and the get-out-of-jail-free card it offers. Inside is a bottle of Jem's sloe gin. I smile as I hold it in my hand, remembering her gran's cottage, how she listened, the way an oldest friend would.

'Here.' I hand it over. 'I thought we could drink it together, maybe go down to the park one night.'

'What is it?' She looks suspicious.

'You'll like it. It's sloe gin, my friend Jem made it.'

Steph's face slips from suspicious to downright angry.

'And who's Jem?' Her voice could split rock.

'Jem's a friend. She's Hillbrand's cousin or something. She calls him 'Dicky'.' I try for a grin but Steph isn't budging. Worse, her cheeks are reddening up to her eyes, which are filling with liquid. Oh God.

'First this Emeline person, then Jem — '

'I'd never like Jem in that way,' I say desperately, 'she's way older than me, and she's a hippy, you should see her hair.'

I hate myself as soon as it's out of my mouth,

but Steph's face softens a bit.

'A hippy?' she gulps, almost smiling. 'Really? Did she wear those silly dyed tops? And sandals?'

I force a smile. 'You have no idea.'

'Did she . . . ?' Steph leans forward to whisper, and I'm engulfed in perfume, strong enough to mask the scent of the fryers. 'Did she take *drugs?*'

I wonder what it would be like to tell the truth. Horrible, I realize. Steph would tell my mum, who would tell my dad, who would snarl about responsibility and the youth of today.

'Look, I was there to work,' I snap. 'How should I know? I barely got outside the bloody house.'

I drain the drink to the halfway mark in one, hoping it covers my red face. By the time I look back, Steph's staring at her hands in her lap.

'Sorry, Bill. I know you'd never do anything like that. I just missed you, and you didn't call.' She smiles and shuffles closer on the carpeted bench. 'I'm dead proud, you know, you doing so well on your first big case.'

I raise my arm and tuck it around her, feeling like a terrible person.

'Thanks, Steph.'

That night, in the lounge, my parents grill me for what seems like an age. I try to answer their questions, using bland lies to cover a skeleton of truth. The cold gas fire looks like a toy after the huge grate in Jem's gran's house, stained by the smoke of generations. My dad claps me on the shoulder when I finally escape towards my room, and Mum doesn't even comment on the state of my suit. It just makes everything worse. If they knew . . .

Knew what? They're allowed to be proud, I tell myself, as I trudge up the stairs. *You should be proud. You went to Hallerton, you got the evidence, did the job, like you were meant to. That makes you a solicitor, sort of. Maybe Hillbrand will make you a partner one day.*

But all of those thoughts die at the sight of the briefcase on the bed. Carefully, I take out the photograph of the group outside The World's End. Jem said I could keep it for the time being. Emeline gazes back at me. The sight of her face is jarring so far from Hallerton, out of place in a suburban bedroom. I take out the diary and smooth its stained cover, wishing I could write back.

What are you going to do? Jem asked.

I could present a solid case to Hillbrand: use the doctor's bill, Emeline's words to prove she was not in her right mind, that she no doubt met with an unfortunate end by her own hand, that there is nothing to stop the sale of Hallerton from going ahead. Take credit for a job well done. Take a bonus, turn away as Mrs Mallory and her brother shake hands with a developer and sell Hallerton from under their father's nose, to be torn down for ever, for Emeline to be forgotten. It's not my business after all. I should be pleased. I should buy a new suit. I should be planning for my future.

Or, I could never go back to Hillbrand & Moffat. I could finish what I've started and find Emeline: take off, with nothing but a bag of clothes and hope. I could change everything with one decision . . .

But I know I won't. Not Bill, not brave enough. I'm sorry, Emeline. Resignedly, I pack the diary, the photograph, the doctor's bill back into the file, ready to place into Hillbrand's hands on Monday morning.

March 1919

It was a smell that brought me to, a putrid stench that filled my nose, made me pull away and cough. By the time I opened watering eyes, a stranger was leaning back, a wooden pail in her hand.

'Fish guts,' she said, matter-of-factly. 'Stink would wake the dead.'

She was small, shorter than me, but looked a good deal stronger. Her face was round, deeply tanned. Although lines creased her eyes and mouth, she did not look old. A headscarf was wrapped tight to her brow.

She was speaking French, I registered belatedly, not the strange language of the women at the station. The station ... what had happened? I remembered the young man, his silver eyes, but then?

'Where am I?' It came out as a whisper, but I saw her frown at my accent.

'You're in my kitchen. My son dragged you in here, like something from the bottom of a fishing net, or don't you remember?'

'Your son?'

She opened her mouth to answer, but was interrupted by a noise of protest. I looked around for the first time. We were indeed in a kitchen, rough but homely and warm. The young man from the station was seated on a stool near the stove. He caught my eye and smiled. I felt my cheeks flare.

'Your son tried to detain me at the station,' I told the woman, trying to muster some decorum. '*And* he refused to answer me, even though I was clearly distressed.'

The young man did something strange; he caught his mother's eye and made a series of gestures, pointing at me, then himself, tapping at his hands where the bandages were on my own palms. He finished with a shrug, half a smile.

When the woman spoke next, she angled her body so that he could see her face. Her manner was still brusque, but her expression had changed.

'He said he saw you hiding at the station, and thought you were scared. When you fainted he decided to bring you here, in case you were in trouble.' She slid a glance at her son, who was watching her face carefully. 'He said he is sorry if you hurt your hands.'

The young man nodded at me, made a gesture.

'I don't understand,' I said, feeling more lost than ever.

'Aaró is deaf,' she told me bluntly. She crossed her arms over her chest. 'Now, I think you should explain yourself before I report you to the railway officials as a runaway. Then they can send you back to your family if — '

'I'm not a runaway!' The lie dropped from my mouth before I could think. 'And I don't have any family. At least, none to be sent back to.'

The woman's eyes were calculating. The young man made a noise and she absent-mindedly gestured at him. Evidently they had their own way of speaking. I tried not to look at either of them in the silence, but I could feel her hard stare.

'Do you have any money?' she said.

I shook my head, gaze fixed on the tiled floor.

'Are you in trouble with the army or the police?'

'No. I have done nothing wrong. But — '

She nodded impatiently. I could see her feet agitating within her worn leather boots. There was a third question on the other side of her lips; I could sense it. Finally she turned to her son and made a few signs. He looked indignant, but eventually got to his feet. I didn't realize I was watching him go, until he glanced back from the door and we locked eyes. He frowned slightly, half-amused, half-searching, and was gone.

'I don't want him listening,' the woman said. I looked back at her, trying not to blush.

'I thought you said he couldn't hear?'

'He hears in other ways.' Her feet rested, perfectly still upon the floor. 'Tell me the truth now, are you with child?'

The question was so sudden, so unexpected, all I could do was stare. It had never occurred to me that someone might presume . . . Is that what Puce thought? And this woman's son?

'I . . . ' I shut my mouth, opened it again, 'no, I — '

'All right.' The woman looked relieved, though a frown still lingered. 'You are red enough to cook an egg on, obviously you're ignorant of such things.'

She brushed past me and took up a coffee pot,

153

clanged it down on the stove.

'This is not a charity,' she said. 'If you truly are in trouble, you may stay here while you consider your options. Two days. I can't afford to keep you any longer than that.'

I started to stammer my thanks.

'And you will have to tell me your name.'

You can find another, Puce had said, *the world has ways of giving you another.* My eyes fell on the wooden pail, waiting by the door.

'Fischer,' I told her, 'my name is Emilie Fischer.'

★ ★ ★

The woman, I learned, was called Clémence Fournier, but everyone knew her as Maman.

'We all have our roles,' she told me as she leaned against the doorjamb. We were in the scullery, separated from the kitchen only by a threadbare curtain.

'What makes you their mother?' I said, wishing she would leave me to undress alone. 'Are they all orphans?'

'Many of them. That's the way with border towns.'

'What border?'

She smiled curiously.

'We're the last town in France. Spain is all of a mile or two away, over the hills. Funny for you not to know that.'

I said nothing. Although I had been vague about my circumstances, my clothes gave away too much. Beneath the grime, there was no

154

denying that they had once been expensive, with their velvet and embroidery.

'And your son's name is Aaró?' I said to fill the expectant silence. 'I have never heard it before.'

'It's Catalan. Like half the people here.'

'But not you?'

Her accent, though rough around the edges, sounded like the French I had learned from my tutors: urban, respectable. She frowned at me. Impossible to guess at the thoughts gathering behind her brown, lined face.

'No,' she said slowly, 'not me. But I speak it. Aaró does too, in his way.'

She held out a hand for my clothes. Between us, water steamed in a tin bath. It had been heated on the huge kitchen stove, carried through to the scullery in pans.

'Better get in,' she told me as we stood, eye to eye, 'before it gets cold.'

I had no choice but to strip off the rest of my clothes, trying to cover myself with my bandaged hands as I did so. Her eyes lingered over my ribs, showing through the skin, the bones of my hips.

'Thin,' she observed, before bundling up my garments and sweeping back into the kitchen.

The hot water stung as I lowered myself into the dented tub. She'd left a sponge and a block of hard soap and I scrubbed myself pink. With that layer of grime came away a layer of Emeline Vane. Emilie Fischer, I repeated, working the name into my skin. Emilie Fischer.

I unwound the sodden bandages. After three days, the cuts were still raw in places, but in others they were scabbing, knitting slowly into

155

new skin. I flexed my fingers carefully.

Clémence had left me some clothes, old ones of hers. There was a dark red skirt, too big around the waist, a much darned cotton blouse, a shawl. I didn't have any pins for my hair, or a mirror, so I plaited the tangled strands and left it at that.

The smell of coffee drew me back into the kitchen. Clémence was removing a pot from the stove. The young man, Aaró, was there, slicing bread at the table. His hands paused when I walked in. I got the impression he was studying me, from my wet hair down to my scarred hands, holding the skirt at my waist to prevent it from falling down.

He made a noise to catch his mother's attention and a couple of signs, before brushing the crumbs off his hands and taking off his belt. I watched in confusion as he used the sharp point of the bread knife to bore another hole in the leather.

'He said you don't look so wild any more,' Clémence translated, placing a jar of honey on the table.

Aaró strode towards me and the next thing I knew, his arms were encircling my waist. His head was bent close to my own, and I saw every strand of his black hair. It was matted in places, with sea-salt, I realized. I could feel the heat radiating from him; he smelled of coffee and faintly of tar.

When he pulled back, it took my mind a moment to catch up. The skirt was now secure; his own belt cinched about my waist.

'Thank you,' I said, forgetting he could not hear me. The blood rushed to my face. 'How do I tell him . . . ?' I asked Clémence.

At first I thought she would not answer. Then she lifted her fingers to her lips and extended them towards Aaró. Awkwardly, I did the same.

He laughed, a strange breathy sound, and nodded. Not knowing what else to do, I sat down. Aaró was scooping honey from the jar on to a piece of bread. Some pooled stickily on to the table, and Clémence slapped at his hands, but he only winked, stooped to kiss her on the cheek before disappearing out into the morning, eating as he went.

A trio of cats sauntered in when he left. They milled around the stove, obviously waiting for their breakfast. Clémence put a bowl of fish scraps on the floor and they fell upon them.

'They're his handiwork,' she said, hacking another slice from the bread. 'He's always been this way, bringing home lost things. He's got sharper eyes than most, sees things trying to hide themselves. Half-starved cats, gulls tangled in fishing line.' She pushed the food towards me. 'I feed them, so I might as well feed you too.'

Part of me balked at her words, but I didn't have the energy to argue. Perhaps it was the warmth of the kitchen, or the bath, or the fact that I was safe beneath a roof, but weariness was washing over me.

'Go on, girl, try and eat before you sleep,' she said gently.

I barely saw the room she showed me to, only knew that it was up a dark, narrow staircase, at

157

the very top of the house, where closed shutters kept out the light. There was a wooden floor and a creaking iron bed that had seen better days, but it was cosy and there were sheets and blankets smelling of soap and the sea air that had dried them.

Whatever she told me next, I don't remember. I sank into the blankets and slept the dead sleep of fugitives and runaways.

June 1969

The break in the weather doesn't last and by Monday, London is back to its old, sticky self. Between the buildings, the sky is a strip of perfect blue, like the posters that advertise holidays to Spain. Can solicitors afford to go to Spain? Hillbrand only ever goes to his sister's caravan at Bognor. Maybe he'll get a cheap deal at Hallerton when it's finally turned into a holiday camp.

The streets are crammed, all sputtering buses and swerving messenger bikes; nothing like Saltedge with its endless reeds that are one long *husssssssssh* and a sky so big and empty it makes you feel like you've been turned inside out.

I pause at the door of Hillbrand & Moffat. Emeline's diary is in my briefcase. Time and time again over the weekend I've tried to make sense of why I feel so bad, without success. Now, all I'm left with is a sense of unease, dogging me as I trudge up each stair.

'Billy!' Jill exclaims as I round the corner. She beams up at me, in her eternal blue twinset and pearls.

'Morning, Jill.'

'And what time d'you call this, lad?'

'Sorry, Mr Hillbrand, that A13 was a right mess — '

The answer drops from my mouth before I see that he's grinning, hands on his hips, or at least

159

hands on where his trousers fasten around his belly.

'No clock-watching today, Perch, not from my man in Havana! You got it there? All the bits of business?'

The leather of the briefcase is warm. I place it on the table.

'Yes, sir.'

'Good lad! Sit down, sit down, let's see it.'

He uses his belly to shepherd me towards his own chair. I sink into it with a vague sense of horror. It's more comfortable than mine, the leather pummelled into submission by years of his weight. He leans over me, all eagerness as I open the clasp of the briefcase.

My instincts are yelling for me to stop as I take out the diary, but it's already too late. Hillbrand snatches it up, pores over the pages, and all I can do is watch as Emeline's secrets, whispered into the darkness of her room, are laid bare.

'I know a diary doesn't really prove any-thing — ' I start.

Hillbrand brushes my protestations aside. 'It's just what we need, lad. I'll get us a doctor's statement to back it all up. Lithium bromide, was it? Jill! Get Dr Berger on the phone, he'll give us a quote.' He seizes the photograph of the group in Saltedge. 'Which one is she then?'

I have to point out Emeline, sitting there, so real and sad in the middle.

Hillbrand whistles. 'Bit of a looker, wasn't she? Pity she was out of her tree.'

I jam my hands between my knees, fighting

160

the sudden urge to punch him in his big, red face. 'Yes, sir.'

'Perch, this is sterling work, lad. Really is. Won't go unrecognized.'

Last week I would've jumped for joy. Now, I just feel wretched.

'Thank you, Mr Hillbrand.'

'Well, shift yourself,' he bustles. 'Got some calls to make before we can go for a victory pint.'

The towering stack of triplicate forms is almost a relief. Perhaps the repetitive typing will drown out the shame I'm feeling. That's the idea, anyway. By the time Hillbrand puts down the receiver half an hour later, I've barely managed to complete one.

'That was Mrs Mallory,' he says, cracking his neck with relish. 'She's delighted, lad. Delighted. She's meeting the property developer at her club for luncheon, asked us to join them.' His face is shining at the prospect. 'How about that, eh? Jill, any appointments this afternoon?'

'You've got Mr Parminter at three, Dick.'

'Cancel him, will you? These business lunches take time. Perch, we leave in half an hour. Bring all of this lot with you. Her ladyship and those property folk will want to see it. And *try* to get that hair to lie flat. You look like a hippy. This is a fancy place we're going to.'

After fifteen minutes pressed up against Hillbrand on the sweaty, crowded tube, I feel anything but fancy. As he knocks on the door of a quietly opulent Belgravia townhouse I search my pockets for a handkerchief, and not finding one, wipe my face surreptitiously with my tie.

161

I'm drying off the reservoir under my nose when the door swings open.

A butler in white gloves watches as I drop the tie, mid-dab.

'Here to see a Mrs Mallory,' Hillbrand announces. 'She's expecting us.'

The butler mutely inclines his head as if to say, *How unfortunate for her*, and sweeps before us into a grand entrance hall. I try not to gawp. It's like Buckingham Palace. Steph would go mad. There's a wide, carpeted staircase, and a slippery-looking marble floor and plants everywhere. Even Hillbrand looks surprised.

'Could be a top client for us here, Perch,' he says through the corner of his mouth.

I wish I could tell him that once this business with Emeline and Hallerton is done, he'll never see Mrs Mallory or her brother again. I want to point out that the only reason they even set foot in Hillbrand & Moffat is because he has Great-uncle Durrant's files, because they were too greedy and impatient to try to transfer them to their own *respectable* family solicitor.

But I can't, not least because the butler is ushering us into a cloakroom, where a second man divests Hillbrand of his hat and me of my briefcase. From there it's on to a dark-panelled dining room. Tables spread with pristine linen stand a discreet distance from each other, populated by men in expensive suits and women with perfect up-dos.

Mrs Mallory is waiting, along with a thin, bald man. His head is so shiny it looks like it's made from Bakelite. His blue suit is cut perfectly to his frame and she's wearing a tailored cream dress that probably cost more than my month's wages.

'Gentlemen,' she says, serenely, 'how nice to see you. This is Mr Remington.'

The Bakelite cracks as the man lifts his mouth in a smile. I shake his hand. It's dry and weightless.

'Mr Remington,' Hillbrand beams over his own handshake, 'an honour. I hear you have some grand plans for Hallerton, sir.'

I know what he's thinking. Remington Camps are one of the biggest holiday businesses in the country: a game-changing client for Hillbrand & Moffat.

'Would you like a drink?'

Mrs Mallory's looking at me. Oh God.

'Ah,' I say, 'a pint of — '

'Sherry,' interrupts Hillbrand. 'We'll both take a sherry.'

The waiters vanish as though they never existed. Mrs Mallory is up to her old trick of not blinking. I try to loosen my collar and almost knock a knife flying.

'Well, Mr Perch,' Remington says over my fumbling, 'you have good news for us, all the way from Hallerton.'

The name sounds wrong in his voice, smooth and artificial as sweetener. I look at his immaculately pressed jacket, his gold cufflinks. I can't think of anyone less suited to Hallerton, or to the remote green marshes of Saltedge, but I attempt a smile.

'That's right.'

'Like I said, we'll have this case sewn up by

the end of the month.' Hillbrand flaps his napkin importantly. 'Mr Perch has discovered that your aunt's mental state, Mrs Mallory, was less than stable at the time of her disappearance.'

'Indeed. And while I don't mean to sound ungrateful, we knew that already, Mr Hillbrand. Our great-uncle Andrew told us as much before he died. I do hope Mr Perch has managed to obtain some hard proof?' She smiles. 'Without it, all of this is just family gossip. Not enough for a declaration of death, as I'm sure you know.'

Hillbrand nods indulgently. 'Not only did Mr Perch manage to obtain it, ma'am, but we've brought it along with us today. He'll be only too happy to show you later, won't you, Perch?'

The waiters return, bringing amber liquid in little cut crystal goblets. I stare into mine and all I can think of is Emeline, pouring drinks for the men come to buy up her past, trying so hard to hold on to herself. Emeline, heart-broken, her hands full of shards . . .

'In that case, here's to a rewarding end to this whole business.' Mrs Mallory raises her glass in a toast. 'You can't imagine how grateful my brother and I are, Mr Perch.'

'Or my board of directors,' says Remington, and they laugh.

I've never had sherry before. I take a gulp so that I don't have to join in. It's dry and cloying all at once, with a taste that sticks at the back of my throat and won't be swallowed away. Hillbrand is talking. I force my attention back to the conversation.

' . . . obviously due to the lack of progeny on

Emeline's part, Hallerton reverts solely to your father, Mrs Mallory. As for the timing,' Hillbrand sluices down some more sherry, 'I don't think any court would disagree that fixing Emeline's death at the time of her disappearance is in keeping with any suicidal — '

'She didn't kill herself.'

I close my mouth, to stop any other words escaping of their own accord. Hillbrand throws me a disbelieving look.

'No, indeed, Mr Perch is right, we'll phrase it more sensitively than that,' he rushes. 'But based on the documentation we have gathered, the court will, without a doubt, declare her death and grant probate.'

'Let us hope that's the case,' Mrs Mallory murmurs, exchanging a look with Remington. I can tell he's studying me, even while he pretends to peruse the menu.

I don't recognize any of the words written there, beyond 'salad' and, inexplicably, 'turtle soup' and nod when Hillbrand offers to order for me.

'Ever tried pate, lad?' He winks, whilst Remington questions the waiter in detail about salad dressing.

The prospect of food seems to have cheered Hillbrand up enough to let my previous outburst slip. Perhaps he thinks I'm just nervous. Am I nervous? My breathing is quicker than it should be. For some reason, I want to grab the flimsy glasses and fling them across the room, want to yell at the three of them, until they understand that what we're doing is wrong.

165

I manage to get through the next few minutes with a series of nods and noises, but by the time the food arrives, I feel like I'm going to explode. I watch the waiters place a bowl of perfectly clear soup in front of Mrs Mallory.

'It'll be our biggest camp yet,' Mr Remington is explaining to Hillbrand. 'We've found a way to double the accommodation within any given area. Not as much space, of course,' he leans back as a waiter slides a plate before him, 'but that's not a problem.' He smiles at me, mistaking my deathly silence for interest. 'They all want a holiday, Mr Perch, that's the beauty of it. They'll pay more for newer, better attractions, and at the same time, by building at Hallerton we take custom from our rivals at Great Yarmouth and Southwold.'

With a flourish, the waiter lays a plate before me. It contains an artfully curled bit of toast, next to a rectangle of something mottled and meaty and yellow. It glistens in the light, repulsive and expensive. It has a cost, I realize, all of this has a cost . . .

My chair squeaks as I push it backwards. Hillbrand looks alarmed, Mrs Mallory and Remington quizzical, but I put on my best sheepish grin.

'Excuse me a minute, would you? Nature calls.'

Hillbrand chortles at my clueless manners and Mrs Mallory gives me a pained smile before turning back to the conversation. I follow the waiter out of the dining room, heart pounding.

'The gentlemen's room is this way, sir,' the

waiter-butler tells me. Ahead I can see the marble entrance hall. I mumble something to him about needing air and stride off before he can correct me. The cloakroom attendant looks confused, but hands over my briefcase when I ask. I clutch the worn leather to my chest, manage to make it across the hall and out the front door before I break into a run.

I don't know what I'm doing; I only know that it's right. With every step away from the restaurant my anger is being replaced by something else, bright and frightening and fragile. I think it's hope.

Outside the tube station, I slow to a stop. All around me workers are pushing their way back to offices, suited, hatted, hurried. A man is heading towards the nearest telephone box but I get there first. I dial a number from memory. It rings. Once, twice, three times. Please don't be on lunch, please . . .

'Hillbrand and Moffat?' Jill answers, her mouth full.

'Jill, it's me.'

'Billy! Aren't you meant to be at your fancy lunch?'

'Something's come up, I need to check — ' I swallow hard, but there's no going back. 'Jill, Timothy Vane . . . which hospital is he at?'

March 1919

For the second time that day, a scent pulled me out of sleep. At first I was confused in the darkness, but it found me again, impossible to ignore: onions, frying fish, spices that hovered at the edge of recognition. I pushed myself up on to my elbows and sniffed. I had no notion of how much time had passed, or even what day it was. All I knew was that I was ravenous.

I crawled from the blankets. Tiredness clung to me as I found the wooden shutters and pulled them open. Outside, it was dark. Carefully, I shunted open the frame, too. The noise of the sea rushed up to greet me. I had no idea it was so close. I could smell it, mingling with the scent of cooking from below.

And there were voices, many voices, talking, laughing. Light spilled from the ground floor of the Fourniers' house, stretching across a dirt road and down on to what looked like a beach. Occasionally, a wave would catch the edge of the light.

I crept down the creaking staircase, like a child at a party. The smell grew stronger, the heat of cooking wafted up to greet me and my stomach growled. My body had definite ideas about what it wanted and that was food, and drink — and soon. I stepped into the kitchen.

Clémence stood at the stove. It dominated the space, a huge black range fuelled by wood, which added its irresistible scent to the cooking. Dozens of pots and pans and skillets hung from the walls, blackened from use. Shelves on either side held jars and tins, bunches of dried herbs, bottles of liquid. A shallow bowl sat near Clémence's elbow, filled to the brim with glistening sea salt.

She was tending to three pans at once. In two, chunks of white fish were frying, a coating of flour turning them crisp and golden. In the third, I could see onions and herbs bubbling in oil. A heavy *thud* from the table made me jump and I turned to see Aaró, a mallet in his hand, crushing something on a wooden board.

'It smells wonderful,' I called over the sizzling. 'What are you cooking?'

Clémence flipped the fish deftly with one hand, reaching for a tin with the other.

'Dinner.'

I watched, fascinated, as she shook a bright red powder into the onions. Immediately a scent rose, sweet and smoky, turning everything in the pan a deep crimson. Swiftly, she added the fish, a slosh of wine from an unmarked bottle, a ladleful of broth from a pan at the back of the stove.

I'd never seen anything like it. No weights or measures or hesitancy. She cooked by instinct, moved like lightning, as if her hands knew what to do on their own. At my cooking classes, we had been taught to work slowly and prudently, in pinches and thimbles and tiny slivers.

She slurped a bit of the bubbling sauce from a wooden spoon, nodded once and pushed it to a cooler part of the stove.

'If you want to help,' she said over her shoulder as she glugged oil into a new pan, 'ask Aaró.'

The young man was still using the mallet to crush something up, making noises to himself that I knew he couldn't hear. It was garlic, I saw, two entire heads of it. The smell was intense; it made my eyes and my mouth water at the same time. We had never used garlic at my classes. The teacher had deemed it 'too coarse' a flavour for the palate of young ladies. She would've swooned at the sight of this. I smiled and Aaró looked up, with his bright grey eyes.

'Can I help?' I pointed to the garlic and to me, hoping that Clémence would step in and translate, but she was busy slapping another half-dozen pieces of fish into a pan. Aaró frowned, looking down at the garlic, not understanding. I tried again, pointing to me, then him, then a bowl, to no avail.

Perhaps it was my useless expression, but abruptly he glanced at his mother, clanging away at the stove, and his face lit up with realization. He beckoned me forward.

He dumped the pulverized garlic cloves into a huge pestle and mortar that stood beside him, threw in a handful of rough salt, and began to mash it all into a paste. He had strong hands, I saw, as tanned as his face and callused across the fingers. I had never known a man who could cook, but Aaró moved like his mother, swift and comfortable. It was wonderful to watch.

He waved his hand before my face to get my attention. I nodded to show I was watching. He took up a tin can with a long, thin spout and dropped a tiny amount of golden-green oil into the garlic. He worked it in, slowly and methodically, then added another few drops, before handing over the tin to me.

We worked that way, heads close, until the mortar was magically filled with a smooth, creamy, yellow substance. Smiling to himself, Aaró stuck his little finger into it and tasted before indicating that I should do the same.

The flavour exploded on my tongue. It was like nothing I had ever eaten, strong and rich and sweet all at once. Forgetting myself, I reached out again, only to find my hand slapped away by Aaró. We smiled at each other, and once again I felt that strange urge to step closer, to study his face.

But Clémence called me over. She was pouring the steaming stew into two enormous serving bowls.

'Take these if you want to help.' She shoved several loaves of crusty bread into my arms and pointed to a tray. I was so preoccupied with hunger and cooking with Aaró that I had forgotten the sound of voices from the front of the house, didn't even consider it until I stepped through a curtained doorway and was confronted by the sight of two-dozen strangers.

They sat squashed together, drinking wine from tumblers, their cheeks flushed and faces bright. The front of the house was a café, I saw then. Long tables and mismatched chairs had been crammed into every conceivable space. The walls were roughly plastered, painted a cheery yellow. A wooden bar ran along the back of the room, stacked with plates and spoons and glasses.

The people were speaking the odd language from the train station again, mixed with French and Spanish. The men wore jumpers and neck scarves, soft caps pushed back on their heads. Others were dressed in overalls. The women wore plain skirts and heavy boots, their black hair coiled and pinned sensibly above tanned necks.

Most of them began applauding when they saw Clémence walk in, only to falter as I appeared behind her. I stuck out like a sore thumb. Even in my borrowed clothes, I looked different, knew I would sound different, with my stiff, tutor-polished French.

I kept my head down, away from those dark, direct stares, wishing I could creep back to the kitchen. I heard more than one voice start to whisper.

'This is Mademoiselle Fischer,' Clémence said to the room, setting a steaming bowl on the counter. 'She will be staying here for a few days. Now, *txin txin!*'

The townspeople forgot me in the business of yelling their approval and raising their wine glasses. They piled up to the front, scrambling to get in front of each other. Clémence ladled portions of stew on to the waiting plates.

Stealthily, Aaró doled out a couple of servings of his own. He topped each with a spoonful of the yellow garlic sauce and a large chunk of bread. I found the bowl pushed into my hands.

He winked at me, made a sign with his closed fingers against his mouth, rubbed his chest and was gone, weaving through the tables towards a group of men in fishermen's clothes, who smiled and waved as he approached.

I was left alone, holding the brimming plate, anxious as a child on the first day of school. Part of me wanted to stride across the room to sit with Aaró but it wouldn't be right, a single woman and a group of men. There was space at the furthest corner of the last table. The townspeople nearby ignored me when I sat down. They spoke in their own language, occasionally whispering and glancing my way.

Concentrate on eating, I told myself, but soon I found that I didn't need to try. The food claimed all my attention. I'd never eaten anything like it. Every mouthful seemed to sing with flavour. Onions cooked to sweetness, fish so fresh it still tasted of the ocean's minerals, fragrant herbs, thyme and aniseed, and most of all the powerful red spice, mouth-wateringly smoky. I forgot myself completely and ate like a savage, tearing off mouthfuls of the bread to soak up the garlic sauce that mingled with the savoury broth.

All too soon I had to sit back, though the bowl was still half-full. The chatter in the room continued over the scrape of spoons, over slurping and noises of appreciation. Clémence sat in the middle, elbow to elbow, laughing at a joke. She looked younger than before. They called her 'Maman', I realized, because she gave them what a mother would: a familiar face, the warmth of a hearth, a meal cooked with love.

We all have our roles, she'd said. Emeline Vane had a role, one that I had never asked for. But Emilie Fischer? Next to me, a man poured himself a tumbler of wine from the communal pitcher, and drank it down. Smiling, I did the same.

June 1969

I follow Jill's directions to a private hospital, in another wealthy area. Before I can talk myself out of it, I run up the steps. In the reception area there are flowers on a table and padded chairs, and a radio playing classical music. No sterile green lino and harsh lights and metallic noises here.

A woman in a nurse's cap is staring at me from behind a high counter. I try to swallow down the nerves that are bubbling up from my stomach.

'Good afternoon.' I put on my best posh accent. 'I'm here to see my uncle, Mr Vane.'

'Your uncle?' the nurse says. Unlike mine, her voice is BBC perfect. 'And your name is?'

'William Vane.' It sounds so strange that I worry I've said it wrong. 'William Vane,' I try again, for emphasis.

'I see.' Her neat smile gives nothing away. 'The lunch round is currently taking place, Mr Vane. Visiting hours will recommence in fifteen minutes. If you'd like to make yourself comfortable . . . ?'

As soon as I walk away she slides her glass partition shut and picks up the phone. I'd wager half a crown she's checking up on me with Mrs Mallory or her brother. In which case, I need a Plan B.

While she's distracted I make a break for it,

175

sidle out and down the steps. These places always have a back door, right? Somewhere to keep rubbish and laundry carts and for people to have a fag. Sure enough, down the street I come across an alleyway, a line of bins. I follow them down. Two porters stand near an open door, smoking cigarettes.

Be like Harry Palmer, I tell myself and put on my best Michael Caine walk.

'Afternoon,' I greet the porters briskly, as though I know where I'm going and don't have time to shilly-shally. They nod in response and go back to their conversation.

I did it! I can't believe I did it! I keep expecting one of them to change their mind and call me back, so I take a set of stairs two at a time, up another flight for good measure to avoid the reception nurse, until I emerge on to a quiet corridor.

It's more like a hospital here, white-tiled and brightly lit. Rooms stretch off left and right. I creep along as unobtrusively as I can, checking the name on each door, without success.

But there, on the next floor up, is a room labelled with two words that make me break into a cold sweat. Through the door I can see a figure lying in a bed, beneath starched sheets. A bag of liquid drip-drips steadily down a tube, into his arm.

I don't know what to expect. To me, Timothy is a little boy with hair as brown as a bulrush, frightened and lonely. There's no answer to my knock, so hesitantly, I step inside and close the door behind me.

The man in the bed looks like someone who has lost a lot of weight in a short space of time. His once-brown hair is almost entirely silver, but is still thick. He's not old, I realize as I stand there, speechless. He's ill, but not old, in his late fifties, perhaps. A handful of fine lines score a handsome face, surround the dark brown eyes that open blearily to look at me.

We stare, both as confused as each other, before his mouth drops open in alarm.

'Mr Vane,' I've never been so nervous in my life, 'please, I need to speak to you. It's about Hallerton.' An expression that could be anger creases one of his brows as he turns his head away, staring at a red cord that hangs beside the bed. 'It's about Emeline.'

His head flops back towards me. It obviously takes great effort. One side of his mouth is slack, saliva spilling from his lip, but as I watch, he tries to form a word. I make out what could be the shapes of 'm' and 'li'.

Trying to put him at ease, I explain who I am, about Great-uncle Durrant and Hillbrand. Mrs Mallory said something about a stroke. Does he understand anything I'm telling him? He's looking at me hard; I think he's listening, but I can't be sure. I carry on anyway. I don't have a choice.

'Mr Vane, your daughter has hired us to prove that Emeline is dead. They're going to sell Hallerton, have it knocked down. Did you know that?'

Timothy Vane moves his mouth an inch, manages a nod, a tiny shake of the head. I don't know what he means, but I can sense his frustration, the fierce struggle of a man against his body.

'Mr Vane, I went to Saltedge.' I pull up a chair to the bed, fumble through the briefcase. 'It's beautiful there.'

I tell him about the first time I saw Hallerton, about the garden and the rooms and the study and the face I thought I saw in the window. About Jem and her car and smoking on the terrace. One of his eyes crinkles in what could be amusement. When I take out the diary, though, his face changes and I worry what I'm about to say might be too much for him.

'This is where I first heard about you,' I say, opening a page. I read Emeline's words aloud: memories of her brothers, the Blackberry Day and the February marshes, her conversations with Andrew, tucking Timothy into bed. I stop abruptly as a strange, strangled sound comes from Vane's throat and I realize that he is crying.

For a moment I'm racked with guilt, but then I remember Mrs Mallory, Mr Remington, raising a glass to the end of it all.

'I don't think Emeline is dead,' I tell him. 'At least, I don't think she killed herself all those years ago.'

The tears are spilling from Vane's closed eyes, his nose beginning to run. After a second's hesitation, I take a tissue from the box beside the bed, and wipe his face. His bloodshot eyes open wide in shock. Then, I see a flicker of the businessman he must have been, as he comes to a decision.

Laboured noises emerge from his throat as he twitches a finger, pointing. There's a cabinet next to him, a key in the door. I open it. Inside there's an expensive hat, some keys, a silk handkerchief and a large leather wallet. Vane must have been carrying them when he was brought in. Hesitantly, I bring out the wallet.

'This?'

Half a nod.

I open it. Inside are banknotes, more than I've ever seen in one go, must be nearly fifty pounds.

'I don't understand,' I murmur, staring at the absurdity of all that wealth.

He's trying to speak, gesturing with his finger, and then I see it, tucked away behind the notes, paper that's brown and fuzzed at the edges, as though it has been carried for a long time.

I lift it out. It looks like a letter, coming apart at the creases. My heart starts to beat faster. Is this the hidden letter Mrs Mallory mentioned? *He's always said that it proves she's alive somewhere* . . . But before I can ask, Vane starts making noises again. He's peering at the table by his head. There's a notepad lying there, and a pencil.

'You want . . . ?'

It's a struggle to wedge it under his unmoving hand, a dead weight on the sheet. It seems he can only move his fingers, and the pencil falls again and again from his frail grip. He's exhausted but determined. Finally, I place my, hand over his and hold the pencil steady for him.

The writing is tortured, barely decipherable. By the time the pencil drops on to the blanket and Vane's head sinks into the pillow, there are just two words:

FIND HER

March 1919

The waves washed against the shore. In the dawn light they were the same colour as the inside of a shell, blue-white and flushed with pink.

Behind me stood the Fourniers' house. It was tall and narrow, its peeling shutters painted a bright blue against the ochre walls. Above the folding doors, a sign explained everything. *Café Fi del Món*, it pronounced in hand-painted letters. *Café at the World's End*.

It stood at the very heart of the town, only a few paces from the beach. Hills rose up on either side, sheltering the bay like a pair of cupped hands holding water.

Strange, to have come from one world's end to another. The last time I had visited the public house in Saltedge, it had been Armistice Day. There had seemed little to celebrate, but I had hoped that the occasion might mark the beginning of our healing, Mother and Timothy and I. I hadn't known that the world would crumble further before three months were out.

I wondered at the café's name. The town here certainly felt removed, perched on the very edge of France, in a forgotten corner that I had never noticed on any map. Although I knew now that Spain lay just over the border, it still seemed a thousand miles away. Cerbère was its own place: neither one country nor another.

I shivered. The dawn air held on to night's chill. England would be trapped deep in frost, but here I sensed that the rising sun would bring warmth, a bright spring day. Out of nowhere, a sharp breeze blew, snatching at the shawl I hugged around my chest. It was cold, smelled inexplicably of ice. From the station above the town, I heard a long, melancholic hoot, a train's whistle as it came to a halt at the last station in France.

Now? It seemed to ask. I watched the foam break and dissolve on the shore. The answer to that question had kept me awake since the early hours, tired though I was. A possibility had chased its tail around my head, until I was forced to throw back the blankets and venture into the dark kitchen in search of paper and a pen. With my feet tucked up on the bench above the cold tiled floor, I had written the letter.

It fluttered in my hand. I had seen a tiny post office on Cerbère's one main street, but I didn't dare to send it that way. A post office used stamps, which in turn gave a location. Besides, I had no money, and did not want to beg any from Clémence. There was one other way, one person I might be able to trust to see the letter safely home. Even so, it had taken me a long time to write the seven words on the front of an envelope.

Jean-Baptiste Gosse
Depot
Gare d'Austerlitz
Paris

The noises of the station grew louder as I walked up the steep hill towards it. A dozen times, I almost turned back. What if someone knew I'd stowed away and was waiting to have me arrested? What if someone suspected that I was running and decided to make enquiries in Paris? Andrew must have been searching for me there. By fleeing the train I'd proved his every fear about my mental state. A bleak thought surfaced. *What if he was right?*

I tried to shake off my anxiety as I approached the station. One day at a time. No one knew I was here, no one knew who I was; as far as the townspeople were concerned, I was Mademoiselle Fischer.

It wasn't difficult to find the conductors and the drivers of the trains, smoking and lounging outside the company office. They stared at me as I approached, and I smiled, hiding my trembling hands in my skirts.

'*Bonjour*,' I said, trying to soften my precise French. 'Are any of you going to Paris?'

A man in uniform shifted his posture a few inches.

'Paris, *non*,' he told me. 'Lyon for me, mam'selle.'

'I'm going to Bordeaux,' a soot-stained driver said, finishing his cigarette, 'but it'll be someone else taking the train from there to Paris. Why?'

'Would you mind passing this on, please?' I held out the letter. 'It must go to the depot, at Austerlitz.'

I thought he would refuse but he glanced down, saw the man's name written there. He

183

smirked at me, tipped a knowing wink.

'Leave it with me, *ma petite*,' he said, shoving the letter into his pocket. 'I'll see that it finds its way.'

⋆ ⋆ ⋆

By the time I returned, Clémence was already up and starting the work of the day. I lingered in the doorway, summoning my courage, watching as she raked out the ash from the stove. One of Aaró's cats strolled in and bumped against my legs. I bent to stroke its soft ears.

'Whatever you've got to say,' Clémence called, 'you might as well get on with it. I'm not a mind-reader.'

She stood, pushing her headscarf back with ash-covered hands. I straightened up too. The letter was sent. I had no excuse for hesitation, now.

I tried to keep my voice calm. 'I . . . '

'Want to stay?' she finished. When I didn't reply she gave a hard laugh and turned back to the stove, shoving in a handful of twigs and wood shavings, lighting them with a match. 'I knew it. It's the way with strays. You feel sorry for them, show them, charity, and they move in, eat you out of house and home — '

'I'm not an animal.' My temper flared, from fear as well as anger. I didn't want to think about what might happen if she refused. 'And I'd appreciate it if you stopped comparing me to one. I do not want charity.'

'What then?' She faced me again, hands on

184

hips, formidable. 'You told me you had no money, and I certainly can't afford to keep you.'

'I could work.'

'But you're . . . ' *A lady.* The unspoken words hung between us. *Respectable. Well-bred. Useless.* 'You've never worked a day in your life,' she concluded. 'What would you do?'

Here was the second battle.

'I could cook.'

'In *my* café?' Clémence drew herself up.

'I want to learn,' I said, before she could protest. 'Where I came from, they used to say I was good at cooking.' My eyes lingered over the huge, black stove. 'But what you do here, it's different. Last night, when I ate, it was like tasting for the first time. Like discovering colour. It made me want to — '

I cut myself off. *Live*, I'd almost said.

She was staring at me, with her silver-blue eyes so like her son's. I had to look away.

'It made me happy,' I murmured. 'I wasn't sure I would ever be happy again.'

The fire popped and smoked behind her. She turned away to tend it, adding more kindling, logs, propped carefully against each other. I could see she was thinking hard. All I could do was wait, standing in the open door with nothing but hope.

'You say you can cook?'

I still couldn't see her face.

'Yes.' I took a step forwards. 'I took a few lessons. Nothing like you, but some basic — '

'What can you cook?'

An easier question. 'Quail, partridge, soups,

185

beef, pies, cakes, custards . . . '

Clémence wrinkled her nose in distaste.

'Fish?' she asked.

'Yes, of course.' I tried to sound confident.

'Fine. You can make us lunch today. If you know a spoon from your elbow, I might consider it.'

★ ★ ★

Later that morning I stood alone in the kitchen, staring at a squat-looking fish, a 'dorade' Clémence called it. Aaró had brought it in earlier. He was a fisherman, his mother told me, had been since he was a boy. Out there, he did not need to hear. Every day, before dawn, he took to his boat with the other men. What they brought back depended on time, and tide, but a large amount of it always found its way into the kitchen of the Café Fi del Món. Dinner was created from whatever could be found that day, fresh from sea or land.

Mid-morning, Aaró had brought the day's fish, in a box filled with seawater to keep them fresh. His feet were bare, trousers rolled up to his knees, tanned arms streaked with salt. As Clémence inspected the catch, he looked up at me, his black hair damp with spray. I wanted to ask him who had taught him to fish, about the sea, about himself, but I didn't know how. So I only smiled, and stepped to join them, looking down at the dozen or so fish, their scales silver and pink as the waves at sunrise. They were so beautiful it seemed a shame to cook them.

Clémence picked one out for me, sealed the others away in the scullery for dinner, and left me alone to prove myself. I did not have much to work with. At my cooking classes, everything had always been prepared, cleaned and scrubbed of mud, skinned or gutted or plucked. Such dirty jobs should be left to the domestic help, we had been told.

Here, I had a whole fish, a bucket of offcuts from the night before, onions, garlic, unfamiliar spices . . . It was nothing like the cooking I had done at home, with bottles of Madeira or sherry to hand, with blocks of fresh butter and churns full of cream. But I pushed back my sleeves and selected one of the sharp knives.

Hesitantly, I cut into the belly of the fish. It looked at me accusingly as blood and juices ran free. *You're going to make a mess of me*, it seemed to say. Clémence came in behind me, holding a bundle of linen.

'You're going to make a mess of that,' she said.

I ignored her, tried to lift up the belly of the fish. Some of the guts spilled out.

'Here.' She strode over, and took the knife from me. 'Lift his fin, cut like this.'

Soon, a perfectly cleaned fish sat before me. Clémence wiped her hands and went back to the table and her darning. 'Head in the pot with the scraps,' she said, 'tail for the cats, guts in the bucket for the fishermen.'

As I cooked, I tried to remember what I had seen Clémence doing the night before. I was too afraid to use the hot, red powder that had been so delicious. In the end, I rubbed the fish with oil

187

and salt and garlic and dried thyme, and set it to cook in a dish on top of some sliced onion.

It looked good enough, but was nothing like the symphony of flavours that Clémence had produced. I caught her appraising glances over at the stove from time to time. I had never been so desperate to please anyone, but what could I do? I felt like a child with a toy violin in the presence of a great composer. It wasn't enough. Perhaps if I had been at home, with ingredients I recognized . . .

Out of nowhere, an idea crept upon me. The fish baking in the oven was almost cooked, but there was still time. I took a knife and raced out of the back door without a word to Clémence, around the corner and on to the beach. I had seen the clumps of green plants that morning, growing out of the shingle, but it hadn't occurred to me to look closer.

Down on my knees, I ran my aching hands through the fleshy stems. Tentatively, I broke one off, and bit into it. A salty, juicy taste flooded my tongue, taking me straight back to Saltedge, to the marshes and to picnics with my brothers.

Clémence stared at me as though I was mad when I returned with a handful of the stems and dropped them into a pan of water.

'You're planning to feed us weeds?'

'Not weeds,' I told her, with a flicker of pride, 'it's called crest marine, or glasswort. At home we used to eat it raw, sometimes.' I didn't mention that my mother would never have allowed it on our plates, that she used to say it was only fit for paupers. Clémence sniffed, and turned back to her darning. Her expression plainly said, *We'll see.*

I could barely watch when, a short while later, Clémence lifted out the fish and separated it on to three plates. I put a few of the salty green stems on each. Aaró had come in from his work, mending nets, Clémence said. His cheeks were whipped pink and he brought the scents of the shore with him. He looked ravenous.Clémence put a plate in front of him, pointed to me, made a few signs.

He raised his eyebrows in surprise, then grinned and fell upon the fish. Hesitantly, I tried a piece. It was good, but that was thanks mostly to the fish itself. I watched the pair of them chew, Aaró quickly, Clémence thoughtfully.

'Well?' I forced myself to say, when the plates were cleaned. Seeing my hopeful expression, Aaró deliberately tore off a piece of bread to mop up the oils from the dish, nodding his approval. I smiled at him gratefully. Licking the oil from his fingers, he signed something. Clémence snorted with laughter, and signed back.

'What did he say?' I couldn't contain the impatience in my voice.

'He said it wasn't bad, for an Englishwoman.'

A smile lingered around her eyes as she leaned forwards over the table.

'You have a lot to learn, girl.'

Hope, fluttering in my chest, too easily crushed.

'You mean . . . ?'

'We shall have to serve more people in the

evenings, to make up for another mouth to feed. *And* I have a few conditions. But yes, Mam'selle Fischer, if you wish to, you may stay. For now.'

June 1969

In the park everything is normal, but I feel like a fugitive. The ducks quack gently at the edge of the pond, children shriek and tear about in games of tag or leapfrog, watched with one eye by their mothers. Nannies, more like. It's posh here. Their mothers are probably drinking sherry and eating turtle soup.

The thought of the three of them — Mrs Mallory and Remington and Hillbrand — makes my stomach squirm. How long did they go on eating before they realized something was wrong? Will they guess what I've done?

What *have* I done? I press my fingers into my forehead and try to make sense of it all. What will my parents say? I can see their faces now, flabbergasted and angry that I've blown my big chance because of some . . . instinct. But I can't ignore it; the strange connection I feel with Emeline, the certainty that no one will be able to find her except for me.

Slowly, I take out the letter I got from Timothy Vane. Folded around it are a bundle of banknotes. The sight of them makes me feel even queasier. I didn't want to take them, but he kept gesturing until I put them in my pocket. If the nurse from reception had arrived a minute earlier than she did, she definitely would have assumed the worst. As it was, she made it quite clear that if I didn't leave immediately she'd have a pair of porters drag me out by my ears.

What was Vane trying to say as I left? He was red in the face with the effort. I nodded to him over my shoulder and he nodded back, twitched his fingers as if to say, *I'll be here.*

The yellowed paper flutters in my hands like wings. Typewritten, dated April 1919. What's this about? The sheet separates in my hands and I swear, thinking I've ripped it. But it isn't one letter; it's two. The first is thicker, worn at the edges, topped by a letterhead: *Chemin defer du Midi.*

Master Vane,
Please forgive my English. This letter
was wait for me when I return last week,
with a note, ask me to send. It is late
— please forgive. I been away. When
you read, you will write and say, 'Where
is she?' but I not know. I know your
sister short time only, then we part. That
is all I say.

A votre service,
Jean-Baptiste Gosse
Depot, Gare d'Austerlitz, Paris

I've never heard the name before, but whoever it was claims to have known Emeline. Quickly, I turn to the second letter. It's written on cheap paper, the ink paled by time, but I know the writing. I know the loops of those 'e's, the curve of the capital 'T'. It's Emeline.

192

Dearest Timothy,

*I do not know what you will think of me,
or how much Uncle Andrew has told you
about what has happened. Frankly, I am
not sure I know myself. But I wanted to
say that I am safe, somewhere a long way
away, so far it might as well be the end of
the world.*

*You must not worry about me. You
must let Uncle Andrew and Aunt Olivia
look after you, like Mama wanted, and be
a good boy, and work hard at school and
try to laugh again.*

*I wish I could tell you this myself. I wish
we had been left alone at Hallerton.*

*Please try to keep this letter a secret. I
cannot tell you where I am, or give you a
return address, in case someone else does
read it, I don't know if I will still be here,
in any case. I've asked a friend to deliver
this for me: I hope it finds its way to you
safely. I hope that you will understand,
one day.*

I am sorry.
All my love,
E

Later, I stand inside a telephone box, staring at
the receiver. It's the end of the working day and
business-people stream around me, jostling
towards home. I watch them through the little
glass panes. A coin is growing clammy between

193

my fingers. Who do I call? My parents? I can imagine my mum's anxiety, telling me that she doesn't know what I'm playing at, to get home this instant; my dad's anger, saying that if this is how I intend to live my life, I can bloody well do it under a different roof. I dial the only other number I can think of.

'Hello?'

The voice sounds harassed. There are kids shrieking in the background.

'Hello, Mrs Johnson, is Steph — '

'You've got some bloody nerve calling here!'

For a second I'm speechless. Does she know who I am?

'Mrs Johnson, it's Bill.'

'I know who it is. She's been crying her eyes out all afternoon over you, missed her shift at the chippy. I've a mind to — '

There's a scuffling at the end of the phone, voices arguing, then footsteps before Steph says: 'Bill?' The word trembles and cracks.

'Steph, what's going on?'

A strange pause. 'You know what, Bill.'

'No, I honestly don't.'

I hear her swallow. 'Your dad called earlier, to see if you were here. Mr Hillbrand called him. He said you'd . . . that you . . . '

'That I ran out of a meeting?' My face grows hot. 'That's hardly a crime.'

'No, that you stole money from one of your clients. An old man in a hospital. That you lied your way in.'

'What? I didn't steal anything!'

'You didn't?' Steph's voice quavers between

194

hostility and hope. 'Then why would they say it?'

My heart is pounding. This is Mrs Mallory's doing. She'll be furious that I've spoken to her father, told him about the developer, about Emeline. That I've run off with the evidence I collected from Hallerton — the diary and the doctor's bill — just as she was about to sign with Remington.

'Look,' I wipe away a prickle of sweat from my upper lip, 'I didn't *steal* anything. He gave me the money, Timothy Vane.'

'Who?'

'Emeline's brother. Steph, he wants me to find her — '

'Emeline?' She spits the word and I feel my hand tighten around the phone. 'Bill, what the hell's wrong with you? Why do you care about what happened to her? All you've done since Norfolk is go on and on about some mad, dead woman.'

'Don't talk about her like that!'

'You see!' Steph's voice wobbles, higher than usual. 'You're obsessed! You care more about her than you do about me!'

'That's — '

How can I find the words to describe what I'm feeling? How can I tell her that, despite everything, I've never felt more alive than I do right now? That I don't want the life I had before; that there's something else waiting for me, something vital, if only I'm brave enough to look. The silence on the line stretches longer and longer. In the end, it answers for me.

'Steph,' I manage to say, 'I'm sorry, but I don't think this — '

'I don't want to hear it, Bill.' Her anger is edged with tears. 'Go and get yourself locked up for no reason. See if I care.'

'Steph — '

The line goes dead. *Now?* the whining dial tone seems to ask me.

I already know the answer:

Depot. Gare d'Austerlitz. Paris.

Part Three

March 1919

'You want to cook for the people here, you'll need to forget most of what you know,' Clémence told me, tying an apron around her waist. I followed suit, already excited. 'We work hard here, all day. We want food that fills our bellies and warms our blood, makes us forget our aching feet. You understand?'

'Like that spice you used, in the fish?' I asked. 'The red one, that smelled of fire?'

'*Pimentón.*'

'*Pimentón.*' I repeated to myself, remembering its taste. Hot like flames, sweet like sun-ripened fruit.

'What else?' I bumped into her as she stopped before a tall, wooden door.

'*Lentement*, we start at the beginning,' she said, stepping inside.

It was a pantry, dark and cool and lined with shelves. Every house had one, but this was like nothing I had ever seen. The light from the doorway caught upon hundreds of glass jars, upon the colours encased within: brilliant reds, sun-drenched yellows, even slivers of purple and bright, jade green. Strings of shrivelled peppers and tomatoes festooned the ceiling like party decorations; sacks of grain stood waiting in the corners. I ran my fingers across the top of a bag of beans to feel them, hard and cool and mottled.

'We cannot afford to waste anything here,' Clémence was saying. 'We eat skin to bone, nose to tail, and everything in between, understand?'

I nodded, trying to take everything in.

'Where did all of this come from?'

'We are lucky,' she said. 'We have some land in the hills, where we grow vegetables. Aaró will show you. And neighbours bring what they can spare in the summertime, for us to put away.' She smiled mischievously. 'They know they'll eat better in winter if they do.'

The smell inside the pantry was making my mouth water. I picked out spices and the faint tang of fruits and vegetables dried in the hot sun. If it was like this at the end of winter, I couldn't imagine what summer would be like, brimming with the fresh produce of the Mediterranean.

'What are we making?' I asked, as Clémence prowled the shelves, seizing jars and packages.

'*Suquet de poisson*,' she told me without hesitation, 'fish stew.'

'The same as yesterday?'

She snorted at the question.

'No. That was a *picada*, with a little *pimentón* for spirit. Onions, garlic, parsley, nuts. Today, we need something different.'

'What do you mean?'

'Bring a handful of those,' she told me, pointing to a string of dried tomatoes. 'Yesterday, we needed to remember that spring is here. There's planting to be done, winter gloom to shake off. Herbs, nuts, they remind people of the harvest. So today, people will have been outside, in their gardens or on their land.'

I followed her out of the pantry. She dropped the jars and bottles and ingredients on to the table, like a robber's hoard.

'*La Tramontana* will make people cold,' she said, almost to herself. 'They will ache from digging, they will need comfort and warmth and sweetness to remind them that their work is worth it.' Her hands were sorting through the jars, confirming everything she had chosen. 'Fetch the fish from the scullery. There's a basket of potatoes there, bring those too.'

The fish made the small stone space smell of the sea, as though the tide had crept under the door. It made me think of Aaró, working in the waves day after day, fulfilling an ancient agreement with the ocean. I picked up the crate with difficulty, my hands still sore. Perhaps one day he would take me with him on a fishing trip, so I could watch him pull these treasures from beneath the water.

The thought of him, smiling at me from across a small boat, our knees touching, made my cheeks warm.

'What's *la Tramontana*?' I asked as I dropped the crate next to the stove. Not for the first time, I felt as though I only understood half the conversation in Cerbère.

'What?' Clémence was already focused on cooking, rapidly slicing an onion without even looking at it. 'Pass me that head of garlic.'

The fish scraps from yesterday, including the heads, were back on the stove. I tried to stop my nose from wrinkling in distaste. I was here to learn, after all.

201

'La Tramontana?' Clémence tipped the chopped onion in. 'You must have felt it. It is the wind that comes down from the mountains and tastes of snow, all year round.'

I remembered the icy breeze that morning on the beach, snatching at my shawl and making me shiver.

'Your best friend in summer, your enemy in winter, *la Tramontana*,' she said decisively. 'Now, shall we cook?'

The fish heads and bones were soon simmering away with garlic, onions, *pimentón*, wine and herbs, cut from pots on the kitchen window sill. Before, I would never have eaten old fish scraps, but now, it was all I could do to stop myself from grabbing a spoon and scooping up the fragrant broth.

Next came the jars of preserved vegetables. Many of them I had never eaten, even in London. The slices of dense pale flesh with an outside strip of purple were aubergine, Clémence pointed out; the bright yellows and reds were peppers. The jade green ones were courgettes, preserved with basil.

I sliced them up, and soon my hands were glistening with herb-infused oil. I sucked some from my fingers and the taste stopped me in my tracks: peppery and smooth and pungent all at once. I licked every finger clean, like a child scraping a pudding bowl, until Clémence laughed at me, and sent me to wash my hands in the scullery.

When I came back, the vegetables had gone into another pan, their aromas mingling.

Clémence was reaching for a small wooden box.

'This is only for certain dishes,' she told me, lifting the lid and taking out a small, stoppered bottle. 'You know what it is?'

Saffron. In better times at Hallerton, Cook had made saffron cakes or buns, which we ate buttered at teatime. I watched as Clémence took a doll-sized skillet, and began to toast the threads. It smelled exotic, almost medicinal, and brought with it the memory of home, a pang of sorrow.

But the feeling ebbed away. There was stock to be strained, the liquid poured into the vegetables. The left-overs went into the slop bucket, 'for Oriol's pigs'. Soon, we were preparing and filleting the fish Aaró had brought in earlier. I was nowhere near as fast as Clémence, but I was learning.

The stew smelled intoxicating; powerful and salty from the fish, sweet from the vegetables, heady with wine and spices, earthy with potatoes. *This is how food should smell*, I thought. I hadn't noticed the time passing as we cooked, and it was with alarm that I heard noises from the front of the house, the bell on the door tinkling over and over as the townspeople began to pile in.

I peeked through the curtain. Clémence was right, they looked chilled to the bone, hunching coats around themselves and wrestling the door closed when *la Tramontana* howled across the seafront. Even Aaró looked glum when he appeared, his hair windswept, but his face brightened as he stepped into the kitchen and inhaled deeply.

He wrapped his arms around himself and cupped his hands, signing eating from a bowl.

'He says it is comfort food,' Clémence translated, smiling. 'It will be done soon; help Aaró with the dessert there.'

He had brought a large basket with him. From it came tumbling oranges, impossibly bright against the old, scrubbed wood.

'Where did these come from?' I asked Clémence, fetching a clean knife to copy Aaró's peeling and slicing. 'I haven't seen any groves.'

'Spain. They are why this town exists. Buy an orange or a lemon anywhere in France, or England for that matter,' she slid a look at me, 'and it will have come through Cerbère.'

'How so?'

The air around me was a spritz of juices, fresh and sweet.

'The trains,' she said. 'Oranges have to travel somehow. Some idiot made the tracks in Spain and France different sizes, so all the freight must be unloaded and reloaded on both sides of the border. Still, we can't complain. It keeps the women of this town in work. *Les transbordeuses*, they're called, the women who work the citrus freight.'

Aaró's eyes were flicking from his mother to me, even as his hands cut off an orange's skin in four deft movements.

'How do I explain what we're talking about?' I asked Clémence. It must have been strange for him not to know, I realized.

Her smile was crooked as she stroked the side of her face with the back of her fingers then moved her flat palm in a circle against the other one. Though small, in her movement I saw wheels, the might of a train moving along a track.

Aaró watched as I turned to him and repeated the movement. He nodded seriously, laying his hands together in a cross and pushing them down.

'He said they have a hard life, *les transbordeuses*,' Clémence told me, as I went back to slicing. 'His sweetheart Mariona is one.'

My hand slipped, sending the tip of the blade slicing into my finger. For an instant I didn't move, then the blood welled to the surface and with it came the pain.

'Damn!' I dropped the knife. Instinctively, I put my finger in my mouth. *Stupid*, I told myself, as the sweet, cold citrus juices stung and mingled with the taste of warm iron. *Of course he has a sweetheart.*

Aaró was looking concerned. He pulled a handkerchief from his pocket and before I knew what was happening, he had taken my hand, and wrapped my finger in the cloth. I winced as he knotted the ends, but managed to smile apologetically.

'I am sorry,' I told him, and he must have been able to decipher the words from my lips, or my expression, for he smiled too and shook his head minutely as if to say, *It is nothing.*

Then he reached out and ran his thumb along the edge of my lip. It came away streaked with the blood I had obviously smeared there. For a breath, I felt as though the heat of the stove was

205

inside my body, spilling out towards him. Did he hesitate too, his eyes on mine, before he stepped away? Or did I imagine it? He was wiping his hands on a rag, picking up his knife to continue slicing, as though nothing had happened.

My cheeks burned as I did the same, trying to keep my hands steady. I didn't look up, but from across the kitchen, I could feel Clémence's stare.

It is nothing, I told myself. *It is nothing.*

June 1969

Outside the window, tall buildings and a grubby glass roof glide overhead as the train shudders to a halt.

Paris.

Fatigue and excitement make for a weird cocktail. It's been a long night of trains and railway benches and the dark waves of the Channel, but I am here. I am *actually* here.

I stagger on to the platform with the rest of the passengers. Businessmen with thick glasses walk purposefully, swinging their briefcases; a group of girls wearing shorts exclaim in what sounds like German over their rucksacks. I think back to the Bill Perch who nervously boarded the train to Norwich. If someone had told me two weeks ago that I'd soon be standing at the heart of the busiest station in France, I would have thought they were completely bonkers. Perhaps I'm the one who's bonkers. Right now it's easier to grin at the sheer absurdity of life than to dwell on the consequences.

Above the concourse, the huge announcement board is clacking, revealing destinations that all sound mysterious and thrilling. My stomach gurgles with hunger. I could murder a bacon roll. At a kiosk across the way, people are smoking and drinking from minuscule cups, managing to look bored and rushed at the same time. No bacon rolls, but some moon-shaped buns. I point to one and the man behind the counter says something in rapid French. I hold out a handful of unfamiliar coins and he mutters to himself, grabs a few.

The bun he gives me is soft and falls into flakes as I try to eat it. Whatever it is, it's delicious. It tastes of butter and leaves me licking my fingers and wishing I'd bought another six.

What would they say at home if they could see me, eating French food in Paris? When Louise brought my passport to the station her face was a picture. I wonder if she'll keep her promise not to say anything to Mum and Dad, whether our sibling agreement of *I'll scratch your back* still holds, or whether I should've given her another pound note for good measure.

Too late now. I'm here and so, once, was Emeline. *Depot, Gare d'Austerlitz, Paris*. One down.

Outside, it's baking already. The traffic is honking and scooters are zipping between the buses and cars like insects. The sun is bright; the front of the Gare du Nord is grimy. I watch the crowd, trying to get my bearings. A girl wearing huge sunglasses is weaving through the chaos. An old woman shuffles towards the metro in a housecoat, a group of young men with long hair and silk shirts and bizarre hats stride past, talking loudly. It's unruly, it's elegant, it's *glorious*.

Steph always talked about coming to Paris one day, for the fashion, but I bet she never imagined this. The thought of her brings a wave of guilt, remembering our telephone conversation. *You* care more about her than you do about me. I grimace to myself in the middle of the thoroughfare, at my inability to explain. No wonder she's broken things off. She deserves better. Part of me feels awful, yet at the same time, I know it's probably for the best. I made the choice to come here, to follow Emeline. Now I have to see it through.

The metro is packed, sweltering and confusing, but there's a stop called 'Austerlitz' and doggedly, I ride the lines towards it. *Depot, Gare d'Austerlitz*. It isn't until I'm ejected into the station that I realize: I have no idea what comes next. What does a depot look like? Through the crowd, I see a sign that promises 'Information'. If there's one thing I need . . .

The woman at the booth is dressed in a smart burgundy uniform, a matching hat on her cropped hair. She trills out a well-used '*bonjour*' and looks expectant, her hand already on an English tourist map.

'I'm, er, looking for the depot.'

Her smile falters. '*Pardon?*'

'The depot? Gare d'Austerlitz?' She still looks blank. Maybe I'm saying it wrong. I unfold the letter. 'Here, it's this address. I'm looking for someone.'

Frowning, the woman peers at the page. Her eyes flick across the words, the date.

'Sir,' she says, using a careful *he might be a lunatic* voice, 'this letter is fifty years old.'

'I know that, I was hoping the depot might have employee records, be able to give me the home address they had on file for this person.

It's a long shot, but it's all I have to go on, and — '

'The *Chemin defer du Midi* does not exist. Not for thirty years now.'

'Yes, but what about the depot? Is that still here?'

I must sound increasingly desperate, because a man in a similar uniform sidles into view and mumbles something to the woman in French. She whispers back before turning a cool smile on me.

'The depot is for train staff only, *monsieur*. I'm afraid we cannot help you.'

This can't be happening. 'Please, you really don't understand — '

'*Bonne journée, monsieur,*' she reels off, already stepping away from the booth.

'Wait!'

She's gone, and what's worse, the supervisor man reappears to make a *shoo* motion at me. I have no choice but to wander out of the station. Even if there were signs to the depot, I wouldn't know what to ask when I got there. Idiot, Perch. Idiot. Throw your life away on a whim, why don't you? Like a piece of paper from fifty years ago was going to help you find Emeline.

There's another kiosk selling the crescent-shaped buns. This time, I buy four. I sit in the hot sun against the station wall, watching cars and taxis battle it out on the forecourt. Three and a half buns down, and I start to feel a bit sick.

'They will make you fat,' a light voice tells me. The burgundy-suited information girl is standing above me, a half-smoked cigarette in her fingers. I try to swipe away some of the crumbs clinging to my mouth and chin.

'What?'

'In France, we say *pardon*,' she tells me, crouching down beside me, careful not to scuff her shiny court shoes. 'I am sorry, back there. My boss was watching. But you have me wondering.' She smiles around another drag of her cigarette. 'What is this letter, from so many years ago? It is a mystery, *non?*'

For a minute I wonder if it's a trick, but she only raises her eyebrow at me, smoking politely. I reach for my jacket.

'This Jean-Baptiste Gosse,' I tell her, handing the letter over, 'I need to find him. He knew someone, a woman I'm looking for.'

'Ah, an *affaire de coeur?*' the woman says delightedly, throwing away her cigarette. 'A love affair?'

'Not exactly.'

The woman just gives me a knowing look and begins to read the letter.

'Ah, *bon*,' she says after a while, 'so you look for someone at the depot who knows this Gosse?'

'*Oui*,' I tell her. 'I mean, yes. I know it's crazy, but . . . '

'*Allez*.' She jumps to her feet. 'We will go and ask.'

I stand too, shedding crumbs. 'What about your boss?'

She just shrugs.

I follow her through the station, along an empty

platform and eventually out on to the edge of the track itself. As we walk, she asks more questions about what I'm doing, about Emeline. I find myself describing her, what she looked like, things she wrote in her diary. We eventually come to a big wooden shed, open at one end. A group of men in oil-stained overalls are lounging on pallets and old metal chairs, smoking. Most of them have muscles the size of tree trunks. I'm suddenly very glad to have a guide.

But they seem friendly enough, especially when the girl offers around her packet of cigarettes. They talk casually for a while, until one of the older men exclaims something and there's a flurry of activity, as one produces a pencil and another a scrap of paper. I find it pushed into my hands.

'What's this?' I ask her.

'They say they don't know any Gosse, but the old union men, they have a little club. They meet at a bar every day over in the *Butte-aux-Cailles*. Some of them work for the railway their whole lives, so they might remember. You can ask them.'

'Thank you,' I nod to them, 'I will.'

One of the men comes forward, grips my hand with his huge fingers.

'*Petit à petit, l'oiseau fait son nid.*'

'What did he say?' I ask the girl.

'He wishes you luck.'

★ ★ ★

The day is getting hotter, and whatever fanciful notions I had about Paris being a city of cool refinement are fast disappearing. No Eiffel Tower or posh shopping streets here, instead an entire district that looks like a building site. Tower blocks are going up. The sun bounces from the hot concrete and makes my mouth feel dry as a bone.

The girl's directions finally take me away from the baking tarmac and into a quieter neighbourhood. This is more like it; the Paris I've seen at the pictures. The buildings are older, crooked and weathered with wooden shutters and balconies and pots of flowers, tiny attic windows sprouting haphazardly from the roofs, thrown open to the summer weather. Music pours down into the street below. I hear familiar words and realize that it's the Rolling Stones, making themselves at home even here.

I find myself on a street lined with shops, awnings protecting goods from the fierce heat. There's a cobbler, a cheesemonger, a wine merchant, all squashed together.

The girl's directions have run out, so eventually, I show the piece of paper to a man selling fruit. He nods in recognition. I've got no idea what he is saying, but he points the way. Around the corner, there's a park that isn't much more than a dirt square, shaded by trees. A faint *toc, toc* noise comes from the centre. I catch sight of a group of men there, playing a game that looks like bowling. At the edge of the park there's a bar, with the name I'm looking for. I take a deep breath. Second time lucky.

Outside, a group of old men sit, keeping their drinks company. The bar has definitely seen better days; the same goes for the men.

'*Bonjour*,' I try. They peer up at me. Some are beetle-eyed beneath huge, hairy brows, others look tough as old beams. 'I, er, I'm looking for someone.'

They answer in French, and I answer in English and none of us has a clue what's going on until one of them goes to fetch the bartender, who speaks a smattering of odd American English.

With his help, I finally explain what I'm after. Then, they're all excitement. They usher me beneath the awning. I find myself sandwiched into a chair, between two men who introduce themselves as Jean-Paul and Paul-Claude.

While they pass around the letter from Gosse, the bar owner brings me a drink, a glass with an inch of some clear spirit in the bottom. It smells powerfully of aniseed. Not wanting to be rude I try to take a sip, but the men all around me exclaim and laugh and take the glass away, pour a measure of water into it. The liquor turns cloudy white, like what they're drinking. It's sort of refreshing.

Inside, the walls of the bar are thick with photographs. They're all railway related, pictures of trains, of work crews, of men in overalls on unfinished stretches of track, posing with the sleepers and rails, in the act of knitting the country together.

I'm feeling almost drowsy by the time the bartender waves to catch my attention.

'Michel say he work the depot for forty year,' he translates for a man with a huge grey beard, 'and he never know no one call 'Gosse'.'

'*Attendez!*' a man in a crushed felt hat exclaims. 'Maybe . . . ' He waves his gnarled hands, searching for the words. '*Un chevalier d'industrie?*'

The men around him guffaw, but one of them looks thoughtful and starts speaking slowly, squinting as though he could peer back through each decade to see the past more clearly.

'What did he mean?' I whisper to the bartender. 'A 'chevalier'?'

'A *chevalier d'industrie*, it is funny way to say someone is . . . ' He racks his brain. 'A crook, a thief, you know? Someone who make money on the black market.'

The thoughtful man interrupts, explaining something in detail to the bar owner who nods and purses his lips in agreement.

'Carlo say,' he repeats for my benefit, 'that in those days they have an agreement, all the men who work the depots. Maybe they do not see when things go missing from the train.' He shrugs meaningfully. 'Maybe in exchange they get some money. He think your 'Gosse' was maybe a black-market man, on the freight trains.'

Carlo's eyes are screwed tight. He's muttering beneath his breath. The old men around him are all shouting out helpful words at the same time.

'He think he remember a man like this,' the bartender says over the noise, 'but with different name. Something like a bug, he say — '

'Puce!' Carlo's head shoots up like a decrepit jack in the box. '*Bien sûr*, Puce!'

' 'Puce'?' my head is reeling.

'It means 'flea'.' The bartender smiles, listening again. 'Carlo say the Puce he remember was from Belleville. *Bellevillois*, they are proud. If your Gosse is alive, and is in Paris, he is there.'

April 1919

One by one, the days trickled into weeks, and Cerbère shrugged off the last of winter's hold. The days dawned brighter, the sun shone warm, and though *la Tramontana* still sent people hurrying for cover and turning up their collars, summer was undoubtedly on its way.

I felt myself changing, the good food working upon me. I was less gaunt than before, I noticed, when my reflection flashed across the copper pans; there was colour in my cheeks. My palms healed. The criss-cross of scars was ugly, but they rarely bothered me, except on wet days.

At Hallerton, I had not slept properly for what felt like years, at least not without the help of morphine. In Cerbère I worked so hard that most nights I fell into bed and did not stir until the sea birds started up their racket at dawn.

Sometimes the chores seemed never-ending but I did not complain, because every day, after lunch and the traditional rest, Clémence and I would start cooking. Soon, I was able to gut and fillet all manner of fish, could tell a dried *bixto* chilli from a *noria*. I was learning to make a little go a long way and to waste nothing. Every night, twenty or thirty townspeople piled in to the Café Fi del Món, and Clémence cooked what she thought they needed.

When a dispute between two neighbours raged through town, dragging whole families into the mess, she cooked a huge communal rice dish. We filled it with lemon and saffron, flakes of salt cod, mussels and cockles and soon people were crowded around, scooping it straight out of the pot, swapping shellfish and laughing over which mussel shell made the best pair of tongs. When a much-loved grandmother of the town died, we made chicken stew, warming and savoury, rich with brandy and herbs, to soothe grief.

Clémence could tell where a *llangostin* had come from by the colour of its shell, where a goat had grazed by the taste of its cheese. She knew the town in the same way: as a collection of individuals, each influencing the complex whole. As for me . . . I did not yet know what my role was. For one thing, I could not forget the rush of heat that came with Aaró's nearness. The more I dwelt upon it, the more the feeling intensified, until I was barely able to return one of his smiles without flushing.

Do not think about it, I told myself severely, but simultaneously another voice whispered, *Why not? This is not England, you are not Emeline.*

'Sauce,' Clémence announced, snapping me out of a reverie. For a horrible moment, I wondered if she could read my thoughts.

'Pardon?' I could feel my cheeks turning traitorously pink.

We were sat on the kitchen step, descaling the fish that Aaró had just brought. 'Sauce,' she demanded again, 'what are the essential sauces?'

'Butter?' I said absent-mindedly, scraping at the fish. A shower of scales flew off. The dirt beneath our feet sparkled with them.

Clémence threw her fish into the box and picked up another. 'You think we have butter to spare? How many cows do you see around here?'

Not many, I had to admit.

'Bread?' I ventured, trying and failing to keep my thoughts on track.

'You English . . . I do not even want to know what that is.' Clémence flicked her knife over the fish. 'No. There are four sauces you must remember. *Picada, allioli, samfaina, romesco.*' She ticked them off on her fingers with the knife. '*Picada* you have tasted. It is garlic, herbs, nuts. And *allioli*. Aaró makes that.'

'The garlic paste?' Even the memory of it made my mouth water. 'It was delicious. He's very good.'

'Of course he is. I taught him.'

'What are the other two?' I picked up another fish.

'*Samfaina*. It is the taste of the sun. Ripe tomato, aubergine, peppers, stewed together like a ratatouille. *Romesco* is chilli peppers, almonds, pine nuts, garlic, and something secret. That we will make soon, for the *calçotada.*'

'For the what?'

She only smiled mysteriously. 'You will see.'

My head spun with questions, but there was work to be done, food to prepare, floors to sweep, thoughts to avoid. Later, Clémence taught me how to fry onions, so slowly and gently that they melted into a rich, dark ooze. *Sofregit*, she called it, and told me that it was not a sauce but the backbone of every dish. She

219

showed me how it went hand in hand with a *picada:* the sting to the sweetness, the thorn to the rose. I fell asleep with the scents of the kitchen clinging to my hair.

But that night my sleep was far from untroubled. I dreamed of Timothy, of Hallerton. It was crumbling and collapsing as though decades had passed, rather than weeks. I could hear him crying somewhere, and I raced up the stairs towards his bedroom, only to emerge in a different part of the house. I ran past peeling wallpaper and rotting floorboards only for the same thing to happen again and again. I couldn't reach him, and his sobs became quieter, and I knew that if I didn't find him soon, I never would.

I opened my mouth to shout his name and found myself awake, sitting up in bed, my heart pounding, eyes stinging with tears. The feeling of guilt was more than I could bear. I buried my face in my hands and tried to rid my mind of the sound of those sobs.

But they did not disappear. I lowered my hands to listen. Whoever was crying, they were in the house, the sound of their tears echoing up from the floor below me. Hesitantly, I crept out on to the landing. I heard it again, above the muffled snores that came from Clémence's room.

The floorboards groaned as I made my way down, one careful foot at a time. Light was flickering from beneath the door of a room I had never been into. Slowly, I pushed it open.

Aaró was sitting on the edge of his bed. Light

from an oil lamp wavered across the bare skin of his chest and arms, across his face, wet with the tears. His mouth was open, the noise of sobs coming ragged from his throat. *Of course,* I realized, *he cannot hear himself.*

There was something in his hand, a rectangle of card that looked like a photograph. He was staring at it, face contorted with sorrow. Sympathy washed over me and I forgot myself, stepped into the room.

His head snapped up, like an animal that does not know whether to fight or flee. I thought he might be angry, thought he might rush to close the door in my face, but I was wrong. He only looked at me and turned his head away, ashamed.

'Are you . . . ?' I said, before cursing myself for stupidity. I took a step closer, and another, until he was forced to meet my gaze.

You, I pointed, trying to remember the sign they had taught me for 'good'. I bunched my fingers near my mouth and spread them like a starfish.

You, good?

Had I made a mistake? He was looking at me so strangely. But then he sagged down and shook his head. He held up the photograph for me to see. It showed a group of young men, perhaps twenty of them in all. Most of them wore fishing gear, and were posing in and around a boat. A few stood seriously, arms crossed, but others were larking about. I peered closer. Aaró was in the middle of the picture, a devious look on his face as he held something with tentacles over the head of a dour-faced man. It was a joyful scene, and made me smile.

Aaró stood and came to my side. Slowly, he raised a finger to the photograph and drew a cross over the youngest-looking man.

Gone, that movement said. *Gone, gone.* His hand moved across the paper, crossing out one after another, until only four men remained untouched. He was one of them. In that moment, I saw what he saw: not a group of boisterous young men, but a company of the dead, faces that existed now only in memory, in ink on paper. I saw the weight of their lives upon his shoulders, saw the pain that came with trying to remember them all.

I feel it too, I wanted to tell him, *and I couldn't bear it. It nearly destroyed me, so I ran.*

But I didn't know how, except to touch his arm, the lightest brush of my fingertips. He looked into my face, and I tried to show him that I understood. Slowly, slowly, the sorrow ebbed away from us, until something else remained, trembling and tacit. The warmth of his skin lingered, and I felt as though my whole body was thrumming, living furiously because so many had died. My heart pounded against the thin cotton of my borrowed nightdress, as he raised a hand towards my face. I do not know what might have happened then if there hadn't been a creak from the room next door, the sound of an iron bedstead shifting as someone stood up.

He followed the direction of my gaze and his eyes widened, realizing, as I did, how this would look to Clémence, finding us half-clothed and breathless in the middle of the night. And what of his sweetheart, Mariona? Swiftly, silently, I fled the room, my fingertips burning and a feeling like wings in my chest.

June 1969

Late afternoon and Paris is sizzling, and not in a glamorous, open-shirted way. Dust clings to my skin as I toil up the Rue de Belleville. A fishmonger is hosing down the pavement in front of his shop, a group of children in shorts and sandals dashing in and out of the water to stay cool. Wish I could do the same.

Away from the tower blocks, Belleville is old, the buildings leaning and bodged so many times over the years that it's hard to tell where the bricks start and where the repairs begin. On the ground floor there are shops, so many and so varied I can't help slowing to stare at everything. Most are daubed with strange languages. Chinese? Arabic? I have no idea.

People crowd the streets, women in headscarves leaning and chatting in the shade, young men with sunglasses and tight T-shirts, girls in mini-dresses, workmen in dungarees drinking at cafés that spill out on to the road. Everyone seems to have forgotten about work, in the torpor of late afternoon.

It's all I can do to drag myself along. I'm bone weary, would give anything to lie down on a cool bed and sleep and wake up again, untroubled. But the memory of Timothy Vane returns, struggling to write those two vital words: *find her*. I pull myself up. Two more names to check. Then I'll know if this whole absurd gamble has been for nothing.

I find the list that the bartender gave me. He insisted on going through the telephone directory, looking up the name 'Gosse' and copying out the addresses, telling me to start with the ones in Belleville. All the retired railwaymen shook my hand when I left, and wished me luck, and for a while I wondered what it would be like to stay in Paris, to go down to the park every afternoon and drink with them there.

I squint up at the intersecting alleyways, trying to find a name, get my bearings. The bartender underlined four likely candidates within a few miles' radius. So far, I've tried two, with no success. The group of children from the fish shop run past me, their shoes going *slap*, *slap* on the street.

'Hey!' I yell after them, and one turns around, a girl in a faded dress that looks about two sizes too big for her. I brandish the piece of paper, point to the address and wave my arms to signal that I'm lost, saying, 'Rue Piat? Rue Piat?', over and over. She stares at me like I'm insane, before calling one of the other children back. A boy, older, who takes a look at the piece of paper and nods. He beckons me on and I follow, as they rejoin their gaggle of friends.

Eventually they point to a quiet side street, where tall buildings offer blissful shade. I don't know how to thank them, other than by digging out a handful of *centimes*. They grab them and grin and race off once more, their damp footprints drying instantly on the road.

Number forty Rue Piat is a tall, discreet, shuttered building with decorative bars on the bottom windows. It must be flats, but I can't see a concierge or any numbered bells. Instead there's only one, shiny brass, plain and unmarked. I ring it and try to comb my sweat-matted hair into place with my fingers.

The door swings open. Inside, it's dark and cool and smells of flowers. A woman is looking out at me. She must be in her thirties, wearing horn-rimmed glasses and a linen trouser suit. She looks like something out of a magazine.

'*Oui?*' she says.

'*Bonjour,*' I start, again, already knowing that in twenty seconds, I'll be walking away. 'I'm looking for a Monsieur Gosse, Jean-Baptiste Gosse.'

The woman narrows her eyes.

'Why?'

It's not the response I'm expecting, not least because it's in English. I stare at her for a while.

'It's about a letter he wrote, I think he can help me find someone.'

'Who?'

'A woman, who disappeared,' I say. 'Sorry, but is there a Jean-Baptiste Gosse here or not?'

'Are you from Interpol?' she says, renewing her grip on the door.

'Eh? No, I'm looking for a . . . a private client.' It isn't a *complete* lie.

'You're a detective?' She's growing frostier by the second.

'I'm a solicitor.' I open my briefcase to find Gosse's letter. 'I spoke to some people from the

226

railway, and they suggested that I try here.'

'My father is a busy man.' She steps back into the house. 'You're a solicitor? Write him a letter.'

'Please,' I call after her. 'It will only take a minute. I just need to ask him about this woman, Emeline Vane. Please, I'm — '

I'm talking to a closed door. I hear footsteps recede on the other side. Damn it. Why couldn't he have answered the door himself? A minute would've been enough to find out if he's the man I want.

A letter, she said. Fine. I sit down on the edge of the pavement and rummage in the briefcase. At the bottom I find a crumpled piece of letter paper. I've already started to scrawl, 'Dear Mr Gosse', when the door opens behind me.

An old man is standing on the step. He looks like he's been lounging in the sun, with his straw fedora and rolled-up sleeves. I can make out the lines of a faded tattoo upon his arm. He's staring at me, but only with one eye. Beneath the shadow of the hat's brim, the other socket is a mass of flesh.

I jump to my feet, the letter, forgotten. His mouth is open in astonishment.

'Did you say Emeline Vane?'

April 1919

One morning in mid-April, Clémence woke me before dawn. Without speaking, she shoved the window open to let in a blast of chill sea air. I sat bolt upright in bed, looked at her blearily. She was already dressed for work, sleeves rolled up, a scarf tied tightly around her head.

'Get dressed,' she told me, walking out. 'We have a lot of work to do.'

'Why?' I croaked, as the breeze brushed across my neck.

'*La calçotada!*'

That was enough to send me scrambling from the bed. Clémence had been dropping hints about this '*calçotada*' for weeks. All I knew was that it was a special event of some kind; one that had necessitated a *very* large delivery of wine from along the coast. I'd heard the word bouncing from lip to lip across the town, and if the excitement of the local people was anything to go by, it was going to be an occasion to remember.

I clattered down to the kitchen, twisting my hair into a plait as I went. Aaró was sitting at the table, nursing a cup of coffee. Ever since the night in his room, there had been a strange awkwardness between us. We caught eyes, and I felt myself blush as I nodded good morning. He did the same, but I could feel him watching me as I cut bread, drizzled honey on to it.

'What will we be doing today?' I asked Clémence.

'Everything,' she said with a smile. 'I hope you are ready to work, girl.'

I was always ready to work, and I told her so, trying to eat the sticky bread and tie a handkerchief over my hair at the same time. She laughed, and took the cloth from me, tying it tightly at the nape of my neck.

The first knock at the back door came a few minutes later. Aaró stood up to leave. He kissed his mother on the cheek, took half a step towards me too, before raising his hand instead. I watched his retreating back, wondering what it all meant, wishing I was brave enough to ask.

Clémence did not notice. She was busy haggling with the man at the door. He wore a long, stained leather coat, heavy trousers and hobnail boots. A tall dog sat beside him on the step, working at a bone. A smell of decay and fresh blood hung about him, but this didn't seem to bother Clémence. She was exclaiming delightedly in Catalan over a crate at her feet. I peered closer. Soft, furry brown creatures lay in lines.

'Who was that?' I asked when he took his leave, the dog loping off behind him.

'Oriol. He is the best hunter for miles.'

She was a little flustered, I noticed, but I kept it to myself, knelt down with a smile to pick up one of the creatures. It was a rabbit, so fresh that I thought it might leap out of my hands and flee into the early morning.

'What are we making?' I asked, placing it

229

carefully back into the box.

'*Conill aux herbes et vi negre*,' she said, fetching the heavy wooden board she used for meat. 'Rabbit with herbs and wine. People come for the *calçots*, but they expect a decent meal.'

'I suppose you aren't going to explain,' I said, rolling up my sleeves.

'You will see later. Now, I presume you have never butchered rabbit?'

It was bloody work, but it came with a sort of thrill, to be handling something so recently living, so raw and vital. My hands were soon red to the wrist, but I didn't care; I followed Clémence as she sought out the treasures of the bodies, the hearts and livers and kidneys and set them aside, gleaming in an earthen bowl. She added dried, soaked chillies, toasted almonds, garlic, herbs, and then set me to pounding the whole mixture into one heady, earthy substance that had my head spinning and made me almost fearful of its potency.

When the *sofregit* was gently frying, wine was poured over the rabbit carcasses, and brandy, filling the kitchen with musty sweetness. I had to step outside for a breath of air, overwhelmed.

Breathing the clean, salt air, I let my feet take me the short distance to the water's edge. Although it was still spring, and cold in the evenings, at noon the sun blazed in the sky, hot enough to turn my skin pink. I knelt at the surf and washed the blood and spices from my hands, watched the sea swallow them into its cavernous belly. It was a warm day, *la*

Tramontana keeping to the mountains. I unwound my shawl, wiped wet hands over my face and neck and let the sun fall on my skin to dry it.

Once, the cold wind over the North Sea had done the same. For a moment I feared that when I looked down, I would find myself back there, crouching at the edge of the salt marshes. But the sun was too warm for that and when I opened my eyes, it was to the Mediterranean, sparkling blue.

A motorized van had pulled up in front of the Café Fi del Món. It was piled high with bundles of what looked like leeks, green and white and muddy. I hurried towards it. Men were unloading, piling them on to a trestle table.

'What are they?' I asked, like a child at a museum.

One of the men glanced towards me. He was a friend of Aaró's.

'The last of the *calçots*,' he said as he worked. 'From Valls.'

'For the *calçotada*?' I couldn't keep the excitement out of my voice.

He laughed at that. 'Of course.'

The men began building a bonfire at the edge of the beach, piling up driftwood and old crates. A rusted iron bed frame stood nearby, for a purpose I could only guess at. Women started to appear, dressed like Clémence in headscarves, their sleeves rolled back and ready. They began to separate out the *calçots*, rinsing off the mud in buckets of seawater, wrapping them in sheets of damp newspaper.

No one stopped me from joining in, and soon I was working with them: one woman even smiled at me. I asked them questions about the *calçotada* and a few of them switched to French to answer, describing how the *calçots* would be roasted on the fire and eaten with a *romesco* sauce.

'Perhaps I should go back and help, then,' I told them, as we neared the end of the pile. 'Clémence promised to teach me how to make it.'

The women fell silent. A few of them muttered to each other in Catalan. One young woman in particular stared at me from across the table, her eyes like ice. She was small and pretty, with a heart-shaped face and a mass of sleek black hair, barely held back by her headscarf. I felt myself turning red.

'Did I say something wrong?'

'You are very honoured,' one of the older women said at last, wiping her hands on a rag. 'Maman's never shared her *romesco* recipe with anyone, let alone a *forastera*.'

'A what?'

'It means 'outsider',' the pretty young woman snapped, 'someone not welcome.' She dumped the contents of her bucket out on the ground near my feet. I jumped back but not before the sheet of muddy water had soaked my boots and hem.

'It means 'stranger', that's all,' the older woman said softly, as the pretty girl hurried away down the beach. 'Do not mind Mariona.'

'Aaró's sweetheart?' I couldn't stop myself

from asking, though the words were awkward on my tongue.

'She would say so,' the woman laughed, 'though I am not sure whether Aaró would agree.'

So that was Mariona, I thought as I retreated to the safety of the kitchen. Her hostility was entirely unjustified, I told myself, there was nothing between Aaró and me. But however much I repeated those words, I knew they weren't entirely true. By the time Clémence summoned me to make the *romesco*, I was grateful for the distraction.

'Romesco is a sauce for the tongue and the lips,' she told me, as I measured out handfuls of nuts. 'Why?'

'Because of the spice?' I tried, eyeing the chilli peppers that were soaking. 'The sweetness?'

'Yes, but more than that.' She opened the door of the oven and my mouth began to water. Inside, whole heads of garlic and preserved tomatoes were roasting in oil. 'We bake, we simmer, we toast, we bruise; we squeeze every morsel of flavour from these ingredients, until we have their souls. We do not only taste these pine nuts, but the trees where they grew, not only this bread, but the land that nourished the wheat, the herbs of the *maquis*, carried on the wind to ripen the grain.'

She turned to where I stood mesmerized, a handful of almonds suspended above a pan.

'The only secret to a good *romesco*, Emilie,' she smiled, 'is that there is no secret. You have to feel it. That is all.'

As evening descended the kitchen became suffused with the scent of roasting meat, and the mood of the town began to change. From outside, I heard shouts and laughter and even snatches of music. Finally, unable to bear the curiosity, I stuck my head through the dividing curtain.

The folding doors of the café had been thrown open, the tables and benches and stools dragged outside. A huge bonfire blazed on the beach, the iron bedstead in the middle of it, acting as a makeshift grill. Smaller braziers stood at either end of the tables, for light and warmth. Jugs of wine lined the tables, people were gathered around the flames, simultaneously shouting advice and ignoring each other.

I felt a touch on my arm and turned to find Aaró behind me. He was freshly washed and clean-shaven, black hair pushed back from his forehead. He grinned and held out a dish for me to carry, filled with the soft red *romesco* that Clémence and I had made that afternoon.

There were cheers as we walked out into the evening, and applause, and I began to feel welcome at last. The older woman from earlier beckoned me over to her table.

'We work together, we eat together,' she said, her cheeks already rouged with wine. Her name was Agathe, and she introduced me to her family, her young daughter, her elderly mother, her father-in-law. She said nothing of her husband, and as I looked around, I saw what I had seen in Aaró's photograph. People were closely packed together at the tables but between them I saw spaces, voices missing from the chatter, silhouettes missing from around the fire. Fathers, brothers, sons . . .

Looking down the table, I sought out Aaró's eyes and raised my glass. He smiled sadly, the firelight flickering across his face as he too raised his glass. The wine touched my lips and I drank deep.

But that night was not one for mourning. As the sun drowned itself in the sea, a great cheer went up and the *calcots* were pulled from the fire. They were dumped straight on to the tables in their paper bundles, charred and smouldering. I tried to copy the townspeople as they deftly stripped out the tender white cores, smothered them in *romesco* and swung them into their mouths, but soon, I was a dreadful mess, my fingers and chin covered in charcoal flakes and oil and sauce. They were delicious, smoky and fresh. The sauce filled my mouth with its many flavours and I closed my eyes, tasting the land as Clémence had described it.

Agathe poured more wine and soon I was laughing along with her. Before the second course, I had to run down to wash my face and hands in the sea. It was rather unsteadily that I went back to the kitchen to help Clémence. Her eyes were bright too, her face flushed, but together we heaved out the huge platters of roasted, stuffed rabbit in its rich, earthy sauce.

There were no utensils: people ate with their fingers, tearing at the gamey meat with their teeth and mopping up the juices with bread. There was no past then, and no concerns for the

235

future beyond who would fill the next jug of wine, and I was one of them, an outsider no longer, empty no longer.

Stomachs full to bursting, we eventually sat back. People threw bones to the cats and dogs who congregated beneath the tables. I did not even notice when my plate disappeared and the wine in the jugs magically changed. This new one was pale. It tasted golden, like raisins and sun-baked hay. The sweetness clung to my lips, mingling with the salt from the sea wind.

A space was being cleared between the tables and soon the air was filled with the noise of instruments, old guitars, a drum and a kind of clarinet that made a wheezy, quavering sound. The musicians warbled through a few warm-up notes before launching into a song.

I would not have believed that the towns-people who now sprang up to dance had sagged, replete, on the benches only minutes before. Some of the older folk joined hands and held their arms up and paraded in a solemn circle, but the young people were having no such nonsense. With whoops and catcalls to each other, they formed a circle of their own, and they jumped and stamped and spun and raised their arms high and yelled when the song reached its refrain.

It made me smile, alone at my table. Clémence and Agathe were dancing with the older folk, and even if I had been asked to join, I did not know the steps. Mariona was in the circle of younger dancers, her eyes bright, her face flushed as she span, though not with Aaró.

Where was he? It took my eyes time to adjust after the glare of the braziers, but when they did I found him, carefully stacking plates at the furthest table, his head turned away from the dance. I tried to imagine what it must be like, unable to hear the music that delighted everyone else. As I watched him the tempo changed, becoming more boisterous, the stamping more frenzied. My feet were twitching beneath the table, desperate to join in. I could feel the rhythm coming up from the ground itself.

If it hadn't been for the wine, I might never have jumped to my feet, might never have made my way through the tables, might never have tapped Aaró on the shoulder. If it hadn't been for the wine, my whole life might have been different.

He stopped what he was doing. I pointed to him, to me, to the dancers.

'Do you want to dance?'

He frowned, with a touch of frustration I thought, that I could make such an elementary mistake. He started trying to explain, gesturing to his ears and spreading his fingers, but I reached out and took hold of his hands in mine. At that touch, my heart trebled its pace, but I bent down, pulling him with me.

I tried to think as he did, to block out the sounds of the band and the voices, the crash of the waves and the swish of clothing. I placed his palm on the dusty ground and put mine beside it. Sure enough I felt it, the beat of the song, like a metronome, the *thud, thud, thud* of feet, keeping time.

I watched his face grow alert, as he began to tap his fingers. I tapped mine too. We both smiled, nodding along to the beat and I couldn't tell the rhythm from that of my own heart. With an exuberant noise he leaped up, pulling me with him, and we began to dance, galloping wildly to and fro. His hand was clasped about my waist, fingers keeping the beat as mine did, marking out the rhythm on his shoulder as we span, kicking up the dust with our feet, each of us laughing in our way.

There came a cry from the group of dancers as we were spotted; they cheered and clapped and Aaró winked in response. There were only two people who did not look so pleased. One was Clémence. The other was Mariona. We locked eyes, and the resentment I saw in her face made me falter. But then Aaró spun me around and I found I didn't care for anything except the feel of his hand in mine and the pulse of the dance and the joy — so long held back — that rushed through my body, like a flood.

June 1969

'Emeline Vane,' the man murmurs. 'I have not heard that name for thirty years.' He squints, as though seeing something far away with his one good eye.

'Mr Gosse?' I prompt after a long pause, and he smiles, seems to come back to himself.

'Call me 'Puce', young man. Only the tax inspector calls me Mr Gosse.'

'You knew her, then? You knew Emeline?' I have to ask it, unable to believe that this is the man who forwarded her letter to Timothy, fifty years ago. My voice is tight with hope.

'Yes,' he says. 'I did.'

I don't know whether it's the heat of the day or the shock, but my head is spinning. I feel as though I'm about to faint.

'Come,' he says, taking my elbow and ushering me inside. 'My daughter says I should not speak to you, but I take the risk. Anyone who remembers Emeline is worth my time.'

I follow him along a cool hallway and up a wide, curving staircase. The building isn't divided into flats, I note vaguely as we climb, but is one huge townhouse. Must have cost a fortune.

He leads the way on to a wide balcony, lined with potted flowers and shaded by a parasol. Even in my woozy state I can see that the vista beyond is breathtaking. Paris stretches in every

239

direction. Over a mess of rooftops and crumbling chimneys, churches and opera houses, I can see all the way to the Eiffel Tower.

'Welcome to Belleville,' Puce says. He takes out a pair of round sunglasses and puts them on, hiding his bad eye.

'It's beautiful,' I manage, wondering how on earth a crook dealing in black-market railway goods was ever able to afford it. He must see what I'm thinking, for he smiles.

'We have, I think, a lot to say to each other. But first . . . '

He disappears, and I'm left waiting, trying to keep my wits about me. When he returns he's carrying two drinks, clinking with ice cubes.

'To Emeline,' he says, and raises his glass.

'To Emeline.'

The afternoon drifts slowly by as we talk, the noise of the city a distant hum. He listens patiently as I tell him how it all began, about Hillbrand and Hallerton, about Mrs Mallory and her brother, trying to get power of attorney before their father recovers and the offer on the land expires, wanting to prove that Emeline killed herself, fifty years ago. Puce shakes his head when he hears that, spits off the balcony.

'When you met her, did she say what had happened,' I ask tentatively, 'why she was running away?'

He is silent for a while.

'I know she was frightened,' he says. 'I know she was running, but she did not say why. And I do not ask. At the time, it does not matter.'

I tell him about Andrew, about the accident

with the glass, and he rubs his wrinkled knuckles absent-mindedly. We finish the drinks. He pours out more and tells me the story of how he met Emeline, *his* Emeline: a terrified stowaway on a freight train out of the Gare de Lyon.

I listen, rapt, as he talks about her sadness, her spirit, how they ate stolen food and talked and rode the tracks together.

'It was only a day or two,' he says eventually, 'but they are bright in my mind, you know?' He stares into his drink, into the melting ice, smiling.

'Did you ever look for her?' I ask. There's a tightness in my chest; I need this old man to tell me something, anything, that will help with my search. 'Did you ever write back? Try to find her?'

'*Mais oui*, I ask, all the way down the line, but no one has seen her. All I know is that she took a train south from Nîmes. After . . . ' He spreads his hands. 'Nothing.'

'Then where did she go?'

'She only said 'south'. Maybe Carcassonne, Perpignan. Maybe Spain. When I return to Paris, to the depot many weeks later,' he nods at the fifty-year-old letter lying on the table, 'I find this waiting. It passed through so many hands, no one can say where it comes from. I tell this to her brother, when he asks.'

At first I think I've misheard. Puce is draining his drink.

'Timothy Vane? You met him?'

The old man nods, rolling the cool glass between his palms.

241

'Yes. In . . . 'thirty or 'thirty-one. He finds me through the depot too. I work in Customs then,' a glint of tooth, 'good days. I learn good English there.'

'What did you tell him?'

'What I tell you. He is not supposed to be in Paris, I think. He says his uncle will be angry when he finds out. He says he will write to me if he finds her, but I never hear from him again.'

'So he just gave up? He didn't keep trying?'

Puce doesn't rise to the frustration in my voice, only shakes his head slowly.

'The war,' he says, his weathered face calm. 'A different time. So many things lost and never found.'

The silence stretches between us and it's a silence of years, of a thousand brutal days. Yet lasting through it all, untainted in this old man's memory, are a handful of happy hours when a boy and a girl rode a train together.

'I'm sorry,' I say, feeling very young.

'Do not be.' Evening is falling across the city, the fierce heat softening into balmy stillness. Puce takes off his glasses and his good eye creases in a smile. 'You are hungry?'

In a kitchen that overlooks the whole of Paris, Puce begins to lay the table. He hands me a long loaf of crusty bread, a bottle of wine, a bowl of tiny pickles, a plate of a kind of soft cheese. Finally, he reaches around the side of the stove and pulls out a cured ham.

'My daughter says I must use the refrigerator,' he says, dropping the whole thing on the table, 'but I don't like it. Things taste better as nature intends.'

'That was your daughter at the front door?' I take a seat.

'Yes, Melanie. She does the business. She tells me that we are a respectable family now, investing our money in ships that travel to the moon.' He smiles slyly. 'Not like old times.'

I'm ravenous, and try to stop myself from grabbing at the food and stuffing it into my mouth. I needn't have worried; Puce rips himself a chunk of the bread, smears it with cheese, loads it up with slices of ham before taking a hefty bite.

Eagerly, I do the same. It tastes wonderful, a world away from Hillbrand's soggy egg-and-bacon baps. Puce glugs wine into two tumblers and takes a slurp. I follow suit. I've never drunk wine before.

'You do not ask me,' he says, his mouth full, 'how I lose my eye.'

Before I have a chance to, he launches into the story of his childhood in Belleville, of the time he spent in prison during the first war, how during the second he worked for the Resistance on the railways; passing messages, 'redistributing' freight, sabotaging the tracks, smuggling escapees.

My glass of wine disappears too easily, and soon I'm working on my second.

'They catch me in 'forty-four,' he says, helping himself to another pickle. 'They imprison me, interrogate. Put out my eye. I manage to escape, in the end.'

'How?' I'm clutching the glass, enthralled by his story. I think I might be drunk.

Puce leans forward, eye narrowed. 'I make friends with the women prisoners. They are not so well guarded as the men. They sneak me a dress. Then, I use stuffing from my mattress to, you know . . . ' Seriously, he mimes a pair of large breasts.

I stare at him, totally at a loss for words.

'That was . . . brave,' I say, before I realize Puce is grinning, ear to ear. He begins to mime the breasts again and I can't help snorting with laughter, until my eyes are streaming and I have to put down my glass for fear of spilling it.

Eventually, the food and wine are finished. Beyond the open windows, Paris is a carpet of lights, the sounds of summer revelry rising up from the quarter below. I close my eyes, overcome by the strangeness of it all, and almost fall asleep, sitting there.

'What will you do?'

I force my eyes open. Puce is leaning back in his chair, twirling the dregs in his glass. The kitchen lights are dim, and the shadows gather in the lines of a face that has seen the hard edges of the world.

'I don't know. To be honest I was hoping you'd tell me.' I shake my head, trying to think. 'You said you last saw Emeline at the station in Nîmes?'

'Yes, going south.'

'Then I suppose that's where I'll go too.'

'Why? I do not think you will find anything. Why go, when there is no hope?'

In the semi-darkness, in my exhausted state I have nothing left to hide behind. How can I explain that, since first hearing Emeline's name, something has been changing in me, that because of her, and Hallerton and the case, everything I thought of as certain has shifted; that even if it weren't for my promise to Timothy Vane, I would have to keep searching, going forward, until I found *something*?

'I just . . . can't go back home,' I tell him. 'Not yet.'

Puce's face is kind.

'You know,' he says, leaning across the table to pat my hand, 'she tells me the same thing.'

April 1919

The next morning my head was heavy from the wine, but my heart was light. I rolled over in the blankets and pressed my fingers to my lips, remembering. The taste of sweet wine, the dust from the road, the salt spray, the secret place on the cliffs, the cherry tree and the song of a nightingale all around, but most of all, *him*.

When I emerged, I saw Aaró sitting at the kitchen table, his head balanced on one hand, looking a little green. Ordinarily, he would have been out fishing at this time. I guessed the rest of the town would be similarly nursing sore heads and enjoying a rare late start. I watched him from the doorway for a while, unseen. Last night we had been electrified, fuelled by wine and music, the blood rushing through our veins, but this morning we were human again.

I forced myself to step into the kitchen. Aaró looked up as soon as I did, as if he had been waiting. He smiled, somewhat sheepishly, as I sat down opposite him. How much did he remember about what had happened between us? Had anyone seen us leave? What would he tell Mariona? Despite the girl's unfriendliness I felt my face redden with guilt and shame. How could I ask him?

'Good afternoon,' Clémence said sarcastically, and thumped the coffee pot down on to the table. We both winced. 'Don't expect a day off,' she told me, simultaneously signing something to him. 'There's work to be done.'

Aaró gestured back indignantly, but evidently Clémence was having none of his objections. Finally, he rolled his eyes, pushed back his chair and took his leave, but not before giving me one unfathomable look that left me more confused than ever.

'Where's he going?' I asked, busying myself with the coffee.

'To get some more *botifarra negra*. We have run out.'

'Some what?'

'*Botifarra*, it is a type of sausage. Madame Casal makes the best ones around here,' I felt her gaze settle on me, 'Mariona's mother.'

Queasiness spread through my stomach as I remembered the girl's icy stare, how she'd watched as Aaró and I whirled through the dancers. I thought about his lips, touching mine on the cliff edge, imagined them meeting hers instead and almost dropped the cup I was holding.

'And me?' I asked. 'What am I to do?'

'You'll tend to the vegetables,' Clémence said firmly, handing me a basket.

The Fourniers' vegetable garden was in the land south of the town. You could see the Spanish border station from there, atop a nearby hill. I laboured along the path through the arid *maquis*. The sun pounded down, making me wish that *la Tramontana* would appear and dry the sweat from my neck.

It was no coincidence, I guessed, that

247

Clémence had separated Aaró and me, sent him to Mariona's house and banished me out here. She, obviously thought that the girl would be a good match for her son, and was reminding him of it. Was she showing me my place, a foreigner, who shouldn't meddle or threaten to change the way of things? She shouldn't have bothered. I was already afraid that, no matter how hard I tried, I would always be an outsider in Cerbère; worse, that one day, I would have to leave.

A wave of the old familiar sorrow crept upon me when I remembered how things had been at Hallerton before the accident, before I ran. The emptiness, indistinct and all-pervading, pulling at everything I was, like a tide that grew harder and harder to resist. I had given in to it on the night of the dinner party. I could see that now. Uncle Andrew had been right to be afraid, to seek out a solution. He was not to know that the solution would never have been St Augustine's. Here in Cerbère, I had found a cure; I couldn't bear the thought that I might lose that too . . .

Tears burned my eyes as I worked. I tried to ignore them as I lugged bucket after bucket of water up from the tiny stream, below. The, land was, banked, into terraces, separated by dry-stone walls like old scars. The arid soil sucked at the water, and I found myself sinking my fingers into the wet dirt, wishing that I could be part of it, that I had been born here rather than on the edge of a cold sea far away, to a name I could not shake loose.

From the path below I heard the crunch of bicycle tyres and I swiped the tears from my face. Whatever the townspeople thought of me, I would not let them see me cry. The bicycle stopped. When there was no shout of greeting, I knew who it would be.

Every part of me ached to meet Aaró's gaze as he approached, but I didn't, not even when he sat down beside me in the dirt. Would he try to apologize, try to make me understand that he and Mariona were intended, that last night was a slip, youthful exuberance and nothing more? But he only sat there until, at last, I looked up.

His eyes were solemn, grey as the winters of my childhood. My own felt red and swollen.

You, well? he signed carefully.

I couldn't lie then. I shook my head.

He frowned, but nodded sadly in understanding. His fingers were twitching, running through all of the words he wanted to express. Finally, he turned to me again.

You, he signed, and hesitated, obviously trying to think of words that I would understand. *You,* he pointed, to my eyes and him, *see me.* He passed his hands over his face, pulled one finger gently down his cheek.

You saw me, crying at night.

I understood, and nodded. A smile broke from him.

You, he pointed again, held up two fingers separately before placing them together. I frowned, and he huffed impatiently through his nose, before picking up two dead leaves, slim and brown and identical. He pointed to one, then the other, then placed them together.

Same. He raised his eyebrows, repeated it.

249

You are the same?

I knew then what he was asking. I had seen it in him, the terrible sadness, the weight of the dead, of trying to keep them alive in his thoughts. Did I feel that too?

Yes, I wanted to tell him, *every day, every day.* My brothers, who would never grow older than nineteen and twenty-two; our mother, who lost the will to keep living, even for Timothy and me. I wanted to tell him everything, to spill it all, but I couldn't, and I felt such longing that I reached out a hand to touch the black hair that curled at the nape of his neck.

He caught my fingers in his, and I thought he would push me away, but instead he turned my palm in his hands, with its fading scars and the earth beneath my nails, and brought it to his mouth.

The sun was all around us, and the scent of growing things, and his lips were like a drug, not the cold kiss of a glass bottle, but warm and grazing, taking my breath and filling me with more all at once. The chores lay forgotten, sorrow forgotten, as we went back again and again, gluttons at a feast.

It was only when my stomach gurgled loudly that I pulled away, laughing. He frowned, until I took his hand and placed it on my belly to feel the rumbling there. He grinned, his hand tightening on my waist before reaching for the basket I had brought with me.

Clémence had given me a few slices of bread and sausage, a little corked bottle of oil, but Aaró bustled around the vegetables, returning with a handful of green tomatoes, and little bouquet of herbs. Thyme, I recognized, as I bruised a sprig, and parsley. Making quiet noises to himself, he took out a penknife and sliced the tomatoes, squeezing the juices into the bread, before tearing up the herbs on top and drizzling the whole thing with golden oil.

Smiling, he held it to my mouth and I ate. Smooth and peppery, singing with herbs, the sting of the fresh tomatoes soaking into the bread . . . I closed my eyes as I chewed, trying to pick apart every flavour, because nothing — not even Clémence's cooking — had ever tasted so good. Even before I finished the mouthful, I felt him leaning in, to kiss the oil from my lips.

June 1969

Jem,

Remember what you said about me being a terrible solicitor? Turns out you were right, I'm in Paris! Right now I'm at the Gare Austerlitz, waiting for a train. I have too much to tell you, and no space to tell it. You've probably guessed already; I'm going to look for Emeline. The train I'm catching will take me south, towards a place called Nîmes, the last place anyone saw her. From there . . . I don't know. I hope I'll work something out.

Bill

PS I hope you don't mind me writing, You're the only one who will understand.

PPS They have these delicious buns here called 'croissants' but you probably knew that already.

All around the city is getting started. Scooters growl past, overloaded delivery vans cough and splutter; businessmen and builders start work on their third cups of coffee. A grimy announcement board clacks out another wave of departures. At last, there's the train I want, one that goes all the way to Nîmes.

In a little kiosk that sells newspapers and cigarettes and all manner of strange things, I wave the postcard around until the woman nods in understanding and sells me a stamp. Beside her on the counter, there's a display of sunglasses. I can imagine my mother's face, grimacing in horror at the little round lenses. I buy a pair. The world is tinted honey brown as I walk up to the platform.

My hopes of finding an empty compartment, where I can settle down with Emeline's diary and try to work out my next step in peace, are dashed by a businessman with a pencil moustache and an old woman in a fur hat, despite the weather. One of them smells overwhelmingly of mothballs. As the train pulls away, I shove down the window as far as it will go and lean my head out, so I can watch Paris disappear into the distance.

Just as we reach the end of the platform, I see a group of people break cover from behind an information board and race for the train. Three of them, two boys and a girl, running with bags on their shoulders. We're going faster now, and it doesn't look like they're going to make it, but one by one, they leap aboard. The last thing I see is a pair of legs flailing as the girl is pulled on to the end of the last carriage.

I sit back. The mothball woman gives me a disapproving look and I realize that I'm grinning stupidly, still wearing the sunglasses. Oh well. I suppose I do look a bit of a mess, in a linen shirt borrowed from Puce and my crumpled suit trousers.

We haven't long been under way when the door of the compartment slides open, I glance up, thinking it might be the ticket inspector, only to find myself staring. I can't help it; the man standing there looks extraordinary, like Jimi Hendrix. He's wearing a pair of tight striped trousers, a threadbare blue shirt and a leather necklace. He even has a battered hat with a feather stuck in it over his wild black hair.

He's asking something in French, but I've got no idea what. The mothball woman's eyes look like they're going to pop out and the businessman only grunts. The young man looks towards me, but shakes his head at my gormless expression and turns away. It's only then that I see the unlit cigarette in his hand.

'Hey!' I jump to my feet. 'Wait, *monsieur?*'

At the bottom of my briefcase is the box of matches I bought at Liverpool Street station, what seems like a hundred years ago. I hand them over at the door.

'Thanks, man,' he says, lighting up. I gawp all over again.

'You're American?'

He takes off his sunglasses and tucks them into his pocket.

'Canadian.'

'Oh, sorry.'

'Sorry that I'm Canadian?'

'No, I . . . '

The man smiles and shakes his head again.

'Kidding. Want one?'

I don't normally smoke. I glance back into the compartment. The mothball woman is looking more and more like an angry toad. I slide the door shut on her.

'Why not?'

At the end of the train, where the corridor widens, two people are sitting on their bags. They're the three who scrambled aboard, I realize. Fare-dodgers. I feel a prickle of apprehension as the cigarette guy takes out a pouch of tobacco.

'I'm Matthieu,' he says, 'that's Lucille, and Javi.'

And I thought Jem was a hippy. The other guy, Javi, looks Italian or Spanish, with long dark hair and a scrubby beard. His lean face stretches into a smile and I smile back.

'Are you both Canadian too?' I ask, for something to say.

The girl snorts dismissively. Her hair is blond and straight with a fringe that hangs into her eyes. She's wearing what looks like a man's shirt, a pair of shorts and sandals that lace up to her knees. The mothball woman would have a heart attack.

'Lucille is *Parisienne*,' Javi tells me as Matthieu hands over a freshly rolled cigarette. 'I am from Spain. You?'

'England,' I say, taking a careful drag on the cigarette.

'You speak no French?'

I shake my head. 'I'd like to learn, but so far I only know '*excusez-moi*' and '*bonjour*' and '*croissant*'.'

The girl laughs at that and looks a little friendlier.

'How are you called?' she asks.

'Bill.' I fumble with my bag and cigarette to hold out a hand. 'Bill Perch.'

'Bill,' she repeats. 'Sit.'

I'm sure we shouldn't be lounging out in the corridor like this, but there's no conductor in sight, so I do. Once I would have worried about my trousers.

'Why are you out here?' I ask, as Matthieu settles back down. 'Don't you have tickets?'

They all laugh. Lucille stretches her legs over Matthieu's lap.

'No money.' Javi shrugs.

'And Paris is too hot,' says Lucille.

'So we're flying south, to visit Javi's homeland and maybe find a sea to bask in,' Matthieu finishes, putting his sunglasses back on. 'How about you, Bill Perch from England? Where are you going?'

'Nîmes.' I try to make it sound casual. 'For a start, at least. Won't it take you ages to get to Spain?'

'It's not that much further than Nîmes, actually. And anyway there's no rush. We're on a summer holiday, sort of.'

'Not like Cliff Richard,' Javi assures me. 'It is a work holiday. My grandparents, they have a finca, in Girona. Times are hard for them, so we go to help.'

'And to fight the good fight,' says Matthieu, 'one in the eye for Franco.'

'We are going to pick beans, not fight.' Lucille laughs, as Javi looks rather pained.

They are students in Paris, it turns out. Matthieu and Javi are studying history and art; Lucille, music. My parents would never have let me study anything so romantic.

'What do you play?' I ask.

'A few things.' She shrugs.

'Anything with strings.' Matthieu nudges her, and her lips soften into a smile.

'Mandolin is my favourite,' she says. 'I like bluegrass, you know?'

I have no idea what she's talking about.

'Cool.'

'And you?' Matthieu finishes his cigarette and chucks it out of the window. 'What's in Nîmes?'

'It's a long story,' I say and sigh.

'It's a long train ride.'

★ ★ ★

Matthieu isn't wrong. There's nothing else to do on the train except talk and smoke, so I tell them the bare bones; that I'm here in France looking for someone. Rather than grilling me, they shrug and nod and the conversation moves on. Soon we're talking about music, and the differences between Paris and London, English and French food. Javi idly sketches on a piece of paper, a little cartoon of me riding a horse, *like Don Quixote*, he says.

The countryside is endless, field after field of cabbages. The warm summer air buffets through the open windows. More than once when we arrive at a station, I find myself bundled into the tiny toilet cubicle with the rest of them, to avoid the conductor. Lucille bites her lips to keep from laughing and I feel like a kid at school playing sardines, trying not to breathe in the smell.

The train rattles out of a place called *Nevers*

and we fall out of the toilet again, laughing as Matthieu mock-vomits out of the window. I realize with surprise that I haven't thought about Emeline, or my ill-advised quest, for hours. Part of me itches to get to Nîmes, to start searching, but another part wishes I could forget all about it, tag along with Luci and Matti and Javi — as they insist I call them — all the way to Spain.

Outside, the land starts to change; clusters of old stone buildings poking up between stands of trees, the ground surging into small hills, like rumpled blankets on a bed. I play about twenty games of 'snap' with Javi, while Luci and Matthieu start a heated debate in French. Whatever it's about, it's resolved when Luci laughs and kisses Matti's cheek. He grins and starts to roll a cigarette, which I suspect doesn't only contain tobacco.

When it comes my way, I hesitate, but only for a second. William Perch, Solicitor, would've refused, but I left William Perch, Solicitor, back in London. Bill Perch can do what he likes. The pungent fumes soon fill the end of the carriage. The movement of the train is soothing. We sit, cushioned by our bags, and the afternoon slides by like honey.

I must doze for a while because when I wake it's to the sound of jingling coins. Javi is holding a handful of change, Luci is digging through her bag.

'Hey, man,' says Matthieu, looking a bit bleary. 'We're going to the buffet car. You want anything?'

Luci drops another small bronze coin into

Javi's hand. He pokes through the pile, a little despondently. Feeling the wad of French banknotes in my pocket, my cheeks start to burn. I've no idea how much is there but I assume it's quite a lot; when I changed the money Mr Vane gave me at the currency booth, the lady was surprisingly nice and called me 'sir'.

'I'll go,' I tell them, standing before they can protest. 'I need a walk anyway.'

It's late afternoon now, a cool breeze rattling down the train corridor, blowing the hair back from my forehead.

'*Bonjour*,' I say to the bored-looking man behind the buffet bar, and point to what I want, holding up a variety of fingers. When I'm done, there's a bizarre assortment of biscuits, crackers, bottles of lemonade and nuts on the surface. The man rolls his eyes when I pay with a note but I don't care. I scoop up the armful of bounty and stagger happily back down the train.

We've come to a stop at another station. The others will be in the toilet. But when I make it to the very end, there's no sign of them. The toilet door stands ajar, the cubicle noxious, but empty.

My briefcase. All of my mother's warnings about hippies and vagrants surge back with force. But there it is, in the corner, exactly where I left it. Where the hell are they? Someone blows a whistle; compartment doors are being slammed, the train is about to leave. Would they really have just gone without a word?

Why would they bother to stay? William Perch, Solicitor, hisses from the back of my mind. *You're not like them. They wouldn't want to be friends with you.*

Miserably, I shove the snacks into my bag. The brakes release, and as the train pulls away, I peer out of the window one last time. A bare, concrete platform, a dilapidated station building and a single sign that tells me this middle-of-nowhere station is *Coteau-Sainte-Thérèse*.

I watch it go, am about to turn away, when I hear shouting, a familiar voice protesting loudly. Through the door of the station I catch a glimpse of Luci, struggling in the grip of a uniformed official, Matti and Javi fighting to keep hold of their bags, as a second man tries to drag them away.

Then the scene is gone, snatched away from view as the train picks up speed. The very end of the platform is approaching. In another few seconds, it will be too late. The evening light flashes upon the window of the station like a beacon. *Stay or go?* it asks. *Stay or go?*

Without another thought, I shove open the door, clutch my briefcase to me and take a leap from the moving train.

May 1919

From that day, we were inseparable, though we could not be seen as such. We nodded and smiled amiably to each other in front of Clémence, then he would go to his work and I to mine. But the afternoons, the quiet time after lunch and before the preparations for dinner began, when the whole town rested in the ever-growing heat, those were our own.

We would meet at the edge of the *maquis*, he with his bicycle, me with an empty basket, and we would flee from prying eyes, into the wild borderland where the only sounds were the droning of insects, the, far-off jingling of goat bells and the hiss of dry plants, baked to husks by the fierce sun.

He took me to secret places, like his cliff overlooking the sea, where I picked crest marine from the rocks. Or we ventured far into the dense scrubland, seeking out wild sage and rosemary. I always tried to collect enough to explain my absence, but it was never long before we sank down together beneath the shade of the twisted juniper trees.

I learned to let go of speech. Instead, he taught me his language, fluttering his hands over my unclothed body, making me repeat signs and gestures, taunting and teasing until I got them right, until I thought I would go mad with waiting and wanting.

In that no man's land between countries, we crossed every border. I didn't care; all I knew was recklessness and joy. Even the sunburn across my cheeks, the scratches on my legs from the gorse, were testimony, were treasured reminders of what it felt like to live.

As the weeks wore on, I grew stronger. My skin turned brown, the sun lightened my hair to gold and when *la Tramontana* tugged it from its pins and sent it flying, I let it.

Every night people came by the café, to drink, to talk, but invariably to eat. The meals Clémence and I produced were becoming more elaborate, with no need to rely on the pantry; summer was coming to Cerbère, bringing with it a rush of produce. Tomatoes ripened by the bucket-load, and as Clémence predicted, someone from the town nearly always left a basket of them, freshly picked, on the back step of the café. The deep, red fruits found their way into every dish, roasted or diced or cooked down with garlic and oil into sauces that stained mouths and fingers orange. For breakfast we even ate them squeezed over bread, slathered in olive oil and sprinkled with salt.

I went out to the vegetable garden every day now, to help with watering, and to gather what was ready to eat. We picked colourful peppers, beans and courgettes, careful to save their crinkled orange flowers. I couldn't believe my eyes when Clémence showed me how to fill them with soft goat's cheese and herbs and pine nuts and fry them until their petals were crisp as autumn leaves.

But I still had a lot to learn. Every time Aaró brought home his catch, he would spend a few minutes, showing them to me. I learned about all manner of fish and crustaceans that way, how they lived and what they ate. Sometimes, his hands would pause in their speech to touch mine, dripping with seawater.

I did not know how much Clémence knew about us. She had made it clear on several occasions that she considered Mariona and Aaró to be a good pairing. Sometimes, she arranged things so that the two of them sat together at dinner. Mariona knew a lot of Aaró's language, I saw, trying to push down a squall of jealousy.

They had known each other since childhood, my friend Agathe told me, though in the last year Mariona had begun to suggest they should be more than friends. I answered as casually as I could, and kept my face lowered so that no one would see the burning in my cheeks. I knew I should try to ask Aaró about Mariona, whether there was anything between them, and dozens of times I almost did. But at the last minute I always stilled my hands, and said nothing. In truth, I was afraid of the answer. Instead, I ate and worked, and willed away the hours until he and I could be alone together.

One morning, he came into the kitchen with a crate of the strangest creatures I had ever seen, mottled and striped with huge eyes. He grinned and waved one at me from the bucket, flapping its tentacles in my face. I laughed and was only just able to stop myself from pushing at him affectionately, from leaning in to kiss his cheek.

'What is it?' I asked, as Aaró sorted through the creatures in the bucket and held up eight fingers.

'Cuttlefish,' Clémence groaned. 'They are good but they make such a mess. We shall have to prepare them outside.'

I went to fetch a knife, but Clémence called me back.

'Leave that,' she said, 'just bring a bowl, and a cloth.'

On the beach, I followed suit as Clémence took off her shoes, rolled up her skirt until it was over her shins and stepped into the surf. The water was balmy in the shallows and I wiggled my toes, enjoying the feel of it. The old fishermen started catcalling, but Clémence yelled what sounded like a few choice insults in Catalan and they soon fell quiet.

'Do as I do.' She slapped a cuttlefish into my hands. It was slimy and chill from the sea. I watched as she pushed an oval-shaped bone out of its skin as easily as shelling a nut. Her fingers dug into the soft flesh beneath and twisted, pulling the head and guts free in one movement. They were dripping with black liquid, but she didn't waste a drop, just threw the inky mess into a bowl on the shore, the now flat cuttlefish into the bucket.

'It should not take you long to do the rest,' she told me with a wicked smile, rinsing her hands in the sea.

Tentatively, I stuck my thumbs into the creature's back. The bone came free, but a jet of black ink spurted up and into my face, leaving me gasping and swearing and covered with briny liquid.

Clémence laughed until her eyes ran.

'*Mon Dieu*,' she gasped, handing me a cloth, 'I remember the first time that happened to me.' A few passers-by had stopped to watch the spectacle and add their laughter. Agathe was there. I waved at her, and only succeeded in splattering myself further.

'What's for dinner?' she called down to us.

'*Arròs negre*,' Clémence called back, 'if Mam'selle Fischer can spare me any ink!'

That set them off laughing again. I smiled sheepishly, only to see Mariona in the crowd, looking satisfied at my clumsiness. I struggled to do as Clémence had done and pull the creature's guts free but the black stuff oozed through my fingers, making a terrible mess.

'Mariona,' Clémence called, 'are you busy?'

I froze, even as her feet came crunching down the beach towards us.

'No, *Maman*,' came her answer, emphasizing the second word. I dug my fingers into the squid a little harder.

'Would you mind showing Mam'selle Fischer what to do? I have chores in the kitchen and I fear she will be here all day, otherwise.'

'*Bien sûr*.' The girl smiled, and began to unlace her own boots.

'You take the bone like this,' she told me politely in her accented French, as Clémence disappeared towards the café.

Though not as deft as Clémence, Mariona made quick work of the fish. Her black hair was piled up on her head. In a white blouse and blue skirt she looked pretty and neat. I thought about the smirks she had thrown my way the night before, as she sat beside Aaró.

'You do not need to pretend for my sake,' I told her sharply, 'she is gone.'

Mariona glanced up at me through her dark lashes.

'I know what you are doing,' she said. 'You think you are so secret, with your baskets from the *maquis*, but I know.'

My fingers slipped, sending the cuttlefish splashing into the shallow water at my feet. I retrieved it, shaken.

'I don't know what you're talking about.'

She shrugged, throwing a handful of innards into the bowl.

'I am not worried. Sometimes, you find a new taste. And you like it, because it is different. But soon, new becomes old, especially when there is no place for it. You will leave and he will forget, return to what he knows is right for him. Right for the town.'

I watched the ink drip from the creature's body into the gently frothing surf.

'He will make a good husband,' she said decisively, seizing up another cuttlefish, pushing out its bone with a wet *snap*. 'There aren't many left here like him. He could not go away to fight, so he is strong. Not like the others who came back. I do not want to be a nurse to a broken man.'

I stepped towards her in the sea, until she was forced to look up, to meet my gaze.

266

'You don't understand at all,' I said, trembling with emotion. 'You don't understand how he feels, what it is like for him to be the one who survived . . . ' I couldn't find the words, could only stare down into her wide, dark eyes.

'What does a wife need to understand about her husband beyond what their bodies can tell them?' she asked innocently.

★　★　★

I told Clémence that the cuttlefish had made me sick. I shoved the bucket and bowl on to the table and fled for the stairs, ignoring her questions. In the cracked mirror she'd given me for my room, I saw my face, smeared with dark ink. I went to the washbowl, scrubbed at the skin until it was red and stinging, and all the while Mariona's words echoed through my head.

You will leave and he will forget.

She was wrong, I told myself feverishly. I could make a home here in Cerbère. But beneath that, stronger than a rip tide, was the fear that she spoke the truth. I was a stranger. What was more, I had lied about who I was and what I had left behind me. How could I stay here, marry Aaró and raise children, when I could not even tell him my real name? It seemed impossible.

And what if you slip? a voice from the darkest part of my mind whispered. *What if you lose yourself again and everything that happened at Hallerton happens here? You think he wants a madwoman for his wife?*

I lay on the bed and dragged the sheet over my head. I did not move when Clémence called me for lunch, did not move when I heard church bells toll the hour, when the heat of the afternoon grew strong and sweat prickled my forehead. I knew Aaró would be waiting, alone with his bicycle, but I only stared, dry-eyed, at the cotton threads, willing myself to make a choice.

Finally, it grew cooler and the scent of onions frying rose from downstairs. I knew a summons when I smelled it. Clémence was kind to me that evening. Perhaps she thought she had gone too far, leaving me alone with Mariona. Perhaps she thought she had finally succeeded in warning me away from Aaró. For all I knew at that moment, she had.

We made *arròs negre*, a rice dish cooked with cuttlefish. It was pungent with lemon and herbs, briny and glossy from the ink, but I couldn't pay proper attention. When we brought it out, I could feel Aaró watching me. Dinner was lively as always, the café's doors open to catch the cool breeze off the sea. I felt questions in his gaze, concern, but I couldn't look at him. Finally, I took my unfinished plate and slipped away, mumbling to Agathe that I was not well.

Heart-sick, I sat in the darkness on the back step, and gave my food to Aaró's cats. I listened to the sounds filtering through from the café, laughter and conversations with fifty years of history behind them.

I should have turned away when I heard that familiar tread come around the corner, but a treacherous part of me refused to move. Aaró stopped when he saw me. His face was tight with hurt.

He tapped his head rapidly, let his hand drop. *Why?*

I looked at the ground, but he stepped forward, repeated it.

I talked, I told him after a while, cycling my hands before my mouth, *me and* . . . I didn't know how to say her name, I realized. In the end, I tapped at my, finger where a wedding ring would be, and pointed back towards the café.

I saw his expression change, and knew that he understood.

You and her, I gestured, *are right. Me* . . . I waved my hands, trying to indicate the whole town and shook my head hopelessly. Not for the first time I wished I still had my old diary, so I could write down everything I was thinking and give it to him to read. It was easier to be honest on paper. But he couldn't read; people learned by sounding, Clémence had explained, and he had never known sound, so had never known written words.

His hand touched my chin, raised it gently until I was looking into his eyes. They were bright as he brushed a finger across my lips.

Enough.

★ ★ ★

His muscles were taut beneath his shirt; they bunched and stretched as we rode away from the town, away from the café. Balanced precariously on the back of the bicycle, I felt the heat of him as he pedalled faster and faster. He swerved and I laughed wildly, gripping him tight. We were in the olive grove, ghost-grey trunks flashing past. Above us were stars, a whole sky thick with them.

I threw my head back, the night air streaming through my hair like ribbons, whisking away the day's sadness and confusion, and I hoped that we would never stop. But stop we did. The dust clung to the sweat of our bodies as we lay amongst the early fallen fruit, their oils locked tight like a merchant's precious cargo.

In the darkness beneath the trees he took my hand, placed it over his heart. The beat rose and fell against my fingers, and those three words, the most important ones a person can say, Aaró told me without a sound.

June 1969

Through a window of the station building I see Luci, Javi and Matti all standing like prisoners at a dock. A railway official — who doesn't look any older than me — stands nervously to one side. In front of them a second man, evidently more senior, sits at a desk sorting through some papers. Javi is nursing a swollen lip; Matthieu and Luci are both glaring with a mixture of fury and contempt.

I take a deep breath, trying to summon my Harry Palmer confidence. It was easier when I didn't look such a mess. I straighten my jacket and grip the briefcase firmly in my sweaty palm. Now or never.

'*What* is the meaning of this?' I demand as I march into the office, trying my best to look both professional and annoyed. The railway men gape at me. They probably don't speak English, I remember. Too late now. 'I demand to know why you have detained these people.'

Matti, Luci and Javi are staring at me like I've sprouted tusks. I feel my terrible act start to waver.

'Well?' I say loudly, to compensate.

The railway official behind the desk has started to recover. His eyes take in my mismatched shirt and sorry-looking suit more thoroughly than I'd like. A sneer crawls up his face.

'What you want?' he says.

'I asked why you are holding these people, who are accompanying me on an important business matter. And I won't repeat it again.'

'Hey, Bill — ' Matthieu starts, but I shake my head at him.

'No ticket,' the official tells me, leaning back in his chair. 'They pay fine.' The three of them burst into outraged French. 'They cannot pay fine,' the official shrugs over their protests, 'so, I call police.' He picks up the telephone receiver.

Deliberately, I take the wad of banknotes from my jacket pocket.

'I'll pay for their tickets. And, er, a bit extra, for taking up your time,' I say meaningfully, hoping I'm doing it right. I've never tried to bribe anyone before.

The receiver hangs forgotten in the railway official's hand. His colleague's eyes look ready to fall out.

'So how much will it be, then?' I ask briskly, separating out a note or two.

The man's double chin stretches into a smile.

★ ★ ★

'Bastards, bastards,' Luci is spitting, before we're even out of earshot. Javi is cursing gently in Spanish and Matthieu is silent, his face like thunder. I trail behind them, shell-shocked.

Behind us, jubilant laughter echoes around the deserted country station, as the officials celebrate their unexpected bonus. What the hell is wrong with me? Why did I take all the money out at once? I should've guessed the greedy bugger would try it on, but threatening to report me to the police for 'bribing an official' unless I gave him the whole lot as a bribe just didn't cross my mind.

'Shit.' I kick at a stone and sink to the kerb. Half an hour ago I had a wallet full of money and a vague, but hopeful, plan. Now I'm stranded in the middle of bloody nowhere with nothing. 'Shit.'

'Hey.' There's a touch on my back and Javi sits down beside me, looking a little haggard. 'Thank you, Bill, you saved our ham.'

'Bacon,' Matthieu corrects, kneeling down as well. 'You did. Thanks.'

Luci squeezes down on the other side of me, and cuts off her swearing to kiss my cheek.

'It was nothing.' I can't help smiling, just a bit.

'Those francs were not nothing,' Luci says. 'Where did you get that money?'

'It wasn't mine, exactly . . . '

As we walk towards what is hopefully a nearby town, I tell them the truth about why I'm in France. They ask questions about Emeline and Hallerton, they laugh when I describe how I found the old union railwaymen in the bar, and then Puce, in his grand Belleville house.

'That's why I was going to Nîmes. It's the last place anyone saw her. I was going to use the money to try to find out something, *anything*, about where she might have gone next.'

I lapse into silence. Tall trees line the road, their dusty green canopies shielding us from the heat. Early-evening birdsong echoes strangely. It reminds me of Hallerton, a thousand miles away. Matthieu stops and puts a hand on my shoulder.

'No 'was'. We owe you, man. We'll get you there, and we'll see if we can't put a bit of money in your pocket at the same time.'

Even if I get to Nîmes, I want to tell him, I don't know what will happen. I might end up penniless on the streets. I might have to turn myself in to the British Embassy and be sent home in disgrace, empty-handed.

'Thanks,' I say instead. 'Do you even know where we are?'

'Probably only a few hours away.' He shrugs. 'Shouldn't be too hard to hitch, even from a place like this.'

Hitchhiking with hippies. Steph would be horrified. Mum would give me up for dead. I still feel guilty, thinking about them, but not for long. They would tell me that I've been an idiot, that all of this trouble has been for nothing.

And they'd be wrong, I think, as the evening sun flashes through the leaves and Javi does a silly walk to make us laugh. *This isn't nothing.*

June 1919

In Cerbère, the seasons did not creep. Instead, mid-summer burst upon us like a drunk at a party: colourful, vibrant, teetering between magnificent and unbearable. The weather was hotter than anything I had ever experienced. More than once I found myself gasping in the shade, my head spinning. Of course, the townspeople were accustomed to it. They adjusted their days to start earlier, resting from noon until the fierce sun began to slip behind the hills. No one ventured outside during this time, except for Aaró and me.

We ruled the countryside. When the trains fell silent on the tracks above the town, and everyone else lay calm behind closed shutters, we ran wild. Those afternoons were like another world, one where there was no need for restraint, for self-consciousness or artifice. Our blood boiled and we were bold. We knew each other's bodies like our own, every blemish and scar.

We lay naked in the deepest part of the rapidly drying streams; we picked cherries and stained our lips red with their juices. We claimed the land, and the fruit and herbs we collected in our uncaring sin were the same ones the towns-people ate, night after night with relish.

The sun began to set later. Often, the sky was still light, people still laughing and singing outside the Café Fi del Món, when in winter they would long be abed. At this time of year, in Saltedge, the people of the village had held midsummer celebrations. Durrant's wife, Annie, had once laughed and told me that it was mostly an excuse for the young people to sneak away together. Perhaps that was on my mind when I asked Clémence whether they observed any such customs in Cerbère.

'The Feast of *Sant Joan*,' she told me as we sat on the back step, sorting through a sack of onions. 'Midsummer's Day, the most distant day from the birth of Our Lord.' She crossed herself with mock piety and I saw where Aaró got some of his mischief.

'What happens?'

'We used to have a *correfoc*,' her eyes brightened, 'a night of fire. We would make *coques*, and drink *cremat*, and build a great bonfire on the beach. And everyone would drink too much and forget to be good Christians, for one night at least.'

'Why 'used to'? Surely it happens every year.'

'Not since the war began.' She reached for the sack again.

'But the war is over,' I said. 'Why shouldn't we celebrate?'

Her hand paused. The papery skin of an onion crackled against her palm.

'Perhaps you are right.' She spoke almost to herself. 'Perhaps it would do us good to remember what it is like to be alive,' she glanced at me, 'what it is like to be young.'

After that, the idea spread across the town like wild-fire. It seemed that if 'Maman' suggested something, it was not long before that thing became gospel. Sure enough, a few days later the mayor of Cerbère sat outside the café, clutching a glass of wine and declaring to anyone who would listen that the following Saturday would mark the return of the *Sant Joan* celebrations.

As the days limped past and the heat grew more feverish, so did the mood in the town. When a delivery cart arrived at the café, laden down with everything from fireworks and sugar to a crate full of rum, my excitement only grew. The Feast of *Sant Joan*, I learned, wasn't simply another saint's day. There were rituals involved, ancient ones from a time before the Church, said Agathe.

'God may be watching,' she told me as we ate *llangostins* one night, our fingers slick with garlic and oil, 'but even He knows it's the sun that gives us all we have. So when it is at its highest, we give it all that we have in return, our breath, our joy, to see it through the winter.'

'We feed him, he feeds us,' interrupted her elderly father-in-law, sneaking a particularly fat *llangostin* from her bowl.

I could hardly wait, and I told Aaró so the next day, as we lay in the shallows of the stream, shaded by juniper trees.

You will see. He smiled and placed one palm flat, sprung two fingers up from it. *People will jump*, he said and made his fingers bloom outwards, waving like flames. *Over the fire.*

Why? I asked.

My hair was wet, clinging to my bare shoulder. He smoothed it away, kissed where it had been, before tapping my nose with a maddening smile.

You will see.

I rolled my eyes.

You are just like your mother, I said.

★ ★ ★

On the day of the feast, Clémence and I were up at the crack of dawn. This time, I was not surprised to find Oriol standing with his dog at the back door.

'*Bon dia,*' I greeted him with a yawn.

He only nodded in return, his eyes on Clémence as he indicated something on the step behind him.

A wild boar lay there, its eyes still open. The musky, feral smell of it reached me, even at the stove.

'We are going to eat *that?*' I asked, forgetting the coffee I was making. I could scarcely comprehend how we would get the meat off the thing.

'Indeed.' Clémence looked pleased, as she handed over some money to Oriol. 'The Feast of *Sant Joan* is no time for grace, Mademoiselle Fischer. It is a night to remember that we have teeth.'

Be that as it may, she dispatched the boar into the care of one of the pig farmers, for which I was grateful.

'We will have quite enough on our hands with all the baking,' she said, and sent me to fetch the flour from the pantry.

'Baking?' I called, feeling sweat spring out on

278

my forehead as I manhandled the heavy sack.

'*Coca de Sant Joan*,' she said. 'It is a special cake, more like *brioche*. Made with lemon zest, candied fruits, nuts, *anisette* . . . ' From the scullery she took a large and precious pat of butter. 'We'll use olive oil too,' she said firmly. 'This is no time to skimp.'

Soon, she had me stirring a huge bowl, into which she poured in more sugar than we used in a month, dozens of eggs, whisked to froth, rich goat's milk and lemon rind and yeast. She showed me how to work the flour in, how to knead the dough until it was soft and silky to the touch.

While it proved, she taught me how to make candied orange and lemon peel. They reminded me of the sugared flowers that had once decorated my mother's teatime confections. When they were done, my other task — far more difficult — was to stop the local children from stealing the candied treats as they lay on a sheet, drying in the sun.

Noon approached and the heat of the day increased, but still we worked. No stolen hours for Aaró and me, today. The kitchen grew hotter until Clémence and I were forced to strip off our blouses and tie scarves about our hair, to keep the sweat from running into our eyes. We formed a production line, shaping the dough into ovals, scattering each one with sugar and candied peel and pine nuts, drizzling them with olive oil and perfumed anise liqueur, before shovelling them into the oven; a seemingly never-ending stream.

'Enough,' Clémence declared, when the final

one was set to cool on the table. 'We have done our part.' Her face was flushed and perspiring, flour clinging to the fine hairs of her cheeks.

'What about the boar?' I wiped my face on my discarded blouse and smiled, wondering what the cook at Hallerton would say if she saw me now.

Clémence waved her hand dismissively.

'We will cook him on the bonfire, with some good brandy and a *picada*. The men can see to that. It is time we had a chance to enjoy ourselves.'

Long before dark started to fall, I felt the anticipation. A strange, simmering quiet had descended on Cerbère, as the townspeople hurried home to wash and change and prepare themselves, body and soul, for the revelry that was to follow. Slowly, I dragged a facecloth over my arms, behind my neck, between my breasts. I stood near the open window, watching the sea turn pearlescent, letting the scant breeze dry my skin, savouring the moment, when everything was yet to come.

I heard footsteps on the stairs; someone trying to be quiet, unaware of how each step creaked and groaned like a ghoul. Smiling, I crept to the door and threw it open.

Aaró leaped in surprise, but soon his face fell into a smile. His black hair was combed neatly back from his face and he looked handsome in his best shirt and neckerchief, smelling of soap and clean cotton. I, on the other hand, was bare from the waist up, my skin still damp, hair a tangle down my back. But I smiled, for what did a pair of sleeves or a row of buttons matter, between us?

He had something hidden behind him. I asked him what it was, and he laughed his irresistible laugh, dodging back and forth out of my grasp before finally he brought it out and placed it in my hands.

It was a wreath, woven from silver-green olive leaves and white myrtle blooms, sprigs of flowering rosemary and thyme. It filled my room with the scent of the *maquis*, and I found myself blinking away tears, that he had made something so beautiful.

For you, he said and rested it gently upon my hair.

Impulsively, I caught at his hand, and pressed it to my heart.

For you, I told him in return.

★   ★   ★

I wore Aaró's wreath that night, as darkness fell and the spirit of midsummer was awoken. It came hurtling into town in the form of the local children, all shrieking and whooping, dressed as devils and carrying tiny burning torches, which they used to light the grand bonfire on the beach, bigger even than the one at the *calçotada*.

Clémence presided over a ritual on the shore, where a huge earthenware dish was being filled with bottle after bottle of rum. I asked if I could help but she waved me away, tossing cinnamon sticks and coffee beans and sugar into the mixture like a witch. Then, with a flourish, she struck a match and the whole thing was ablaze, flames leaping high into the gathering dusk, turning the waves orange.

'What is going on?' I called, watching as Clémence struck a pose with a long-handled ladle.

'*Cremat!*' one of the fishermen yelled over the local band, who had taken this as their cue to burst into song. 'Burned rum! Watch your cups, though, Mam'selle Fischer, this stuff could knock a bishop off his feet . . . '

But there was no time for caution, for watching or waiting. The boar had been roasting on its own fire for hours, wearing a garland of herbs, an onion in its mouth. As the men continued to baste it with brandy and garlic and oil the smell grew irresistible. I found a cup of *cremat* pushed into my hand and took a sip. Hot, fiery, caramel sweetness flooded my mouth, made me gasp for breath. No wonder the Feast of *Sant Joan* was said to be wild.

There was nothing so conservative as an order to the night; the cakes we had made earlier were laid out along the tables, and people helped themselves, balancing slices of it on their cups of *cremat*, waiting for the meat to be cooked. Aaró was near the bonfire, laughing with a few other young men. I caught his eye and we shared a smile across the darkness.

'During the feast, someone told me that people leap over the fires,' I asked Agathe's daughter, who sat alongside me, 'why is that?'

Before she could answer, Agathe appeared out of nowhere and flopped down between us on the beach, juggling three slices of *coca.*

'It is tradition,' she told me, taking a bite. 'A leap over the fire turns a bad year to good. Then,' she waved the cake, 'it is into the sea.'

I must have looked nonplussed, for Agathe's daughter laughed.

'The fire is to purify, the water to wash clean, the herbs to heal,' she explained. Behind her, the boar was being lifted from the spit, to delighted shouts. She smiled wickedly. 'Of course, tradition does not say *which* herbs, or how to eat them.'

Over my shoulder, I watched Aaró, signing something to one of his friends. *A bad year to good . . .* It did not seem possible that a year ago, all of this was unknown to me. A year ago I had sat in the silence of Hallerton, in the green stillness of Saltedge, mourning a brother, wondering if the war would ever end. Since then, my whole life had been turned on its head, from darkness to light. I wanted it to remain that way.

I clambered to my feet, rum and summer heat and music flowing through me. The bonfire had started to die down, the embers glowing white hot at the centre, soft flames licking at the charcoaling wood. On the far side I stopped, and kicked off my shoes. For a heartbeat I faltered, as my mind warned me of all the things that might happen if I did not jump far enough, if I could not make it across.

But then, through the heat, I met Aaró's gaze. His eyes were full of laughter, full of life. I felt myself grinning wildly as I took a step back, threw myself into a run, and leaped.

June 1969

'Where are we?'

A village straggles down the hill before us, a mess of ginger-coloured roof tiles tucked between old, weathered stone outcrops.

'Somewhere in the Haute-Loire?' says Luci. 'Or the Ardeche?'

'Eh?'

She waves her arm vaguely to indicate the shape of France. 'South is the Méditerranée, west is the mountains, the Cévennes. We are in the middle.'

'Wherever it is,' says Matti, 'I hope it has a bar.'

Coteau-Sainte-Thérèse does indeed have a bar, a tiny one that looks like it hasn't changed since the turn of the century, the only nod to modernity being a few greasy Formica tables. Nevertheless, it's full of people, mostly wearing work gear, apart from the old men in their obligatory soft hats. All of them, without fail, turn to stare as we walk up.

'How much money do we have?' Luci murmurs as we take a seat outside, trying to look casual.

'Enough for one drink each.' Javi hands over the meagre handful of change.

'All right.' She picks up one of her bags, disappearing into the bar's dark interior.

'Will she be OK?' I ask. Several of the farmers

are leering at her bare legs.

'Fine,' says Matti, 'you'll see.'

He is just handing me a cigarette when I hear it: the sound of strings being plucked, high and clear and lively. The three of us scramble to our feet to peer inside.

Luci is seated at the bar, her mop of blonde hair pushed over one shoulder, a round-bellied instrument resting on her legs. Her fingers are dancing over the strings, her other hand strumming and picking in time. Whatever the song is, it sounds Irish, and instantly my toes are twitching, my knees jigging like they want to go dancing off without me.

I'm not the only one. Throughout the bar downturned lips have risen. I see one booted foot tapping, then another, and beside me, Javi starts doing a sort of hopping dance. Matti doesn't join in, but his face is softer than I've ever seen, glowing with pride.

Luci's fingers move faster and faster, until the woman behind the bar lets out a whoop and starts to clap her hands in time. As she strums the final note, the whole place breaks into applause. Luci smiles, and thanks them, and one song becomes another, until people are calling out suggestions and thumping their glasses.

The sun has gone down by the time Luci emerges with the instrument over her shoulder, red-cheeked and sweaty.

'You were amazing!' I tell her as she places a jug of wine on the table. 'That was amazing.'

'Thank you.' She pushes back her hair. 'In return they will give us dinner, and tomorrow a nice man called Manou will take us to Mende. From there it is,' she mimes a straight line, 'to Nîmes.'

'Bravo!' cries Javi.

'Bravo,' says Matthieu. 'I thought for an awful moment you were going to play the Paganini.'

Laughing, she thumps him on the arm, drains a glass of wine.

'Dinner' turns out to be four bowls of thick stew. I dig around with my spoon and unearth beans and carrots, a round of sausage and some oily, yellow meat that sinks to the bottom.

'What is it?' I poke.

'Cassoulet,' Matti says, slurping experimentally. 'If it tastes good, it's best not to ask for the details. Could be anything.'

It does taste good, even the weird yellow leg, which I guess once belonged to a duck. Bellies full, and with night well fallen over the valley, we troop around the corner. The landlady's generosity doesn't stretch to letting us stay in the bar, but she does give us a pile of musty-smelling blankets and cushions and tells us we can camp in the barn.

'She is worried we will steal her liquor.' Javi winks.

It's a warm night, and soon I'm lying on my back, with nothing but a blanket between me and the bare ground. Smoke from one of Matti's more exotic cigarettes spirals up towards the barn ceiling. Through the gaps in the roof I can see stars appearing, more than I've ever seen in my life, a whole sky thick with them.

'It's not like this in London,' I murmur. Night

insects click and chirp.

'I would like to see London,' Luci says sleepily, her head on Matti's shoulder.

'Maybe after Spain,' he says and they laugh softly.

'How will you get there?' My eyes are drifting closed. 'Spain?'

'Hitch,' says Javi, 'maybe look for a big truck in Montpellier. Or we jump a train again. We avoid the *policia* at the border if we walk across the *maquis* from Cerbère.'

'Cer-where?'

'Cerbère. A little place, on the sea. The last town in France,' Javi yawns, 'it is like the end of the world there.'

That makes me smile. How could anything feel further away from reality than this does, right now? I'm half asleep, but Javi's words stick in my head. *The end of the world, the end of the world . . . Where have I heard that phrase before?* Something sparks at the back of my mind, making a connection. My heart picks up pace.

'Javi,' I ask slowly, afraid that if I speak too quickly, the thought might burst and disappear. 'Cerbère, is it south of Nîmes?'

'Yes, why?'

'And you can get there on the train?'

'From Nîmes? Of course, but it is the end of the line — '

With a lurch I'm on my knees, scrabbling for my briefcase. Crumpled packets and bits of rubbish go flying as I drag out the file of papers.

'Bill?' asks Luci in alarm, but I don't reply.

287

Instead, I pull out Timothy Vane's letter, almost tearing it in my haste to find the words that Emeline wrote to her brother, fifty years ago: *I wanted to say that I am safe, somewhere a long way away, so far it might as well be the end of the world.*

'Cerbère,' I whisper, hardly daring to believe it. 'Emeline . . . I know where you are.'

July 1919

'Where are you off to?'

Clémence was dressed for an outing in her best skirt, a black hat despite the heat, and a pair of short gloves. I had never seen her looking so smart, and I told her so, pausing in my task of transferring salted anchovies to buckets of brine.

'Thank you,' she told me, with a smile.

I had started to sense a gradual change in her attitude towards me, ever since midsummer and the feast. The day after, while everyone else was still abed, Mariona had left town. According to Agathe, she had gone to stay with her aunt in Beziers. She had told everyone that it was for a holiday, but I knew it was because she had finally confronted Aaró, and he had told her the truth about us. Part of me felt bad, guilty for elbowing my way in on the life she had imagined for herself, but it was a small part. Honestly, I was delighted not to have her dark eyes boring holes in my back every night at dinner.

Ever since then, Clémence had begun to talk more of the seasons, of how at the end of summer the village children would collect snails, which we would cook in garlic and dill and wine. How in autumn, once the first rains fell, we would go to the foothills and hunt for wild mushrooms, gathering some to pickle and dry for winter, some to eat then and there, rolled in oil and charred on a bonfire. It was her way of telling me something important, I realized. She was teaching me how to be part of life in Cerbère.

But we had yet to speak openly about Aaró and me. For all its pagan ways Cerbère was still a Catholic town, where people turned a blind eye, so long as things went unsaid. Every day, I thought about raising the subject with Aaró, but every day, something stopped me; perhaps I was unwilling to break our happiness with the possibility of conflict.

'So where are you going?' I asked Clémence again, as I sorted through the tiny, pungent fish.

'Banyuls-sur-Mer.' She pushed her hat a little higher. 'There is a market today and I have errands to run.'

'Something special?'

She paused, and shared a smile with me. 'Today is Aaró's birthday. His twenty-first.'

'He didn't say!' I burst out. 'Nobody said,' I tried to recover, though she looked amused by my slip. 'That's wonderful. Are we to have a party?'

'Yes. I should have liked to make it a time to remember, with a grand dinner tonight, and a lunch tomorrow but . . . ' She sighed, and I saw her then as I rarely did: as the mother of one rather than many. 'After the expense of *Sant Joan* we simply do not have the money. Not until there are more vegetables to trade. We shall have to make do with what we have.'

'Wait.' I stepped back from the table so fast that I scattered salt all over the floor. 'Wait there.'

Wiping my hands on a rag, I ran upstairs two

steps at a time and into my room. There, wrapped in paper on a high shelf, was my velvet travelling suit, the one I had worn the day I left Hallerton. I had not looked at it for months. It had been cleaned and folded, but as I ran my hand across it I felt a chill, a breath of the shadows that had plagued Emeline Vane, that still lived, buried deep within Emilie Fischer.

'Here.' I thrust the garments at Clémence, glad to be rid of the feel of them. 'Can we not sell these? The embroidery alone should be worth something.'

Clémence turned the velvet, admiring its dull shine.

'I thought you wanted to keep them.' Her voice was careful.

'For what? They are hardly suitable for Cerbère, you said so yourself.'

'For . . . another time.'

For when you leave, she meant. *For when you go back to where you came from.*

I stepped closer. I felt no fear, no hesitation as we stood, holding the last remnant of my old life between us.

'I have no more need of them,' I told her, 'and cannot envisage ever having need of them again.'

She held my gaze for a long moment then nodded briskly, turned away, so that I would not see how her eyes filled.

'Very well,' she said, 'you had better come along to the market too. But go and do something with that hair, and for God's sake wash your hands, or you'll spend the whole day smelling of anchovy.'

We took the train to Banyuls with empty baskets, my travelling suit packed carefully in the bottom of one. I felt a flicker of apprehension as we waited on the scorching platform. The last time I had ridden a train, I had been a runaway. *Not any more*, I told myself.

The third-class carriage was packed to the seams, children shoving their heads out of the windows, getting soot in their eyes; women and men dressed in their best for market day, in clean neckties and wilting hats.

During the short journey, we chatted with our neighbours, squashed six to a four-person bench. I found myself perching on the very end with Agathe's daughter Louise, who was taking a basket of their apricots to sell. They were beautiful, each a perfect sunset, luminous orange and red. She gave me one to try. Its flesh was downy and warm against my mouth, the juice like honey, but lighter. I would have to get some for Aaró. I could see him now, licking the juice from his lips as it mingled with the salt there.

All in a rabble, we poured off the train at Banyuls, trooped down the hill towards the marketplace and the sea. I told Clémence that I would try to sell the suit if she had chores, but she was having none of it.

'They will take one look at you and,' she snapped her fingers dismissively, 'give you half what it is worth. They won't try that with me, not if they know what is good for them.'

At the best haberdashery in town, the

neat-looking proprietor sweated beneath the ferocity of Clémence's stare. He was absent-mindedly stroking the nap of the velvet, back and forth, like the ears of a beloved dog, even as Clémence wrung every last centime out of him.

'Are you certain of this?' she asked me, when the price was finally to her liking and the haberdasher was looking a little pale.

I nodded and watched the last pieces of Emeline Vane disappear beneath the counter. The notes and coins we received in exchange made a bright day even brighter.

'Keep it, please,' I laughed when Clémence tried to press it into my hand. 'I owe you that, and more.'

Judiciously, she counted out half and dropped it into a twisted napkin, gave the rest to me.

'Aaró shall have quite the feast tonight,' she said. 'Now, I think we deserve something for ourselves.'

It felt decidedly odd to sit opposite Clémence outside a little café, with the sea glittering behind the market stalls that lined the front. We had never spent any time together in idleness, I realized. To anyone else we must have looked like two women gathering their strength for the day's shopping, or perhaps even mother and daughter . . . I took a hasty sip of the eau-de-vie in my glass and coughed at its strength. It tasted of almonds and herbs.

'What will we make, this evening?' I asked to cover my awkwardness.

Clémence had her face turned up to the sun, her eyes closed.

293

'A dish called *es nui*,' she said, her voice slow and dreamy, 'the nest. It is a rich thing, the stomach of the sea, the throat of the mountains, the earth between, bringing them together in an instant of pleasure.' Cheeks colouring, she looked down at me. 'I have made it only once before. For Aaró's father.'

I had assumed that Clémence was a widow, but the opportunity to ask more had never arisen, or she had never let it. Aaró, too, told me he knew nothing of his father, save that he was long dead. Now, Clémence was looking at me, her face a strange mix of defiance and expectation.

'A long time ago?' I asked quietly, not wanting to say the wrong thing.

For a breath or two she held herself apart, still. Then something within her shifted; the tough exterior rolled aside, making way for the past.

'Yes. A long time ago. In Perpignan.' She swirled the eau-de-vie in its tiny glass. 'My parents owned a brasserie there. They hired a man from Girona, as domestic help. He could do anything with his hands.' She smiled at the memory, and I saw the shape of youth in her face, in her weathered skin that must once have been city-smooth. 'I had a brooch,' she was saying, 'and the pin broke. He fixed it for me, just like that, with wire as fine as a hair. My parents treated him like a vagabond, had him washing dishes, mending pans, but he was a better cook than any of their chefs.

'He taught me *real* food. About the flavours of the world, the senses. And I wanted more. The food on my parents' table started to disgust me. It was food for the wealthy, dressed up and primped beyond recognition. So one night, when my parents slept above, I crept into the dark kitchen and started to learn on my own, to cook the food that he described. It would have made them shudder.

'One day, he told me about a special dish, *es nui*, and I knew I had to make it for him. It took me a long time to find the right ingredients. I practised it in secret, over and over, until finally, I got it right. And then I took it to him, in his room beneath the old city walls, in the quarter my parents told me never to go to alone.'

She was lost in the memory, her face taut with longing. Abruptly, it came back to me, the question she had asked that first morning, when I stood in her kitchen as a stranger, a runaway.

Are you with child?

She had not taken me in through kindness alone, I knew then, but because twenty-one years ago she too had stood, empty-handed, at the end of the world. Impulsively I reached out and took her hand in mine, squeezed it hard.

'We do not have to make it, if it brings you pain,' I said softly.

She shook her head, and I saw the past retreating in her eyes.

'No. That dish brought me Aaró, and he is my happiness. It is only right that I make it.'

She pulled her hand away and drained the rest of her eau-de-vie in one gulp.

'Enough of this dawdling,' she coughed, 'we have a thousand things to do.'

With that, the moment was broken and I hurried away to one end of the market, while she trawled the other, searching for the ingredients she needed. Alone, I wandered through the bustling stalls, lost in her story. Like me, she had left her home, come to a place where outsiders were mistrusted. No wonder she had wanted Mariona and Aaró to be married. He would be a true citizen of the town then, wed to a local. Yet she had forged a new life for herself, made Cerbère her own, even in the worst of situations. Who was to say that I couldn't too? We were more alike than I realized.

I froze on the promenade, mid-step. A woman tutted and pushed past me, but I couldn't move. A terrible thought was crawling down my neck and into my stomach, where it sat, prickling and clenching. I had been so caught up, so unthinking of anything else, that I had not considered . . . When was the last time I had my monthly cycle? Not this month, I realized in horror, or the last.

The prickling in my stomach became a rolling, then a wave that threatened to push me from my feet. I staggered over to a tree and braced myself there, the bright sea a blur through my flooding eyes.

No, I thought over and again, *no, it is nothing, it is your imagination, running away with Clémence's story, that is all.* But an instinct told me otherwise, one that spoke with Mariona's voice, saying, *What does a wife need to understand about her husband beyond what their bodies can tell them?*

Not my husband . . . my lover, but not my husband. How could I have been so foolish? Clémence had been right, all those months ago; she had spoken from experience. I *was* ignorant. I had not given the consequences of being with Aaró a moment's thought. Or perhaps I had, but pushed them away, living all the more for the risk. Had he done the same?

A woman from one of the stalls was asking me if I was all right, but I could not answer her. I walked blindly away from the seafront, pushing through the crowds and paying no heed to motor cars or carts until I found myself on a quieter street. A deep doorway offered shade and I pressed my forehead against the cool stone, feeling my heart pound and knowing that within me, another heart was doing the same.

June 1969

I wait for the phone to connect, imagining the shrill noise echoing from thick stone walls, from threadbare rugs, maybe even reaching out into a green garden . . .

'Hello?' a voice says blearily.

'Jem?' I can hardly believe that I'm hearing her voice, a thousand miles away from Saltedge.

'*Bill Perch?*' Her voice has a faint Norfolk twang that I hadn't noticed before. I hear her swear at the other end.

'Yes! Hello! Are you all right?'

'I stubbed my toe. Where the hell are you? You sound like you're at the bottom of a well.'

'I'm in France.'

'France?'

'Yes, I sent you a postcard, guess it isn't there yet. Anyway, it's — ' The landlady of the bar, whose phone I'm using, has clocked that I'm on an international call, and has started to tap her fingers impatiently. 'It's a long story. Listen, Jem, I think I've found her.'

'What?' Jem's voice is hesitant.

'I've found Emeline.' Those words bring the same shiver of disbelief, of elation. 'At least, I think I know where she went, all those years ago. I'm on my way there.'

'Where?'

'A tiny place called Cerbère. At the end of the world.' The phrase makes me smile.

'Look, Bill — '

'I know, I know. There's no reason she should still be there, but I have to try. I have this feeling . . . ' I give up. 'I just have to go. I can't explain it.'

There's a pause, a sigh. 'You don't need to, man.'

'Thanks.' I would never receive that answer from anyone else.

Briefly, I try to tell her as much as I can about what has happened, while Javi attempts to distract the landlady.

'What a trip!' Jem laughs. 'So what do you want me to do? I'm guessing this isn't just a courtesy call.'

'I need you to get a message to Timothy Vane,' I say hurriedly, leaning backwards as the landlady makes a grab for the phone cord. 'I need you to tell him that I think I know where Emeline went. That he has to hold on. He's at the Royal Cromwell, in London. You might not be able to talk to him — '

'I'll get through to him somehow, don't worry.'

'You're the best.'

'What're friends for? Anything else?'

The landlady is swiping like an angry cat, Javi jumping about in front of her.

'Keep an eye on Hallerton!'

'I went past the other day, you know it's — '

Her voice snaps into silence. The landlady's hand is pressed triumphantly over the telephone.

Outside in the bright morning sunlight, a pick-up truck stands juddering and wheezing, belching out diesel fumes. Luci and Matti are sitting in the back, among grimy tarpaulins and farm equipment, sharing a morning cigarette. They look more dishevelled than ever. I can't look much better after a sleepless night in the barn.

'What's this?' I yell over the noise.

Matti pats the side of the truck.

'All aboard the Manou Express to Mende!'

Any remaining shreds of William Perch, Solicitor, are blown away by the dust of that journey, left behind on a country road in the rugged, green heartland of France. That day, we hitch and hike and blag our way south. By the end of it we look like a bunch of desert explorers, grit-blasted and sunburned but happy.

We camp for the night on the shore of a green river. An old bridge arches over the water, its reflection forming a perfect circle, disturbed only by the tremor of insects across the surface. My shoes lay abandoned near our camp fire. Were those the same soles that raced to catch the bus every day? That first walked up the front steps of Hallerton in trepidation?

My skin smells glassy with river water. My clothes are dripping dry from a tree branch and nothing seems further away right now than London, with its triplicate forms and Steph's chip shop and Hillbrand & Moffat . . . They're like names from a film I saw a long time ago and can barely remember.

What about Emeline? Did Hallerton fade for her, and Saltedge with its marshes and memories of better times, memories that now feel like my own? I lay back, arms behind my head, and try

to sleep, but my head is full of tomorrows, full of
the past and one name that keeps repeating.

July 1999

I do not remember what came next. I went to meet Clémence, as arranged, but I couldn't focus on the array of food stalls that passed before my eyes, the samples she gave me to taste or the meats she haggled over. I tried to make the right noises, ask the questions I would have done had my world not shifted on its axis, with the barely formed life inside my body as its centre.

Luckily, she was distracted by her purchases, by the money in the handkerchief that she weighed and weighed again. She bought quails and doves, a brace of young pigeons, their soft feathers ruffling in the sea breeze. Finally, she had a fervent discussion in Catalan with a man who had just one basket on his stall. It was full of what looked like long, fleshy white flowers. Cod innards, dried and salted, Clémence told me, placing the newspaper-wrapped package carefully in her basket.

'What for?' I managed to ask, trying not to let my hand stray towards my stomach.

'You will see,' she said, pleased. 'This dish will be like none you have ever tasted, believe me. But what about you? What have you been doing? You haven't bought a thing.'

'I was thinking of a cake,' I said, trying to cover my uncertainty, 'in England we make them for birthdays.'

'Does it sound like I shall have time to bake, girl?' Clémence said, though her eyes were amused. 'I dare say you'll do as you like, though. The sweet stalls are down that way.'

It was after lunch by the time we returned to the café. With so much to prepare for the evening, there was no time for Aaró and me to be alone. What would I have told him anyway, with only my hands and my face, out there in the intense heat of the *maquis?* How would he have answered, with joy or dismay? I did not know and was almost glad for the reprieve, for a chance to think before I had to share the knowledge with him, or his mother.

When he appeared in the kitchen, I copied Clémence's sign to wish him *happy birthday* and when he kissed my cheek as well as hers, she pretended not to notice. But soon she sent him away, to round up his guests for the evening. There was much to be done. We plucked and cleaned the birds, skinned the rabbits, sliced dark *botifarra* sausage, soaked the dried fish, gutted the squid that Aaró had brought in that morning. I stared at the wildly different components, my mind reeling. I had no idea how anyone, even a cook like Clémence, would be able to make it all come together.

She pushed me away when I tried to help further, saying that this was her dish now. I could see the memories rising in her as she went back to the stove. I did not try to interfere; I had my own dish to see to. Slowly, I unpacked the items I had bought in a daze at the market.

They told a story, I realized. A bottle of golden

wine was the night of the *calçotada* and a sweet, burning flavour on my lips. A twist of aniseed and a bag of pine nuts were the Feast of *Sant Joan*, the taste of sugary *coca* and a leap of pure joy. A tiny bottle of brandy was the study at Hallerton, and my cold train journey with Puce through the darkness of France. A jar of honey was the night with Aaró in our secret cove. A single pale cheese, almost cream, wrapped in layers of muslin was as pure and white as a christening gown.

Lost in thought, I began to bake, the way Cook had taught me a lifetime ago in the bustling kitchen at Hallerton. Only I had no recipe, no restrictions, no one to disapprove. I folded into the mixture the flavours that had given me life again. I poured myself into it, as did Clémence at the stove, both of us filled to the brim with memories.

The cheese was fresh and white as new milk. It tasted like the curds I had eaten as a child, sitting with Albie in the nursery. He used to keep me company there, though he was a boy of ten and old enough to be playing with soldiers. He chose to sit with me instead and I loved him for it. I was lonely, when he and Freddie were sent away to school, before Timothy was born.

I couldn't help but rest my palm on my belly, trying to feel the imperceptible flutter of life there. Unwed and with child. What would my parents have said, or my brothers? If they had survived, I would never have come here, never have met Aaró, or Clémence. Would I have been happier, if Hallerton was still my home? An impossible question . . .

My hands moved in time with my thoughts. I toasted pine nuts and aniseed in a pan, tossing them until they grew fragrant. I stirred and poured and whipped until finally, the frenzy and clatter of pans and spoons began to lessen. I found myself licking a last dusting of sugar from my thumb, the cake finished. Beside me, Clémence was wiping her brow.

The scent of her dish filled the kitchen, spiralling out through the open door and into the evening, so delicious and extravagant it would have woken the dead. It was a sort of stew, with a *sofregit* of onions darker than I had ever seen. It was deep and earthy and spicy with roasted rabbit and wild birds, but running through it all was the strong, salty tang of the ocean.

Outside the café all was mirth; empty wine bottles already cluttered the ground. Aaró sat among the other fishermen, his tanned cheeks flushed, a paper crown upon his head and a wreath of seaweed about his neck. As I stepped out, his hands paused in their signing, and the love I saw in his eyes frightened me and filled me with joy at the same time.

Still, we did not sit at the same table, for Cerbère was a place of rules. Again and again, my eyes strayed to his face. Once, I almost rose from my seat, almost took his hand and led him away, desperate to tell him what I knew. Minutes later, I found myself gulping down wine, desperate to forget, as if scrubbing the knowledge from my thoughts would make the reality disappear too, would mean we could carry on as before.

But when Clémence's dish was brought out, all the chatter faded. The guests knew that this evening's meal would be something different, something extraordinary, and they gave it their complete attention. I let the flavours mingle on my tongue, overwhelmed. All around me, people were eating reverently, spoons lingering in their mouths, chasing every last drop of oil from their lips. Feet began to nudge others beneath the table and I saw Agathe cast a suggestive look at the widowed mayor, who turned pink as he chewed on a piece of squid. Seated apart from the rest, the trapper, Oriol, nodded to Clémence, who stared brazenly back.

The wine disappeared faster, plates were scraped clean, and if I had not been so distracted I would have been in a similar state to the rest of them, would have been burning to steal away with Aaró, as we had done so many times before. I could feel his eyes upon me from the other end of the table, like mercury in the dying light. It took every ounce of my self-control to stand, to excuse myself and retreat to the kitchen.

I waited until the chatter began to swell again as Clémence's dish released its hold on people. Hesitantly, I took up the cake I had made. The people of Cerbère didn't often eat sweet things, let alone confections like this one, but they applauded nonetheless when I brought it out, for it was Aaró's day.

He beamed as I set the cake in front of him to serve. For an instant, his hand brushed the backs of my legs through my skirt, and I had to fight to stop myself from reaching out to touch him, to smile politely and return to my seat.

As soon as I tasted a spoonful of the cake, I knew. Clémence's dish was darkness and desire, luxurious and reckless, but mine was something quite different. It started sweet, tasting of cream and honey, of walking in the afternoon with the one person you could share the colour of the sky with. It became the fields, a grove in late summer, warm aniseed and olive oil and ripening nuts and days spent harvesting, saving for the winter. Finally, it fell into the warm sting of liquor, like a candle flame flickering far into the night, where no words were needed and time itself dissolved in the touch of skin on skin.

It was love, and it could not be hidden.

The townspeople had fallen quiet. I raised my eyes. Agathe was smiling gently at me, and Aaró put down his spoon to brush one hand across his heart. Then he was standing, pulling off the paper crown and coming towards me, bending down to reach for my hand. He was going to ask me, I thought feverishly . . .

But a murmur was rippling down the tables, and not because of us. Heads were being turned away towards the door of the café. I followed their gaze. A figure dressed in plain travelling clothes stood there, clutching a roll of paper. A high colour rose on Aaró's cheeks. It was Mariona.

'I am sorry to interrupt,' she said politely, 'but I need to speak alone for a moment,' she paused and met my gaze, 'with Emeline.'

July 1969

Javi peers through the broken wire fence on to the train track. 'This time we are careful,' he says, 'no magic Bill money to save our ham.'

'You worry too much.' Matti sounds as nonchalant as ever.

'You would worry too if you grew up with Franco.'

It's meant to be a joke but Javi looks wary. Not for the first time, I feel bad about the risk they're taking.

'You know, you don't need to come with me,' I tell them again.

'*Arrête ton char!*' Luci says. 'We owe you. And we must go through Cerbère anyway.'

'Yes, we walk straight over the hills, catch a lift on the other side. No border, no trouble,' grins Javi.

'*Allons-y!*' Matti slings his bag over his shoulder. 'There it is.'

In the morning sunlight, an engine is trundling past. Behind it are hundreds of freight compartments, identical with their sun-stripped metal and faded logos. Matti puffs out his chest.

'Ready, Bill?'

I feel like I'm in a war film as we slip through the rusted metal fence to race for the train. The back of the final freight container has a ledge, a railing to hold on to. I feel a thrill of disobedience as we sprint after it. I watch Matti and Luci haul themselves aboard. For a second I'm terrified that I'll be left behind, but then I'm leaping, pulling myself up, nearly losing my shoe in the process. A few seconds later I'm standing shoulder to shoulder with the others, breathless and elated as the train picks up speed.

The last container is open at the top, empty like a big, dry swimming pool. We climb up and slide down into it to wait out the journey, unseen. At first it's romantic; I lie on my back to watch the sky, feeling the tracks rattling by below. But soon the fun starts to wear off. It's another scorching day and the metal walls reflect back the light, until we're all sun-dizzy and flagging. Eventually, we have to clamber out and return to the ledge.

I'm perched on the top of the container, about to climb down, when the embankments on either side of the track drop away and I see it: the Mediterranean. More than blue, it's the promise of blue, brilliant and glittering. My brain gropes for a word to describe it, and 'sapphire' springs to mind, except I've never seen a sapphire and I can't imagine any stone ever being better than this. The others are yelling for me to come down in case I'm seen, but even so, it takes me a long time to tear my eyes away.

'Where are we?' I'm panting by the time I make it to the ledge. My legs are jelly and I feel like I've drunk two pints of beer in quick succession.

'Not sure.' Matti is looking at me strangely, fashioning one of his shirts into a bandana. 'Not far now, I guess. You OK, man?'

309

'I'm great,' I say, rolling up my shirtsleeves, 'this is great.'

The train slows, rattling through tiny, two-track stations. We crouch, ready to bolt in case we're seen, but every platform is empty. It's lunchtime now, and anyone sensible will be in the shade, enjoying a cool drink and a nap. The names roll past: *Argelès-sur-Mer, Collioure, Port-Vendres, Banyuls-sur-Mer* . . .

Finally, Javi gives an excited yelp as we enter a tunnel, cut deep into the sea cliff.

'This is it!'

Sure enough, as we emerge into the sunlight, a sign crawls by. *Cerbère*, it says, in sun-faded paint. Like rats, we abandon the train, leaping one after the other on to the rough track, grazing knees and hands as we dash for safety, barely avoiding a second freight train going in the opposite direction. Hearts hammering, we clutch at each other, laughing from behind the safety of the level-crossing barrier.

Then, through the axle grease and grime of the passing train, I think I see something: a face, as familiar and strange as the one I was sure I saw at the window of Hallerton, staring at me from the other side of the track. *Please be here*, I beg it silently, trying to catch another glimpse through the rolling carriages, *please, Emeline*.

The last compartment disappears. There's nothing there, just an empty space and no one watching. But all the same I feel it, stronger than ever, the impulse that has driven me here, that has plagued me ever since I first saw Hallerton, since I climbed the stairs and found the diary, filled with her voice.

'Here we are.' Javi claps me on the shoulder as we stand looking down at the town. 'Cerbère.'

Tall buildings cluster around a little cove, as if staring out to sea. They're painted in bright colours, yellows and blues and dusky pinks, faded by the weather. Other houses stretch back into the hills, petering out as the land rises and scrubland takes over, knotted with parched vegetation. Javi points out a thin track, little more than a footpath, running over a ridge: the border with Spain.

I stare at it all, overwhelmed. I can't believe that I've come this far.

'I don't know where to start,' I murmur.

Matti squints down at the town.

'In my experience, if you have to start somewhere, start at the bar. That place there looks as good as any.'

I follow the line of his finger. He's pointing to a building on the seafront. It's tall and thin, painted yellow. A sign above the door says it is the Café Fi del Món.

'Café at the World's End,' Javi translates with a smile. 'Like I said.'

It's a struggle to say goodbye to them, at the start of the road that leads into the hills. I hug them all tightly without even thinking about it; at home it would've been a curt handshake or nothing. Luci's face crumples a bit as she steps away, and Javi tells me again and again to call if I need anything, giving me the telephone number of the inn near his grandparents' *finca*. Matthieu also scribbles something down.

311

'My address in Paris, man. Let us know what happens with Emeline? If you find her?'

'I will,' I promise, tucking it into my bag, heart full. 'Thanks, for everything.'

He grips my hand tightly.

'Don't be a stranger.'

Then they're gone, and I'm alone. It's long past noon, and I know I should be hungry, but I'm not. My legs seem to float of their own accord, down the hill and into the town. Everything is quiet, not another soul to be seen. In a tiny square, a few dusty trees offer some shade. A grey cat is stretched flat beneath a window sill. It sees me and gives a low purr, rolling on its back in the grit. As I bend down to stroke it, I catch a scent.

The back door of the nearest house stands open. I sniff deeply. The smell wafting out is rich and savoury and spicy all at once. It reaches down into my stomach and sets it gurgling, clamouring for whatever is cooking.

I can't help myself. I take two paces towards the doorway, three, and only hesitate for a second before knocking and stepping inside.

It's a kitchen: that much I can smell from the cooking. Through the sun-blindness I can see a figure moving at a stove, a woman who is tall and slim with dark, waving hair. The breath catches in my throat as she turns.

'Emeline?'

July 1919

Emeline.

Mutely, I followed Mariona into the dark kitchen. What else could I do? That name, dropping from her lips, might have escaped the notice of the rest of the town but it had not escaped me. She was clutching a roll of newspaper in her hand. I felt cold sweat prickle its way down my back. What did she want?

Clémence had followed us too. 'What is it, Mariona?' she said. Her voice was soft, perhaps out of pity for the girl. 'This is not the time for — '

'I'm sorry, Maman, but this is important. I caught the train back here to tell you.' She looked over at me, half-triumphant, half-wary, like a child who has trapped a wild animal and does not know what to do with it. 'My aunt in Beziers takes the Paris papers. She found this, in one of them.' She held out the newspaper.

Clémence looked like she would refuse, but then she reached out, opened the paper to where a page was marked, near the back. I stood watching in shock, still unable to marshal my thoughts. A moment ago, everything had hovered on the verge of joy. Now, here was Mariona, calling me the name I had run from, that I had left behind when I fled Paris. What had she found, that would bring her running back here, full of victory?

313

Aaró came to stand beside me.

What is going on?

I do not know, I said, but my hands were shaking as I signed and he could see that I was not telling the truth, that I was frightened of that little roll of paper. He tapped Clémence's shoulder, trying to make her explain, but she ignored him, reading, not moving. He made a noise of frustration, only for Mariona to step forward.

She signed something to him that I could not follow. His face was wary as he watched, but there was something else in his expression. He looked guilty, I realized, as he watched her small, callused hands try to explain, perhaps thinking of the hurt he had caused her.

'What is she telling him?' I tried to keep my voice calm, but I couldn't stop a tremor of fear from creeping in. 'Clémence, what?'

She looked up when I said her name. Her face was unreadable as a statue.

'What is written here about someone called Emeline Vane.'

It was like missing a step in the dark, hearing that name on her lips. When she finally handed me the paper, the printed words swam and crawled out of shape.

'I cannot read it,' I whispered. 'What does it say?'

From the corner of my eye I could see Aaró looking over at me in shock.

'It says there is a missing woman,' Mariona's voice was defiant, 'an Englishwoman, called Emeline Vane, last seen at the Gare de Lyon in

Paris. It says she was being taken to a psychiatric institution — '

'No!'

The word broke from me. I shut my mouth but it was too late. My voice had cut through the kitchen, and all three of them could see the terror and truth written across my face.

'Are you her?' Clémence's voice was quiet. 'Emeline Vane?'

Aaró was staring at me from behind his mother's shoulder. *Say no*, his face begged, *say they have it wrong*.

'Yes,' I whispered. He followed the shape of my lips and I saw the confusion begin to gather in his eyes. I couldn't look away.

'It says here that Emeline Vane is a danger to herself, that she . . . that she tried . . . ' Clémence's gaze strayed to my hands, to their ugly scars. 'Is that true?'

How could I answer her? How could I think back to those desperate times, tell her of how every day had dragged me further from myself, until I could see no way out, until I had wanted to feel the cold waves close over my head, so that I would not have to face another day of it? I could feel panic begin to simmer beneath the surface of my skin, the way it had at Hallerton, when the only way to stop it had been a draught of morphine.

'They say she should be taken into custody for her own safety, Maman,' Mariona was saying, 'and her family are offering a reward, for information about her. We can send a tele-gram — '

Those words broke something in me. I lashed out, struck Mariona as hard as I could. She fell back against the stove, sending an empty pot spinning to the floor. Everything I had tried to hold back, that I had tried to forget since first setting foot in this town, had come flooding to the surface, and in the confusion I would have struck her again, had Clémence's strong hands not gripped my arms, forced me backwards.

The abrupt silence was broken only by the sounds of Mariona's sobbing and my rapid breathing. The anger drained as quickly as it arrived. I shook my head, trying to free myself from the clash of emotions, trying to see how we could wave all of this away and return to how things had been only a few minutes ago. Even now Mariona, her face red and tear-streaked, was signing something to Aaró.

'Please,' I interrupted, stepping towards them. *Please*, I begged Aaró, making a mess of the sign. 'It's not like they say.'

I reached for him, wanting him to understand, wanting him to see that whatever had happened in my past, he was my future. But he recoiled, and a cry broke from me then, a hurt so deep it was almost physical. I could barely watch as he swiped one finger across his face and threw the gesture towards me.

'I don't understand,' I told him, as he looked away.

'He said you lied,' Clémence's voice was rough.

'No, I didn't mean to.' I tried to sign it to him. *Your family, looking for you?* His face was

316

taut with emotion. *You said they were dead, like my friends.*

I have a brother. An uncle. The rest —

I trusted you.

Aaró, please listen. But he shook his head with a strangled noise and pushed past me, out of the house.

I tried to follow, but Clémence caught my arm. The back door thudded, *la Tramontana* throwing it against the wall. It made the oil lamps gutter, set the baskets on the walls creaking, like old, sad voices.

'Clémence,' I said, turning to her.

The dim light made her lined face look older than her years.

'You should have told me,' was all she said.

★ ★ ★

That night was the longest of my life. I sat in the dark kitchen and waited for him to return, as the wind mouthed at the door and silence flooded down the stairs from where Clémence lay, unsleeping, above. The lamp beside me sputtered and died but still I sat, waiting. I ached for his arms with every fibre, every nerve until I could stand it no more, and wrapped my own arms around my belly and squeezed and squeezed.

Despite everything, I must have slept. A noise shook me awake, footsteps, and I raised my head in hope only to find Clémence standing in the doorway. Her face was puffy, a black shawl wrapped tightly around her chest. The room was ashen with dawn.

317

'He's already gone,' she said, as I opened my mouth to ask.

'Where?' My throat felt gritty with tiredness.

She hesitated. 'Out with the deep-sea boats.'

She knew the pain those words would cause me. Aaró rarely went deep fishing. Unlike the shore fishermen, the deep boats did not put in until afternoon. He was furious with me, that much was clear, but I had to talk to him. There was so much unsaid between us; apologies, explanations, confessions . . . My hand crept towards my middle again.

'Emilie,' Clémence started, but caught herself. 'Emeline.' She smiled humourlessly, shook her head. 'Mariona was not lying last night. There is a reward for information about you. But I have made her promise not to say anything, for now.' She paused, worrying at a thread of her shawl. 'What would happen, if you were to be found, returned to your family?'

I did not want to think about it. Returned to England, to Uncle Andrew, restrained, sedated if I fought. And if they discovered my condition . . . I met Clémence's eyes.

'That cannot happen.'

She gathered the shawl about herself, sat down opposite me with a tired sigh. It took her a long while to speak.

'When I first discovered Aaró's deafness,' she said, choosing her words carefully, 'I thought it was God punishing me for what I had done, for conceiving a child in sin. But when the war came I knew it was a blessing. God saved my precious boy, kept him whole. I don't want him to suffer the way I did. I want him to have a real family, a home.'

'I love him, Clémence.' They were painful, those words, in the light of what had happened.

She shook her head, slowly.

'Love does not always mean happiness, that I know. What if you were to . . . fall ill again? What if next time, it is Aaró that you run from?'

Her words cut into me, right to the heart of everything I most feared.

'No,' I tried to say, 'I would never — '

'If you truly love him,' her eyes were kind, but unyielding, 'you will put his happiness, his future, before your own.'

⋆ ⋆ ⋆

The barriers of the level crossing blocked the path to the station. I stood, staring at the tracks for what felt like hours, Clémence's words echoing through my head. Could I truly leave here, step on to a train and never return, try to forget Aaró, hope that he would find happiness with someone else, with someone whose mind was clear and whole?

A train was rolling by, wagon after wagon, perhaps even the same engine that had brought me here. Then, through the axle grease and soot and relentless pistons, I thought I saw something; a face with wide eyes that begged me to stay, for a moment, a decade, a lifetime in this place, at the end of the world.

The train disappeared and there was nothing there, an empty space and no one watching, but something had changed. It made my choice. *Let them do what they will*, I thought as *la Tramontana* rushed out of nowhere, whipping my skirts as I turned back towards the town. *Let them come, let them try to take me away from here.*

The waves of the bay were agitated, foaming at the shore; the boats too far out to be seen. I dropped to my knees on the beach, and I waited.

I waited all morning, as the sun scorched and the wind cooled my skin, burning it raw. I waited as Clémence found me there, tried to persuade me to come inside, as the shore fishermen put in around me, shaking their heads over their bad luck and saying that there was a squall coming on.

I waited as the wind grew stronger, as the clouds erupted over the horizon, like lines of men running. I waited as the time for the deep boats to return came and went, as other women began to wait, too, staring into the heartless waves for their loved ones, as flotsam was flung upon the strand.

We waited as the rain began to fall, first as frenzied spittle then as a torrent. My mouth had long dried up, my legs were numb, but still I waited, and still they did not come. Impossible to tell, when the darkness of the storm mingled with night, but one by one the women retreated, and one by one, lanterns appeared in windows, turned up high, guzzling oil, bright enough to guide the boats home.

Then I pulled myself to my feet and struggled

through the gale, back towards the Café Fi del Mon.

★   ★   ★

Inside, there was no mirth, no steaming bowls or jostling elbows. Only tightly closed windows and sombre faces. Nobody stopped me as I pushed through the curtain into the kitchen.

Clémence sat, her head in her hand and a ruined pan beside her on the stove. Mariona was pale in the crook of Agathe's arm. I went straight past them towards the dresser, where the storm lantern was kept. My hands were steady as I filled it with oil, as much as it would take, as I lit the wick with a match.

'Where are you going?' Clémence's voice was worn with worry. 'We wait together, it's what is done.'

'To the cliff.' I adjusted the glass to make sure it was firm. 'He'll be able to see me there.'

'Don't be foolish, Emeline. You don't know what you're doing. You will fall and drown.'

The lamp was growing warmer, and outside the storm raged. I pressed my hand against my stomach, in silent apology, in silent hope.

'Then we will drown.'

Her frown slipped as she stared at my belly in horror.

'Wait!'

But I could not. I had done my waiting and I left the kitchen, went out into the night, though I could barely stand against the wind. Clémence's voice, calling me back, was snatched away in an

321

instant. I bent double, cradling the lamp against myself, making for the place where the cliff marked the end of the beach.

Sand and grit were flung up into my face and I tripped more than once before I reached it. I ran my hands across the rock face, the lantern flame bucking and flickering, until I found the footholds that Aaró had shown me.

It took half a dozen attempts before I managed it, before my hands found the ledge above and I was able to push the lantern up, pull myself after it. I stood on the narrow path that ran around the cliff, catching my breath. Below, waves were battering the rocks, but I closed my eyes and felt my way forward, the lantern in one hand. I tried to imagine that I was following Aaró, tried not to think what would happen if my foot slipped. Finally, the path sloped upwards, the waves dropped away and I felt grass beneath my feet, slick with rain and the ripe fruit that had fallen from the tree.

There, where he had first shown me his world, where I had first learned love, I braced myself against the tree's trunk and held the lantern high. Time fell away; hours might have passed between one breath and the next while the storm tore at my clothes and the unknown life trembled within my body.

Come home. I said it like a prayer as I stared down the fury of the storm. *Come home, come home, come home.* Eventually, it became a whisper, my lips stiff, my arms trembling from the effort of holding the lantern. Gritting my teeth, I hoisted it even higher.

Something sparked at the edge of my vision, and my heart contracted. Was that a light, tiny as a firefly in the deluge? I stared desperately as it was lost in the waves, but there, it appeared again, a flash of white, of sail and stern. I waved the lantern back and forth, blinded by tears as I cried his name.

And although I knew he could not hear me, from far away over the dark sea I saw a lantern waved in reply, to tell me, to tell *us*, that he was coming home.

July 1969

Pain. A horrible pounding in my head. A rolling in my stomach. What the hell happened? I crack my eyes open and bright sunlight streams in, a breeze that brings the smell of the sea. There's something wet and cold on my forehead. A cloth.

And I'm being watched. I can feel it. Someone has registered that I'm awake. I look up as a figure steps from behind a bead curtain.

'Emeline?' It comes out as a croak, scarcely audible over the clattering beads.

She frowns, and it's not Emeline. This young woman is darker, her hair is black not brown, cropped scruffily above her shoulders. And yet . . . I can't help but search her face for something, for a spark of familiarity.

'Why do you keep saying that?' She hands me a glass of water. 'Is it the heat, still?'

Water. My body's screaming for it, and I gulp down the glass in one. Liquid life; I can feel it, sliding through my veins and into my throbbing head. The girl fills the glass again from a jug and I drink that too.

'Slowly,' she orders, 'or you will be sick.'

'Thank you,' I gasp, my lips still wet, trying to make sense of her words. My brain feels all spongy. 'What did you mean about the heat?'

She leans back against a table, crossing her brown arms over her chest. 'Heatstroke. You fainted.'

'Oh.' I squint through the headache, trying to look around. I'm slumped on an old sofa, in the corner of an empty restaurant. The tables are mismatched, as are the chairs. I stare around for some clue and a chalkboard on the long bar catches my attention.

CAFÉ FI DEL MÓN

'You speak English?' I ask, realizing that I haven't become magically fluent in French.

'A bit,' she says drily, her voice accented but confident. 'It pays to, working in a hotel. Why?'

'Maybe you can help.' I haul myself into a more upright position. 'I'm looking for someone.'

'Emeline?'

She's picking idly at a thread of her faded sundress, but her voice is guarded.

'You know her?' I surge to my feet, only to flop back into the sagging cushions, my head pounding. The girl clicks her tongue at me.

'No,' she says, pouring another glass of water, 'but you said the name maybe ten times, when you were busy fainting.'

I try not to turn red. 'You're sure you don't know her?' I ask again between sips, in case she didn't hear properly. 'Emeline Vane?'

She shrugs, shakes her head.

'She was English.' I set the empty glass on the tiled floor. 'She came here to Cerbère about fifty years ago.'

Something flares across the girl's face. Recognition?

'What's *your* name?' I ask abruptly. The turn of her head, even the shape of her chin, jutting out defensively, gives me hope. 'Please,' I beg when she doesn't answer. 'I've come a long way looking for Emeline Vane, and you — '

'Núria,' she interrupts. 'That's my name. Núria Segal.'

'And your grandmother?'

She is silent for a long time. She's suspicious, but there's something else behind her gaze; is it guilt or sadness?

'Please,' I say, placing all of my hope in this bad-tempered, barefoot young woman with a face that's so familiar it hurts. 'Please, where is she?'

The breeze from the door blows a lock of hair across her face. Behind it, her expression softens.

'I'll take you to her.'

★ ★ ★

The cemetery is a peaceful one, small and quiet, separated from the town by a high wall, which dips to frame a view of the glittering sea. Núria walks before me, her sandalled feet crunching over the ground.

At the highest point, where the town is hidden from view and the waves spread endlessly towards the horizon, she stops. She does not need to say anything. A simple headstone, inset with two photographs behind thick glass. Even before I look up, I know what I will find.

Emeline Vane looks back at me, her dark eyes still for ever. She's older in the picture, in her forties, perhaps, as beautiful as she ever was. Her face has lost the sharpness of grief, and she is smiling. The man in the other photograph has short black hair, distant-looking eyes that soften the angle of his jaw. Too young for a grave, both of them.

EMILIE & AARO FOURNIER
Beloved parents
D. 2 July 1944

Núria and I sit beneath the shade of a plane tree, looking out across the bay. I feel like a tin can that's been emptied and crushed out of shape. Emeline, dead for all these years. It seems impossible.

No, a voice tells me, *all too possible.*

My eyes begin to burn again, and I swipe a hand across them. Núria sees, reaches out to squeeze my arm.

'They saved people, you know.' Her voice is soft. 'Hid them in the café, showed them how to escape, across the hills and into Spain and so to Portugal and America.' She looks out to sea, her strong face thoughtful. 'That's why I thought you were here, at first. We still get letters from survivors. They must have helped a great many, before they were caught.'

'But they died. They were killed for it.'

'Yes. War is like that.'

The crickets murmur their dry summer song, filling the spaces between our words. Slowly, I pull the briefcase towards me. It feels ordinary now, just a bag full of old papers, like a conjuring trick with its workings exposed. I take out the photograph of Emeline on Armistice Day.

'She lost so much to war,' I say, showing it to Núria. 'Perhaps when it came again, she couldn't help but fight.' The photograph on the grave looks down. In it Emeline smiles, loving, loved. 'Especially if she had found something to live for.'

I look back to find Núria watching me, smiling sadly. Out of nowhere, a great gust of wind scuds across the ground, whipping up dust, smelling impossibly of ice, before disappearing entirely.

'*La Tramontana*,' Núria says, as if that explains it. There's a fleck of bark caught in her black hair. Hesitantly, I reach towards her and pull it free, my fingers grazing her cheek.

At that moment, my stomach lets out an almighty gurgle of hunger. Red to the ears, I clamp my hands over my torso as Núria laughs.

'Sorry.'

'Do not be. I should get back to the café anyway. Dinner is not until later, but if you like, I can find you something.' She climbs to her feet, holds out a hand to pull me up from the ground.

My palm clasps hers, and I feel as though the heat of the sun is inside my body, spilling out towards her. I let go. We both smile a little nervously.

'You cook there, at the café?' I ask, as we walk downhill. Núria nods. 'You must have inherited that from Emeline, she was a good cook.'

'That's right.' She trails her hand through a lavender bush, releasing the scent. 'She taught Mama and Mama taught me. I like it OK.'

'Just OK?'

'I've lived here my whole life, you know? One day I'd like a place of my own. Somewhere new.' She smiles crookedly. 'Maybe at the other end of the world.'

'Why don't you do it?' I say, surprising myself.

I sneak a look at her. There's a tiny dimple on one side of her cheek, I notice, and trip over a stone.

'I would have to find somewhere *to* do it,' she's saying, 'and that won't happen soon. Not much money in the family hotel business.'

I stop in my tracks. Núria frowns at me from the cemetery gate.

'What is it?'

Use your head, lad, Hillbrand is booming from my memory, *can't sell half a house* . . .

'What would you say,' I ask slowly, 'if I told you that your grandmother might have left you something very valuable?'

Núria laughs and strides away, through the gate and down towards the seafront, 'I would say,' she calls back, 'that I would need to get a very good solicitor.'

Before I can answer, *la Tramontana* blows again. I turn and for an instant I think I see someone watching from the shadows beneath the plane tree: dark eyes, a face half-turned.

'Bill?' Núria calls, looking over her shoulder.

The shadows are empty. I feel a grin rising to my face.

'You'd need a very good solicitor,' I say, hurrying after her, 'or a very bad one.'

Epilogue

April 1921

'Clara! Put that down!'

The little girl grinned, a dead crab clutched tightly in her hand. The woman called again and the child's smile widened even further, pure mischief, right down to her tufty black curls. She squealed and ran towards her mother.

The woman laughed as the little girl threw herself forward. A piece of paper lay in her lap, and she held a pencil, which she put down to divest the child of the crustacean.

'Play with your boat like a good girl, *ma petite*, Mama is too fat to run about after you.'

A loose dress hung in folds over the woman's belly, which was as round and hard as a glass float on a fishing vessel. Absent-mindedly, she ran her hand over its contour, staring out to sea. Beyond the calm bay, tall waves crested.

'Where's Papa, then?' she murmured, and the little girl burbled in response. In answer to her question a breeze sprang up, seemingly out of nowhere. It ruffled the girl's hair, caught at the paper in the woman's lap and nearly sent it flying.

Then the day was warm and still again, as though the wind had never been there at all. The woman muttered beneath her breath and tried to smooth out a crease from the paper. Next to her, the child hefted her toy boat and lowered it, hefted and lowered it, sailing on wild seas.

Eventually, the little girl gave a delighted shriek and pointed. A handful of small boats were putting into shore, the fishermen shouting and waving at each other, nets and traps full. The woman smiled and raised a hand in greeting but before she could get to her feet, the child was off, tottering down towards the waves.

'Clara!'

The woman clambered upright as fast as her belly would allow. She hurried after the child, who even now was being caught and thrown into the air by a man with sea-grey eyes, his black hair glistening with water and salt. When the woman finally reached them, breathless and laughing, he tucked the squealing child under one arm and held out the other, to pull her in close against his brine-sodden shirt.

Behind them on the beach, the woman's letter flapped and rustled, forgotten.

On cold days, it said, *when bright blue Mediterranean turns to pewter, when the crest marine blooms pink and the sea birds flash white in the sun, my thoughts fly to Hallerton, to Saltedge, and to you, Timothy.*

The wind blew again and this time it was victorious. It snatched the paper from the ground, turned it end over end as if examining its words before bearing it away, over the heads of the people on the shore, towards the mountains or the sea or the end of the world.

Acknowledgements

This book owes a debt to three remarkable writers: W. G. Sebald for his East Anglia, Alan Garner for *The Owl Service* and Colman Andrews for his beautiful introduction to Catalan food. A strange trio, perhaps, but I like to think they'd enjoy a good meal together.

Thanks go to the indefatigable Ed Wilson, who nudged this book into being; to Harriet Bourton, who took it on trust, and to Bella Bosworth, who stepped in to smooth its rough edges. To everyone at Transworld, in fact, for taking a manuscript and making it into a Real Book.

I have to thank Yves at the Hotel La Dorade in Cerbère for his generosity, his spirit, and for bringing the town and its history to life.

Thanks also go to Becky and Jude, for putting up with my antics. To Dave and Cheryl, for their support. To my mother — and her Auntie Mimi — for an original idea. To my father, for being more of an inspiration for Bill than I should probably admit . . .

To my sister, Lucy: my constant companion in the world of writing and a rock in stormy seas. And to Nick, for being there at the beginning, middle and end of this book.

Wild Cherry Cake Recipe

When it came to creating a cake to accompany *Where the Wild Cherries Grow*, I knew I wanted it to contain three things, Cherries — as might br found on Emeline and Aaró's secret tree — were a must, Almonds too; the medieval Catalan recipe collection *The Book of Sent Solvi* is full of recipes featuring fragrant almonds, in broths, sauces, creams and puddings . . .

Last of all, I wanted it to contain a hint of sweet, heady wine, the kind I drank during my visit to French Catalonia. Banyuls is *vin doux naturel*, a strong dessert wine made in only four places along the Côte Vermeille: Banyuls-sur-Mer, Port-Vendres, Collioure and Cerbère. It's almost a metaphor for the spirit of the place; the vines have to be hardy to grow in the rocky, arid soil, but they're helped along by the bright sunlight that ripens the grapes and *la Tramonontana*, the wind from the mountains, that sweeps any pests out to sea. In my memory, Banyuls tasted honeyed and deep, like peaches and apricots baked slowly in a clay pot over embers . . .

Sadly, Banyuls is notoriously tricky to find outside of France, so I'd suggest using whatever good quality, rich dessert wine you can lay your hands on. Of course, if you do happen to find a bottle, you know who to call if you want to share.

For The Cherries in Syrup:

150g morello cherries, fresh or frozen (and defrosted)
3 tbsp good quality sweet dessert wine
1 tsp ground cinnamon
2 tbsp golden caster sugar

For the cake:

200g butter, softened
200g golden caster sugar
3 free-range eggs
160g self-raising flour
40g ground almonds .
1 tsp vanilla bean paste, or 1 vanilla pod, seeds scraped out
Large handful of dried cherries
1 tbsp flour
Handful flaked almonds
Icing sugar, to decorate

Allons-y!

1. Preheat the oven to 180°C/350°F/Gas mark 4, Grease and line a 23cm, 9" deep cake tin.
2. Place the cherries, wine, cinnamon and sugar together in a bowl and toss gently until combined. Set aside to infuse.
3. In another bowl, cream together the butter and sugar until light and fluffy.

4. Add one egg to the butter mix, along with a tablespoon of the flour (to stop the mixture from splitting) and beat well. Repeat with the rest of the eggs, beating well in between.
5. Add the rest of the flour in thirds, folding in gently until it is just combined and no streaks are showing.
6. Gently stir in the ground almonds, vanilla and dried cherries.
7. Spoon two-thirds of the infusing cherries onto a plate and toss in the remaining 1 tbsp of flour. (This'll stop them all sinking to the bottom.) Put the syrup and remaining cherries to one side.
8. Carefully stir the flour-coated cherries into the mixture, making sure they're evenly distributed. Add a splash of milk if the mixture needs loosening.
9. Dollop into the tin, smooth over the top and bake for around 30-35 minutes, or until golden and risen, and a skewer inserted comes out clean. Leave to cool slightly in its tin on a wire rack.

To decorate:

1. While the cake is still warm, prick holes all over the surface with a skewer.
2. Spoon the cherry-wine-cinnamon syrup over the top so that it soaks in.
3. Lightly toast the flaked almonds in a dry frying pan for 2-3 minutes. Keep your eye

on them, because they'll catch quickly.

4. Decorate the cake with the remaining infused cherries, almonds and a dusting of icing sugar. Eat with a glass of brandy or sweet wine and dream yourself away to a warm summer's night, outside a seafront café, at the very end of France . . .

We do hope that you have enjoyed reading this large print book.

Did you know that all of our titles are available for purchase?

We publish a wide range of high quality large print books including:
Romances, Mysteries, Classics General Fiction Non Fiction and Westerns

Special interest titles available in large print are:
The Little Oxford Dictionary Music Book Song Book Hymn Book Service Book

Also available from us courtesy of Oxford University Press:
Young Readers' Dictionary (large print edition) Young Readers' Thesaurus (large print edition)

For further information or a free brochure, please contact us at:
Ulverscroft Large Print Books Ltd., The Green, Bradgate Road, Anstey, Leicester, LE7 7FU, England. Tel: (00 44) 0116 236 4325 Fax: (00 44) 0116 234 0205

THE SECRETS BETWEEN US

Laura Madeleine

High in the mountains in the south of France, eighteen-year-old Ceci Corvin is trying hard to carry on as normal. But in 1943, there is no such thing as normal — especially not for a young woman in love with the wrong person. Scandal, it would seem, can be more dangerous than war . . . Fifty years later, Annie is looking for her long-lost grandmother. Armed with nothing more than a sheaf of papers, she travels from England to Paris in pursuit of the truth. But as she traces her grandmother's story, Annie uncovers something she wasn't expecting: something that changes everything she knew about her family — and everything she thought she knew about herself . . .